Also by Synithia Williams

Peachtree Cove

The Secret to a Southern Wedding
About Last Night
Waiting for Friday Night
Frenemies to Lovers

The Jackson Falls series

Forbidden Promises
The Promise of a Kiss
Scandalous Secrets
Careless Whispers
Foolish Hearts

For additional books by Synithia Williams,
visit her website, synithiawilliams.com.

FRENEMIES *with* BENEFITS

SYNITHIA WILLIAMS

CANARY STREET PRESS

CANARY
STREET
PRESS™

Recycling programs
for this product may
not exist in your area.

ISBN-13: 978-1-335-43055-7

Frenemies with Benefits

Canary Street Press
22 Adelaide St. West, 41st Floor
Toronto, Ontario M5H 4E3, Canada
CanaryStPress.com

Printed in U.S.A.

For the people starting over. You have the strength and ability to begin again.

1

Tracey Thompson really wanted to hit something. She fought not to let her hands ball into fists as the idea of pinning a picture of her soon-to-be ex-husband's face to the punching bag hanging in her brother's garage played in her head. He was the reason why her life was in shambles right now. He was why she'd had to hire a new desk clerk for her bed and breakfast, The Fresh Place Inn, instead of relying on the perfectly capable front desk attendant who'd once worked for her. Well, reliable except for the teeny little slip of getting pregnant by Tracey's husband. So instead of having a reliable, motivated desk attendant, Tracey had to tap into her very limited amount of patience and let visions of pounding her almost-ex's face on a punching bag go so she could make sure that Jessica, the new unreliable and unmotivated employee, didn't enter the wrong key for the nice couple waiting to check in.

Tracey tried not to be a micromanaging, demanding boss.

She'd been very optimistic when she'd shown Jessica what she needed to do on her first day three months ago. She'd held on to that optimism when, two weeks after her hire date, Jessica said she had no idea what she'd done with the checklist that outlined everything she needed to handle guest registration and check-in. She'd even held on to her optimism three weeks after that when Jessica spilled her cappuccino on her computer's keyboard for the fifth time and asked for another replacement before mentioning she needed another copy of the checklist because she "must have left it somewhere." Despite her tendency to forget everything she was taught and her inability to keep beverages in a cup, she was a body behind the counter, and Tracey needed someone to help her manage registrations.

Which was why she was once again trying to be patient as she watched Jessica ignore the newly printed checklist right next to her at the front desk and apologize half-heartedly to the waiting guests and claim that she was still new and hadn't been trained on the system.

Tracey took a long breath and clenched her teeth. She could go rescue Jessica, but she was pretty sure that's exactly what the young woman wanted. The instructions she needed tended to magically disappear whenever Tracey was around or whenever she called Tracey to help her figure things out.

Yep, Tracey really wanted to hit her ex's face. It was all his fault. She wouldn't be dealing with Jessica if Bernard had kept his dick in his pants instead of sharing it with her previous employee, Monique. Monique had been perfect. She'd implemented the new booking system to make online registrations easier. She'd been courteous and friendly with all the guests. She'd been Tracey's right hand at the inn from the day she'd opened the door.

If only she hadn't also been screwing Tracey's husband on a regular basis.

A hand patted her shoulder. The familiar scent of butter and cinnamon wafted over Tracey before she was pulled into a side hug. Shirley Cooke, the woman responsible for all the meals at The Fresh Place Inn and Tracey's left hand when Monique had been her right.

"Stop scowling," Shirley said in her warm, slow drawl. She was shorter than Tracey and older by two decades. Her pecan-brown skin was lined around the eyes and mouth from her frequent smiles.

Tracey sighed and forcibly relaxed her face. "I'm not scowling."

"Yes, you are. What's wrong now?"

Tracey had watched Jessica fumble with the guests from around the corner of the hall that led to the kitchen. She motioned in that direction with her head. "Jessica."

Shirley rolled her eyes. "She's still struggling?"

"Yes."

"Does she have the checklist?"

Tracey nodded. "She does, and she hasn't picked it up once. I'm going to have to go help her."

Tracey moved but Shirley's arm around her shoulder tightened. "No, you don't. If you go help that girl then she'll never learn."

Jessica was far from being a girl. She was six years younger than Tracey's thirty-five. Maybe she would have been more patient if Jessica were nineteen instead of twenty-nine. At least then she could blame some of the lack of effort on youth.

"She hasn't learned in three months," Tracey mumbled.

"If you have to do her work then what do you need her for?" Shirley's question wasn't rhetorical and was often repeated.

"I need her because reservations are up now that Peachtree Cove got the Best Small Town designation. We're full almost every week, not to mention the reservations for weddings and birthday parties. I can't afford to let her go."

Shirley grunted before shaking her head. "That's what you're telling yourself. You can find someone else."

"I don't have the time to look."

"So you're going to work yourself to the bone by managing this place and doing Jessica's job. While you're at it, can you come and cook for me?" Tracey cut her eyes at Shirley, who just cut them back before grinning. "What? You don't want to also handle the food?"

"First of all, you don't want me in your kitchen. I'll mess everything up. Second, I'll deal with Jessica. I just need to get through wedding season."

Shirley let Tracey go and threw up her hands. "Wedding season is a long time. Go on. Go help the girl. I saw another car pull up so it might be the other guests for the carriage house."

Tracey placed a hand to her chest and took a long, calming breath. "This is a good problem. This is a good problem," she chanted to herself.

Shirley patted her back. "It is. We'll figure it out. Don't worry."

"Thanks, Shirley," Tracey said before going into the reception area to help Jessica.

She didn't know what she would do if she didn't have Shirley there. Shirley had kept things together while Tracey's personal life imploded. She'd made breakfast, lunch and dinner for the guests on time and to perfection. She was always there when Tracey needed her and ran her kitchen like a five-star general. Without Shirley reminding Tracey every day that she couldn't just give up her dream because her husband and employee were assholes, Tracey might have closed the inn. She still wondered how she'd gotten there. How she'd actually opened a bed and breakfast and was somehow keeping it going. Not many people had expected much of Tracey, including her parents. A part of her was still waiting for things to go wrong. Her failed marriage was strike one. Strikes two and three had to be coming.

She slid up next to Jessica. "Is everything okay here?" Tracey asked sweetly.

Jessica sighed and turned to Tracey with a relieved smile. "Ms. Thompson, thank goodness you're here. I can't figure out how to pull up their reservation."

Tracey kept the smile on her face despite the strong urge to roll her eyes. She looked at the guests, a married couple who'd thankfully remained congenial while Jessica fumbled their reservation. "Sorry for the wait. We'll get you checked right in." She reached for the checklist right next to the keyboard sitting precariously close to a half-full cappuccino cup.

Tracey slid the cup far away from the keyboard before pointing to the first step in the checklist. "First let's input their last name here."

Jessica nodded and watched Tracey with wide, clueless brown eyes. Tracey's smile slipped. Jessica wasn't clueless. The woman had graduated from the University of Georgia with a hospitality degree. Tracey had given her the job after someone in the Peachtree Cove Business Guild made an offhand comment about their friend's daughter needing a place to work. No, rather than clueless she was brilliant. She could teach a class on how to feign ignorance and play the damsel in distress so others would do your work. Tracey knew what Jessica was up to, but, again, she needed someone there and some help was better than no help.

Sighing, Tracey turned back to the couple. "Last name, please."

"Davis," the man said.

Nodding, Tracey input their name and proceeded to quickly pull up their reservation. Jessica pretended to watch, but when the second couple came in, she gave up the pretense and moved aside to start scrolling through her phone. Tracey got both couples registered, gave them the keys to their room, and then walked them around the inn to explain where the rooms were, when food was served and their access to the grounds. Thirty minutes later, she went back to the reception area to go through the checklist once again with Jessica, except she was nowhere to be found.

Instead, a man leaned against the reception desk. Tracey would recognize his profile anywhere, and she cursed.

"Shit, Brian, my bad," she said as she rushed over to the desk.

Brian Nelson straightened and turned to face her. His face was a mask of boredom. His usual expression, as if everything in the world were so far beneath his interest. He was tall, with dark brown skin, piercing black eyes and curly hair cut into the sharpest fade she'd ever seen. In short, Brian was a pretty boy. Or at least that's what she'd always viewed him as in high school. When he'd moved back to Peachtree Cove and opened a nursery, of all things, she'd been surprised he would bother getting his hands dirty.

"You doing Jessica's job again?" he asked in a deep, lazy drawl.

Tracey narrowed her eyes. "You minding my business again?" She hated it when he pointed out the obvious. Something he tended to do with her and often.

Brian tapped the watch on his wrist. Not the expensive ones he wore when he got pretty-boy fine and she'd see him at the bar or out with a woman—he was always with some new woman—but an older watch with a worn leather strap. It matched the worn jeans that sagged just enough to make him look interesting, dirty Henley shirt that clung to his broad shoulders, and muddy Timberland boots. He must have come from moving shrubs for another job.

"It's my business when you keep me waiting." He spoke in his you-should-know-this-already tone.

Tracey also hated that tone. It unnerved her and made her feel like he was judging. So she did what she always did when Brian Nelson judged her: she pretended she didn't care.

"Whatever," she said and waved a hand. "Did you bring what I need?"

He raised a brow. "I'm here to go over the plans for the wedding and *you* tell me what you need. You haven't picked anything yet?"

Tracey was speechless that he'd forget. Then she cursed and slapped her palm to her forehead. "Damn, my bad. I forgot to give you that."

Between Jessica, the lack of help and navigating her upcoming divorce she was forgetting to do a lot of things. She wouldn't focus on that now. She would get her life together, but first she needed to make sure the wedding this weekend went perfectly. She needed shrubs from Brian's nursery to make that happen.

She lightly slapped his arm. "Come on out back and let me show you the setup."

2

Tracey led Brian out to the yard on the side of the bed and breakfast where she hosted outdoor weddings and other events. She walked quickly, but Brian had no problem keeping up with her. She wished he would linger behind and take his time. She hated being caught off her game, and she hated it even more when it was Brian who was doing it. Maybe because Brian Nelson had been catching Tracey off her game since she was in high school.

She hadn't liked him back then. The good-looking, popular boy that all the girls in school had a crush on. Her included, but she'd known that Brian wouldn't look twice at her. He was raised by well-brought-up parents, lived in a nice house on the good side of town, was a star in both basketball and wrestling, and had a new girlfriend every quarter. She, on the other hand, was the girl brought up in the Section 8 apartments in town, with the alcoholic father and a mother who cheated on him constantly. Tracey's smart mouth constantly got her into trouble at school, and the only guys interested in her were the ones who thought she was just as easy as her mom.

Every time she was in the principal's office for going off on someone for talking about her family, Brian was also there getting praised. Whenever she stumbled over her own two feet marching in JROTC, Brian was there doing a perfect about-face in a freshly pressed uniform. And when she'd accepted Cornell Murphy's invitation to the JROTC ball senior year because she'd foolishly believed he liked her, only for him to try and shove his hand up her dress in the hallway, Brian was the one who'd witnessed the embarrassing moment and her punching Cornell in the stomach so hard he'd thrown up on Tracey's new shoes. Then, as an adult, he'd been the first person to notice Bernard, her soon-to-be ex-husband, was cheating.

Yep, most of her embarrassing moments in high school were witnessed by Brian, and he'd continued to witness more when he'd moved back to Peachtree Cove as an adult. Which meant it was par for the course that he would be there just as she ran back into the inn, frustrated and flustered from doing Jessica's job.

"Where's the fire?"

Tracey stopped and spun to face him. "What?"

He gave her the same bland I'm-bored-with-this look that he always wore. Except this time a raised brow accompanied it. He pointed to her feet. "You're damn near running. I thought maybe something was on fire."

Tracey narrowed her eyes. "Hardy har har. You're so damn funny," she said in a flat voice.

"Why are you upset? It's your own fault."

"What's my own fault?"

He pointed to the back of the inn. Jessica was on her phone at the back corner. "You should have fired her two months ago."

"I need help right now. You, of all people, should know how busy things are."

"If you're doing her job, is it really help?"

Tracey crossed her arms over her chest. "You were in the kitchen with Shirley, weren't you?"

Brian shrugged his shoulders. "Doesn't matter where I was. My point still stands. Jessica isn't doing her job. Even I know that. You're running around here like a chicken with its head cut off doing her work and yours. Get rid of her and hire a real manager."

Tracey took a deep breath. She was not going to curse out Brian. She was not going to kick him off her property. She needed his help, even if she didn't want his very obvious, unsolicited advice.

After she'd calmed herself she asked in an even tone, "Do I come telling you how to run your nursery? No. So worry about that and not about my inn."

"Then, don't keep me waiting next time," he shot back easily.

Tracey shook her head and smirked. "You'll wait because I'm your biggest customer. Now, shut up and listen."

Brian grunted, but the corner of his mouth lifted. Despite him having a first-row seat to the all things embarrassing about Tracey's life show, Brian also refused to let her sharp tongue cut him. Which was why she couldn't quite go from being consistently annoyed with him to straight up disliking him. Brian witnessed her shame, made the occasional offer of advice she didn't want or need, and then moved on. That she appreciated. Other people took joy in reveling in the messed-up stuff in her life. He never did.

"What's the layout?" he asked.

Tracey looked around the yard and envisioned it with the white chairs set up for a small wedding. "The usual. A small wedding. The happy couple will be in the gazebo." She pointed to the wooden structure at the far end of the yard. "There will be about fifty guests. The colors are red and yellow, so I need flowers or shrubs to go with that."

Brian frowned as he considered the yard. Tracey let him do what he did. The side yard for The Fresh Place Inn was cute and quaint, but it wasn't very decorative. Tracey used Brian's nursery to provide the extra pizzazz needed for events. He brought in shrubs and flowers of various colors and sizes to provide natural decoration. Tracey paid him for the temporary use, and then he hauled them away after the wedding was complete.

"I can bring in some gold zebra and maybe some admiration barberry. We can put those around the gazebo."

Tracey nodded. "I don't know what you're saying, but I trust your judgment. Do it."

Brian turned to her with a quizzical look. "You're not going to hand-select the flowers this time?"

She shook her head. "I don't have time. The wedding is this weekend."

His head fell to the side, and his eyes widened. "Saturday?"

"Yeah."

"Tracey," he sighed, looked heavenward then shook his head. "It's Monday, Tracey. You know I need more time to get the plants in."

"I know, but this slipped through the cracks. I thought I'd already booked the shrubs with you, but I didn't."

"What if I can't do it by Saturday?"

Her heart jumped damn near out of her chest. If he couldn't, then the cute side yard she'd promised the bride would not come true. The bride would leave a horrible review. Others would pile on, and the inn would fail. Probably not immediately, but if she kept this up it would.

She clasped her hands together as if praying and held them out to Brian. "If anyone can do it by then it's you. Please, Brian, do this for me." She may not be as easy as her mom, or half as desirable, but she did know that if she batted her eyes and pleaded, her pitiful look sometimes worked on Brian.

Brian rubbed his temple. "How did this slip through? You used to be better organized than this."

"I used to have a good person working next to me, but now I don't. So this is what happens."

He dropped his hand, and his eyes met hers. "Don't do that."

"Do what? Bring up why I had to hire Jessica and important things like booking the flowers for a wedding at my inn slip through the cracks? Why not?"

"You need to let that shit go," he said easily. As if getting over betrayal and heartbreak were something a person could just wake up one morning and say *Yeah, that sucked, but I'm over it now.*

"Well, I can't. You, more than anyone, should also know why I'm struggling here."

His eyes narrowed. "Don't go there."

"Too late. I'm already there. I've set up a chair and got comfortable." She took a few steps closer until there was only a few inches separating them. "So because you know why I'm floundering, with the increased bookings and popularity of Peachtree Cove, you should know that I really need you to do me a solid and get the shrubs here for the wedding on Saturday."

Brian glowered down at her. He had his hands on his hips and his nostrils flared. She had to fight not to smile back at his frustration. She loved frustrating Brian, mostly because his observations frustrated her. He was also cute when he was upset. She liked watching the cool playboy, down-for-whatever facade disappear when she pushed his buttons. And again, he was cute when he was upset. Teenage Tracey liked to come out and play and remind her of the old crush she used to have on him.

"What time is the wedding?" he asked through gritted teeth.

She didn't bother to hold back her smile. "Two in the afternoon."

His eyes narrowed more but he asked, "What time do you need them set up?"

Her cheeks hurt from the grin on her face. "Can you get it set up by eleven?"

He pointed at her. Tracey grabbed his finger and shook it. "Thank you, Brian. You're a lifesaver. And I'll pay you ten percent extra."

He sighed and jerked back on his finger. Tracey let him go. "Get rid of Jessica, get your schedule under control and don't do this again."

She nodded. "I'll get it worked out."

"I'm for real, Tracey. You can't keep going like this. Losing Monique the way you did was messed up, but don't ruin your life trying to prove that you can keep doing this by yourself."

The smile fell off Tracey's face. In the blink of an eye, he'd reminded her why he stayed on her Annoying Person list. "Quit minding my business."

He pointed around the yard. "This last-minute thing makes it my business." He reached over and tweaked her chin before turning and walking away. Full-on swag with his ridiculously long legs and broad shoulders. Damn him!

Tracey gave his back the finger. He looked over his shoulder at the same time and caught it. Then, in Brian Nelson fashion, he grinned, turned away and kept on walking.

3

Brian parked his truck in front of the small modular build-ing that served as the sales office of his nursery. The usual satisfaction and pride he felt when he drove up and saw the greenhouse and rows of plants and shrubs lined up next to the building didn't hit him. He was too distracted.

He shook his head and turned off the truck. Tracey's problems were not his problems. She made it abundantly clear that she did not want or need his help when it came to her life. He got out and slammed the door. His footsteps were heavy as he marched into the office. His office manager, Natalie, sat with the phone held between her shoulder and ear while she tapped away on the laptop on the desk. Natalie was the best manager he could have hired. She understood the business, could calm down any irate customer or vendor, and even understood enough about plants to help him make selections. A good manager was worth their weight in gold. And if Tracey would get off her high horse and find her own perfect assistant, he wouldn't have to rearrange his schedule to find a way to make this fit. Tracey's last-minute request was annoying, but not something he couldn't handle. He couldn't believe she'd forgotten something so important and that she would rather stretch herself thin than to either make Jessica do her job or find someone else who would.

Natalie raised a brow and watched him with curious dark eyes. She was a year older than his thirty-five, white, with dark brown hair that she wore in a short style that stopped at her ears. She was dressed in her typical denim overalls and T-shirt she put on whenever she was working.

"Okay, Mr. Davenport, I'll be sure to call you back when we get more azaleas. You have a great day. Bye-bye." She ended the call, crossed her arms and frowned at him. "What's wrong with you?"

"Two guesses," Brian said. He went over to the water cooler in the corner and filled one of the small paper cups in the attached dispenser.

"Hmm…did someone order something, and when you delivered they said it wasn't right?"

"Nope." Brian drained the cup in one swallow.

Natalie tipped her head to the side. "Your ex-wife called again?"

Brian scowled but shook his head. "I blocked her number."

Natalie shrugged. "She always finds a way to get through."

She did, which was why Brian consistently screened his phone calls. He didn't know why Renee insisted on calling him and pretending like they were still cool when they were not and never would be. But that was just like his ex. She didn't take no for an answer or back down. Including when it came to accepting that things were over between them. Even though he accepted that he was partially to blame for that.

"Then, I'm out of guesses," Natalie said. She sat back in her chair.

"I'm surprised you can't guess. We've got a surprise order for The Fresh Place Inn."

Natalie sighed and shook her head. "Tracey forgot to call with another order again?"

"She did."

Natalie sat forward and made a few clicks on the laptop. Probably to bring up their inventory so she could quickly check and see if they had what Tracey needed. "When's the wedding?"

"This Saturday." Brian crumpled the cup and tossed it in the trash.

Natalie made a tsking sound, and pity filled her eyes. "I want to be mad, but then when I think about the circumstances..." She balled her hand into a fist.

"Nope. Nah, we're not doing that. Her circumstances happened almost a year ago."

"But still. That's a lot to get over. Her husband cheating with her manager right under her nose. And then getting the woman pregnant! Then she has to get rid of him, hire a new manager and deal with all the reservation requests because of the small-town designation. That's a lot."

"That's life. She can't keep burying her head in the sand. Besides, she's better off without that guy. This is her time to shine."

Natalie narrowed her eyes. "You always act upset when you really want to help her. So stop complaining and tell me what she needs. I'll get with Pat so he can deliver the shrubs."

"I can complain because I'm helping her." He moved toward his office.

"Just tell her you like her and get it over with," Natalie said with a laugh.

Brian looked over his shoulder. "I don't like her. I'm a small nursery, and she's one of my best customers so I can't piss her off. Besides, I can't stand seeing people ruin their own lives."

He went into his office and shut the door before Natalie could give another reply. Natalie was too damn insightful. He did like Tracey, always had. He'd always found her attractive and interesting. She was sexy. Large dark eyes, warm brown skin, full breasts and an ass that would make any man bite his lower lip combined with a sassy attitude that called to a primitive part of him. What was there not to like about her? She spoke what was on her mind, wasn't afraid of confrontation and had overcome so much. He'd been in awe of her brashness and don't-give-a-fuck attitude when they were in school. When he'd returned to Peachtree Cove after his divorce, he hadn't been surprised to see she was opening a new bed and breakfast, despite town gossips saying she would fail. He had been surprised to find out she'd married Bernard Thompson, of all people. A stuck-up, judgmental, boring guy Brian had forgotten existed until he'd moved back to Peachtree Cove.

Then to learn the most boring guy in town was cheating on the most interesting person he'd known growing up had thrown Brian for a loop. A part of him understood how hard it was to leave a bad relationship. He'd been there. His disaster of a marriage with Renee had been nothing but loud arguments and tantrums followed by almost euphoric make-up sessions fueled with sex and weed. He'd sworn that was love, even though his dad told him over and over that it wasn't. Then Renee cheated when he'd come home for his dad's funeral, and Brian realized his dad had been right. He needed to get his life in order, and staying married to Renee wasn't the way to do it.

So why couldn't Tracey do the same? And why was he so obsessed with figuring out why she couldn't break out of the funk caused by her ex-husband?

"You know why," he mumbled out loud.

Guilt. That was why. He'd been the first one to see what was happening. The first person to bring it to her attention. And he'd been there the day it had all come crashing down. He didn't regret her finding out the truth, but he did feel bad about being the one to bring it to her attention. He'd forever be connected with the start of the end of her marriage.

His cell phone rang. He glanced at the screen and cringed. The number was unknown but was coming from Southern California. More than likely Renee. He sent the call to voice mail. If it was her, then he'd block that number, too.

He searched for his friend Quinton's number. Q answered after the third ring. "Brian, what's up?"

"Just got back from a few deliveries. Checking to see what you're up to tonight. Want to check out the game at Cyril's bar?"

"Oh man, I would, but I've got something going on with Halle tonight."

"What do y'all got going on?" He tried to hide his disappointment, but some of it slid into his tone. In the year since Quinton and Halle had started dating, his friend was always doing something with his Halle, or with Halle and their daughter, Shania.

"Well, Shania is staying at her cousin Kayla's house so we're going to go out, have a drink and enjoy the time alone." The smile was evident in his friend's voice.

"Didn't you all go out a few days ago?" Brian remembered because he'd called Q and asked him about going out for drinks then.

"Yeah, when my parents were hanging with Shania."

"Things are better now, right? Now that your parents have their own place. You and Halle get more time together."

When Quinton's parents first moved to Peachtree Cove, they lived with him and limited the amount of alone time he had with Halle. Brian understood wanting to spend time with your lady, but Quinton was never available. Brian was about to think he'd never get a chance to hang with his boy.

"Things are better, but you know how it is. Gotta enjoy the moments we can get together."

Brian struggled not to roll his eyes. He didn't want to hate on his friend and his new relationship. He liked Halle and he was glad that she, Quinton and their daughter were finding a way to make their unorthodox family work. But with the new relationship, Brian had lost his hanging partner. Cyril was his other friend, but he only saw him when he was working at his bar. When he wasn't working, he was spending time with his fiancée, Imani, planning their wedding. Now they were looking at him like he should get paired up.

"I thought you had a date tonight?" Quinton asked in a way that implied Brian shouldn't be upset about Quinton having other plans.

"Angelica," Brian said remembering the woman his older brother introduced him to at a bar in Atlanta the weekend before. Brian had embraced bachelorhood after his divorce, but his brother had completely embraced the life of playboy bachelor from the moment he'd noticed women had tits and that all tits didn't look the same. His brother had never acted foolish over a woman.

"Yeah, I told her I might swing through, but I'm not feeling it."

"Why not? I thought y'all hooked up?"

Brian leaned back in his chair. "We did, but right after she asked me what I wanted from her. I mean, we just met. I don't know where things are going."

Quinton grunted. "So she basically rang the death knell on anything else happening with you two?"

"Aye, man, I'm not that bad."

"But you also aren't trying to answer the where-is-this-going question with anyone either."

Brian shrugged and nodded. His friend had a point. "True, but I'm always up-front about that. I told her that I wasn't looking for anything serious, and she said cool."

"Then, what's the problem?"

"She looked disappointed before saying she was cool. A sure sign that she said she was good with casual but isn't. Which means sleeping with her again is a trap. I'm not looking for a relationship, but I'm also not trying to play with her feelings."

"Well, if she doesn't work out, I'm sure you've got someone else you can call."

Brian did. He had a few women who were just as good with his let's-just-hook-up lifestyle, but he wasn't feeling that tonight. He wasn't going to tell Quinton that. People happy in relationships tended to take any sign of a single person not being completely happy with being single as an invitation to start trying to get them committed to someone.

"We'll see. I just thought we could hang. But it's no big deal."

"Another day," Quinton said.

"Sure thing. Tell Halle I said what's up."

He dialed Angelica's number. It only took a brief conversation to cancel his plans to meet up. She sounded disappointed, but not so much so that Brian felt guilty. He considered calling his brother, but he wasn't in the mood to hear DeWayne say he needed to find a new person to warm his bed. As an investment banker his brother's days were spent making money, trying to help his family get better with money and dating casually. Brian didn't feel like hearing a lecture about how he needed to be saving for retirement or the reasons he should find a casual hookup to blow off steam. Brian wasn't in the mood for a casual hookup either. Maybe it was because he'd been surprised by Tracey at the end of the long day. Seeing firsthand what a bad relationship could do to throw off a capable person soured his mood. He'd rather be alone.

4

Tracey sat with her hands clenched in her lap as she waited
for the judge to decide how difficult or easy her life was going
to become. Her divorce from Bernard should have been easy.
The asshole had cheated and gotten another woman pregnant.
A classic open-and-shut case of why they no longer needed
to be married. Except he'd doubled down on being not just a
bad husband but also a bad person. Not only did he want to
keep their house so he could have a place to raise his kid—the
jerk—but he also claimed that he had a right to claim earnings from The Fresh Place Inn. That's what made her want to
pull a Bernadine from the classic movie *Waiting to Exhale* and
set his car on fire.

Bernard had *nothing* to do with helping her business. If anything, he'd been a hindrance. First claiming that she didn't
have the time or ability to open a bed and breakfast, and then
when she'd figured things out and made it work, claiming her

work at the bed and breakfast was part of the reason why he'd cheated in the first place. For him to dare try and say he had any part in it meant the man she'd been married to and loved for eleven years was a stranger. The Bernard she'd fallen in love with wouldn't do her like this.

Jasmine Evans, her lawyer, reached over and placed a hand on Tracey's knee. Tracey stopped bouncing her leg. Jasmine gave her a soft pat before balling her fist and giving Tracey a we-got-this fist bump.

Tracey tried to smile, but the churning in her stomach made her grimace. Every time her life seemed to be going well, something happened to set her back.

"After reviewing the information submitted by both parties," Judge Feaster said, "I've decided that the house located at 234 Emory Lane is dual property. It is to be sold and the proceeds split between both parties."

Tracey sat forward. "What?" She didn't care about losing the house. She'd moved out and into her bed and breakfast not long after finding out about Bernard's affair, but if this was how things were starting, did it mean they would have to split everything?

Jasmine placed a hand on her arm. "Wait," she said in a *Please be patient* tone.

Tracey swallowed hard and sat back. She glared over at Bernard, but he wasn't looking her way. Instead, he grinned at the judge as if he'd just granted the first of his three wishes.

"This is some bullshit," Tracey mumbled under her breath. Jasmine cut her eyes, and Tracey tried to look apologetic.

Ignoring her outburst, the judge continued talking. "As for Mr. Thompson's claim that he has stake in the bed and breakfast known as The Fresh Place Inn, I see no evidence supporting that claim. The home was sold to Ms. Thompson by Mr. Leon Sullivan. He clearly stated prior to his death that the home was for her use, and her use alone, as long as she saw fit. Ms.

Thompson also received the bank loan to start the business on her own, and there is no evidence supporting Mr. Thompson's claim that he assisted in any way with starting the business."

"Your honor," Bernard's slimy lawyer spoke up. She was sleek and was known as one of the best divorce attorneys in the area. "By virtue of being her husband he supported the business."

The judge shot her a look over his glasses. "Being married to a person does not automatically mean they support the other's endeavors. You and I both see that every day in this courtroom. Either way, his claim is denied. Ms. Thompson keeps all interest and money from the running of the inn. All other assets will be split as follows."

Tracey didn't even pay attention as the judge went through the remaining division of items she and Bernard had owned together. So what if she got the car and he kept the rental property they'd purchased at a tax sale together? She had her inn! It was hers, free and clear, and Bernard wouldn't get to lay a single finger on any of the earnings. It was the only good news out of this entire divorce.

After the hearing, Tracey held out her hand to shake Jasmine's. "Thank you so much. I don't think I could have gotten through this without you."

"You would have, but my job is to make it easier. Tracey, I know he hurt you, but don't let him break you. You're a lot stronger than you give yourself credit for. That and half of the people in town are rooting for you. Never forget that he did *you* wrong."

Tracey smiled. Damn her eyes for burning. She was not a crier. Crying got you nowhere, but ever since Bernard had busted up her life and proven that she was never going to have the kind of supportive, loving relationship that she'd dreamed of, she understood that people supported her in this messy breakup. The good folks of Peachtree Cove had to take a side. But support didn't change the fact that most people hadn't believed it when Tracey, daughter of the town whore and drunk, had married Bernard, beloved straight-A student and all-around good guy. They'd always assumed she and Bernard wouldn't make it, and they'd been right. They just hadn't bet that Bernard would be the reason and not Tracey.

"Thank you, Jasmine. I appreciate that. And that you fought like hell for me to keep the business. I don't even care about the house as long as I keep The Fresh Place Inn."

"You deserve to keep it. All the work you put in. Not only that but being named the best place to stay in Peachtree Cove after we won Best Small Town…that's the only reason he wanted any part of it, and I wasn't going to let him take that, too."

Tracey's cell phone chimed. She lifted the device and smiled at the text on the screen. It was a group chat with her two best friends, Halle and Imani.

How did it go? Did you get it all?!? Imani asked.

"It's good to see you smile," Jasmine said.

"It's my friends. They're texting me about how the hearing went."

Jasmine nodded. "Talk with them. And be sure to celebrate. I'll give you a call later."

"I will. Thanks, Jasmine." She looked back at her phone and texted back.

I got the inn. That's all that matters.

Hell yes! with a fist emoji came from Halle.

We gotta celebrate! came from Imani.

Tracey's hand hovered over the screen. She should celebrate. She was happy to be done with Bernard. She did not want him back, but she wasn't in a celebratory mood. The ending of the marriage she'd shared with her dream man left her feeling a little sad.

Another text popped up before she could reply to her friends. I'll do the wedding Saturday.

From Brian along with a picture of the perfect plant to match her color scheme. Tracey grinned, and tears threatened her eyes again. There was at least one man in the world outside of her brother that she could depend on.

"Brian, you always come through," she said on a shaky laugh.

"Texting your boy again."

Tracey's shoulders stiffened. She straightened and turned to face Bernard. "In case you didn't realize it, the judge literally just broke us up. Why the hell are you over here bothering me?"

She wasn't even going to address his *your boy* comment. Bernard had hated on her working with Brian from the start. He'd never liked Brian. He either called him a washed-up pretty boy or accused him of working with Tracey because he was interested in her. Tracey hadn't believed either accusation. Brian was, and would continue to be, a good-looking man, but he wasn't interested in Tracey. But knowing working with him irritated Bernard, she'd kept their business arrangement. That, and he was damn good at his job.

Bernard gave her the look of irritation that had been a permanent fixture on his face in the last year of their marriage. He still was handsome, the bastard. Polished and refined, with his wire-framed glasses, golden-brown skin and gym-toned body. She'd once believed she was the luckiest woman to have him not only notice her but want to marry her. She'd known for a while they were ending, but her refusal to be a failure at marriage like her parents had kept her holding on. The look hurt now just like it had every other time, but she would never let him see how much he'd broken her.

"I came to wish you well. Despite everything, I don't hate you, Tracey." He held out his hand as if she should shake it. She didn't take his hand. Hell, he was lucky she didn't slap it away.

"Funny, I'm not sure I can say the same thing about my feelings toward you."

He cocked his head to the side. "You don't hate me."

She sucked in a breath. He'd given her *the look*. The look that used to always make her stomach clench and her heart flip. The look he'd given her when she couldn't believe a guy like him would ever want a loud-mouth, ready-to-fight, wrong-side-of-the-tracks girl like her. The look had won her over then and hundreds of times since. But the look no longer had the same effect. Her heart was encased in steel, surrounded by barbed wire and protected by a moat of molten lava. He'd never get close to it again.

"I don't love you anymore, Bernard. Go be with your new family." Her voice hitched on the word *family*. The thing he'd denied them for so long. Always saying the time wasn't right to have kids. That they weren't financially ready or they wouldn't be able to spend as much time together. Problems he didn't have when he'd knocked up her former employee.

The smug look on his face melted into one of disappointment. "Hard core to the end, huh."

"Always," she replied, lifting her chin.

He scoffed, scratched his chin then nodded. "See you around, Tracey." He turned, and then she called his name. It was pointless and foolish, but before she could stop herself, the one question she'd never asked bubbled up.

"Why, Bernard? Why did you do this to us?"

He shrugged before pointing to the chamber they'd just left. "In case you forgot, you filed for divorce."

Tracey rolled her eyes. Yes, she'd filed for divorce, but he'd ruined their marriage. For him to act as if their break was ultimately her fault was the most absurd thing she'd ever heard. "I did file for divorce, but you gave me no choice. Why did you do this to me?"

He hesitated for a second, a hint of the old affection he once felt flashed in his eyes, then they focused on her face and it went away. "You stopped being fun, Tracey."

She frowned. "What?"

"When we first met, you were fun. You were different. Then we got married, and you wanted to be like some fake married couple on TV." He shook his head. "That's not who I married."

"I'm fun." But even she didn't sound convinced. The things that had made her so-called fun back then had been her protection methods. The quick attitude, being ready to defend herself or her family if needed, the I-don't-care persona so people wouldn't get close enough to hurt her. Except he'd gotten close. He'd made her think she could feel safe, protected. She'd been neither.

The look he gave her was pitiful. "Sure, Tracey." He turned and walked away. This time, she didn't call him back.

Although Tracey appreciated her friends' willingness to celebrate her divorce, she opted to tell them there was an emergency at the inn that she needed to handle, and they'd celebrate that weekend. But there was no emergency. Jessica would have to figure out how to handle the couple of guests they had for a Wednesday night. That, and she'd also scheduled her other desk attendant to work. Dinner was going to be covered by Shirley, and she hadn't planned any activities or entertainment for the guests because she'd known that on the day of her divorce settlement she'd either be too upset or too busy celebrating to focus on the needs of any guests.

So instead of hanging out with her friends or going to work, Tracey drove to Augusta and checked out a bar that she'd come across on social media. An influencer she liked recommended their drinks, low-key atmosphere and reasonable prices. It was a place she'd longed to visit for over a year. A place she'd once asked Bernard to visit with her, but he'd refused, saying that they didn't have the time to go to Augusta and hang out at a bar. The words hadn't made sense then, but now that she knew he was spending his time making a baby with a whole other woman, she understood what he'd really meant.

The bar was just as nice as described on social media. The crowd wasn't too big, but not as thin as she'd expected on a Wednesday night. Instead of staying inside she opted to check out the rooftop portion. Up there a guy with a guitar crooned out hits from the nineties and two thousands. A few couples and girlfriends mingled either on the couches or at tables set up by the rectangular bar. Four people lined the bar.

She ordered a lemon drop martini and then snatched up an empty table in the back corner of the rooftop. Away from the soloist and other couples, slightly hidden in the shadows. The spot matched her mood. She was better off without Bernard. She wouldn't take him back if he showed up at her house the next morning with two dozen roses, a hundred pieces of gold and an excuse for bad behavior signed by Jesus. He'd hurt her and done the one thing she'd always asked him not to do.

I'll never blindside you or make a fool of you, Tracey. We won't be like your parents.

Except he had blindsided her. Multiple times. He had turned them into a sequel of her parents' relationship. Not just from the lies or the cheating but by making them a scandal. She'd never again wanted her name to be in the Peachtree Cove rumor mill. He knew how much she hadn't wanted that, but there she was. Back in the rumor mill and because of him.

Sighing, she took a long sip of her drink. She should have ordered a second. This wasn't going to be enough to douse the fire of her anger.

The door to the rooftop opened. Another couple came out. Tracey looked away. She wasn't big on seeing happy couples. But her eyes jerked back then widened. "Brian?" she said. The musician had just stopped his song, and Tracey's voice carried across the rooftop.

Brian looked up from the woman next to him. He had his arm hooked around her shoulders. He'd been smiling at her. The smile of a man who was confident that he knew where his night was going. His eyes met Tracey's and widened then narrowed as his brows drew together. He spoke a few words to the woman. She gave Tracey a curious look, but whatever she saw must not have concerned her because she gave Tracey a *whatever* smile before kissing Brian and going to the bar.

Brian crossed the rooftop to her. "Tracey? What are you doing here?"

"There you go minding my business again," she said, flipping her braids over her shoulder.

He cocked his head to the side. "You're the one who called out my name like I'd done something wrong."

"I did not. I was just surprised to see you."

"This is my hangout spot. I've come here a few times, which is how I know that seeing you here is a surprise."

She sighed. "I can't leave Peachtree Cove and check out a place? I'm good. Go back to whatever you were doing." She turned away and sipped her drink.

Brian sat in the chair opposite of her, concern and curiosity in his eyes as he watched her. She wanted to squirm but settled for shifting slightly in her seat. This man always had an up-close and personal view of her whenever she was at a low point in her life.

"For real, as a friend. You good?"

"We're friends?" she tossed back.

"Quit playing, Tracey. I just changed my whole weekend around to accommodate your need for bushes at that wedding. I wouldn't do that if we weren't."

"You're a businessman. You're doing this because it's a good business move."

"I'm doing this because you're my friend. You were frazzled Monday about covering the wedding, and now you're up here drinking alone in a dark corner. So I need to know if you're good."

"I'm good."

His eyes narrowed. "Tell me the truth. Not that bravado you put up. Where are Imani and Halle? Why aren't they here with you?"

"Damn, do I have to have chaperones when I hang out?"

"Tracey?" he said in a *Quit playing* voice. His patience was growing thin. She could keep pushing him, but she didn't want to. He was being nice.

Sighing, Tracey took another sip then answered. "My divorce was finalized today. I'm celebrating." She lifted her glass.

He let out a breath and grinned. "Good."

"Good?"

"You're better off without him."

"I am." She couldn't deny that, but that didn't mean he had to sound satisfied. As if she'd done something great. She was curious to know what he thought, but Brian's opinion on her relationships shouldn't matter. Plus, she already knew Brian didn't care for Bernard.

"Why aren't you celebrating with Halle and Imani? I heard them planning your I'm Free party at Cyril's bar, so I know they should be up here with you."

Tracey shrugged. "They're in new relationships and happy. I don't begrudge my friends, but I'm not feeling overly confident in love right now. I just needed some time to process before we properly celebrate later."

She waited to see if he'd judge her. If he'd say that she was being petty or jealous because she didn't want to hang with her friends. She was happy for both Halle and Imani. Hell, Imani's wedding was going to be at her bed and breakfast that fall, but while her friends were at the start of new love they weren't the crowd she needed as she mourned the loss of her own love. She'd only bring them down.

"I can understand that."

"You can?"

"Yeah. After my divorce, I didn't want to hang with my boys who were still in relationships. I just wanted to let go and get back out there. They wanted that for me, too, but they were not the best wingmen."

Tracey sat up straight and nodded. "Right! Like, I want to talk about how men suck. They can't do that. They found good men. They're happy. I'm not in a not-all-men-suck mood."

The corner of his lips lifted in a small smile. "I wasn't in a not-all-women-suck mood either."

She was glad that he hadn't taken offense to what she'd said. She understood all men weren't horrible, but right now, she needed a ticket on the Men Suck train.

"What about now?" she asked.

"Now I can admit that not all women are like my ex-wife. But I'm still not ready to tie myself to one until death do us part. Not feeling marriage again."

"Me either."

Again, he smiled. Again, teenage Tracey popped up and reminded her about the crush she used to have on Brian. He looked good tonight. All moisturized and put-together in a tan shirt that clung to his broad shoulders and arms, and dark jeans. She'd heard he'd modeled when he was away from Peachtree Cove...well, heard and then looked him up online. He had modeled, and she had appreciated the way he looked in a pair of briefs.

"You'll bounce back. You always do." Brian reached over and gently nudged her hand.

Tracey blinked and blocked the mental images of Brian modeling underwear. "How do you know that?"

"I've known you most of my life. I've seen you bounce back from a lot of things."

Tracey groaned and rubbed her temple. "I almost forgot, you've been there for all my humiliating moments."

"I saw you go through some things that would bring other people down, but not you. That's how I know you'll get through this."

"I'm tired of being strong," she mumbled.

"Then, lean on your friends when you need to."

She smirked. "Friends like you?" She took a sip of her drink.

His gaze never left hers. "You can lean on me if you need to."

"Really? So if I asked you to dip out on your date and keep me company tonight, you would?" she teased.

"In a hot minute," he said quickly.

Tracey laughed. Brian didn't. He watched her seriously. Was he serious? She glanced at the bar. The woman he'd come in with darted glances their way. Brian hadn't looked to check on her once. His focus remained solely on her. Tracey's face heated. She was tempted. A big part of her wanted to ask him to do just that. Dump his date and be her wingman for the night. Show her that there was life after divorce. That she wasn't boring and that she could find the spark that made her interesting again. The idea made her heart race. And deeper than that, it tapped into a hidden territorial part of her. A part that made her want to pretend she had a claim on Brian and that would stroke her ego to watch the woman at the bar who'd looked at her as if she were nothing realize she'd underestimated Tracey. That Tracey still had enough fire to pull a guy like Brian.

She blinked and shook her head. Those thoughts were dangerous. "Thanks, but I'm good. I'm going to have this drink, maybe another, and then I'm done."

"You sure? You're okay?"

She smiled and nodded. "I'm good. But thank you, friend."

He grinned and sighed. "Alright. I'll call you tomorrow about the wedding."

"Until tomorrow."

Brian watched her for another second then got up and went back to the bar. She ordered another drink and an order of potato skins. She sat in her corner, stared at the sky and finished her food. When she asked for her bill, the bartender told her it had already been handled. She glanced over at Brian, still cuddled up with the woman at the bar. He met her eyes and lifted his chin. Smiling, Tracey nodded and then left.

5

By the time Tracey started work the next day she was out of her funk and ready to look forward. She'd taken a day to mourn the end of her marriage but had woken up feeling light and free. The inn was all hers. Bernard had no say in her life anymore. That was worth celebrating. After making sure the cleaning crew had handled the rooms and that the guests were taken care of, she sat down with Shirley to look over the menu for a wedding scheduled a few weeks out. Shirley had met with the bride the day before to discuss the menu while Tracey was out.

Tracey glanced over the list, frowned, and then looked up at Shirley. "They want spaghetti?"

Shirley shrugged and shook her head. "As an option for the kids in attendance."

"But we don't serve spaghetti."

"I know, but I can make up a little bit. You got the attendee list, right? There aren't a lot of kids coming."

Tracey sighed and opened the portfolio on the large granite-topped island in the kitchen. She scanned the attendee list. "There are about eight, I think."

"I can make enough spaghetti for eight kids."

"What about the other stuff they want for the wedding?"

"Piece of cake. They're doing heavy hors d'oeuvres. It really won't be a problem."

Tracey rubbed her temple. "It can't be that easy. I feel like something will go wrong. If we do a special order for one wedding we'll have to do them for multiple."

Shirley placed a comforting hand on Tracey's back. "Nothing is going to go wrong. Special orders aren't a bad thing as long as we can handle the request. This isn't our first wedding, and it won't be the last."

"I should have been here. I feel like I'm not on top of things like this. If I'd been here we could have told her no spaghetti."

Shirley patted Tracey's back. "You've got a lot going on right now. You're still on top of things. And, seriously, spaghetti won't kill me. Now, if we can get Jessica on top of things, then we'll really be in good shape."

Tracey groaned. She'd gotten an email from her other desk attendant complaining about Jessica the night before. Jessica had spent half the night acting as if she didn't know how to handle customer requests and the other half disappearing to talk on her phone. Something else that wouldn't have happened if Tracey had been there. Jessica at least tried to pretend to care when Tracey was around.

"I've got to do something about her, don't I?"

Shirley nodded. "Eventually, you do. You can't keep doing her job and yours."

"I know. It took a long time to find someone, before she was recommended. Who knows how long it'll take to find a replacement?"

"Having nobody fill the position is better than a person who isn't even trying."

The sound of heels in the hallway preceded a woman's low-pitched voice calling, "Tracey? You back there?"

Tracey closed her eyes and suppressed a groan. Her mother. "Why is she here?"

Shirley gave one more pat on Tracey's back before pushing away from the island. "Probably because she wants to check on you."

"I don't need checking up on," Tracey shot back.

Shirley gave her a doubtful look. "You may not think so, but I think you deserve a little checking on."

Tracey's mom stopped at the door of the kitchen. She spotted her daughter, frowned and put her hands on her hips. "Tracey, you heard me calling you. Why didn't you answer? Hey, Shirley."

Her mom threw up a hand at Shirley before coming farther into the kitchen. Loretta's eyes skimmed over Tracey from head to toe. Her mom looked great, as usual. She guessed happiness did that to a person. Her dark brown skin was slightly lined, and thanks to a late-in-life discovery of a love for CrossFit, of all things, her curvy figure was snatched in just the right spots. Well, thanks to CrossFit and laser liposuction paid for by her latest boyfriend.

"You knew I was back here." Tracey leaned forward to accept her mom's quick hug. "No need to go shouting through my place of business. I do have guests staying here."

Her mom placed a manicured hand over her mouth. "Oh, I'm sorry. It's Thursday, I didn't think anyone would be checked in until later."

"You know people don't just stay here on the weekends, right?"

"I guess you're right. Anyway, Tracey Denise Thompson, why didn't you call me yesterday and tell me what happened at the settlement?" Her mom's eyes narrowed. "That bastard didn't get his hands on this bed and breakfast, did he?"

Tracey shook her head. "No, he did not. Thankfully, the judge realized his claim on The Fresh Place Inn was as bogus as his regret over the end of our marriage."

Her mom squealed and held up a hand. Tracey slapped palms with her mom. The corner of her lip lifting slightly. Despite wishing her mom hadn't just popped in on her, today she was ready to celebrate her divorce and Bernard not getting his trifling hands on her inn.

"Thank the Good Lord above," her mom said and crossed her heart and then looked to the sky. "You know, Raymond and I prayed for you every Sunday."

Tracey held up a hand. "I really don't need your boyfriend praying for me."

Tracey accepted that her parents were never going to be relationship models, but she also wasn't going to cuddle up to Raymond, her mom's boyfriend, as if he were her stepdad or something. She didn't understand her parents' relationship. They kept claiming they would get a divorce but never actually did the paperwork. Their current separation was going on two years, and her mom had been with Raymond since before the split.

Her mom cocked her head to the side. "Don't be like that. We both wanted what was best for you. Especially when it came to that damn Bernard. I told you that man wasn't any good for you."

"You've never thought any man was good enough for me, Mom."

"That's because I know men ain't shit most of the time. Your daddy is proof of that."

Tracey held up a finger. "No bashing Daddy."

Her mom rolled her eyes. "I'm not bashing him. I'm stating nearly thirty years of the truth."

"He's sober now."

Her mom raised a brow. "For how long? I'll believe it when I see it consistently."

Tracey took a deep breath. "He's sober for you." He'd stopped drinking eighteen months after her mom left this last time. She was hoping this time would stick.

"I don't know why—I'm not going back to him."

"Then, you should try this magic thing called a divorce," Tracey said with fake enthusiasm. "I just did it, and it works out fine."

Her mom cut her eyes. "When he pays for it, I'll get it."

Tracey shook her head. Her dad wasn't going to pay for a divorce. He still thought his wife would come home. Why shouldn't he? She'd stuck around and come home all those years before when he'd been drunk and unreliable most of the time. He didn't realize that this time was different. Raymond's wife had passed, and Raymond had moved her mom in six months after that. Tracey's dad still held out hope that his wife was coming back to him, but she wasn't sure if there was any love left on her mom's part.

"Whatever. You and Daddy's messed-up relationship is yours."

Unfazed by Tracey's words, Loretta continued. "What are you going to do now? You about to get back out there?"

"For what? I'm trying to focus on my business. Not get back out there."

Her mom shook her head. Eyes filled with disappointment. "That's your problem."

"I don't have a problem."

"Yes, you do. You left my house, went to college and only dated that damn Bernard. All because he was the exact opposite of your daddy, when I could tell he wasn't worth a damn when it came to the long game. You never figured out who you were and what you liked. You just lost yourself in that man."

"I didn't lose myself."

"Yes, you did. And I know why. I get it. Me and your dad were not the picture of a perfect relationship, but, Tracey, no relationship is perfect. You were trying too hard to be what Bernard wanted when all he wanted from the get-go was to walk on the wild side with you."

Tracey fought not to flinch. Her mom's words hit the sore spot Bernard's accusation the day before had created. "It wasn't like that."

"Yes, it was. He was so uptight even when y'all were in high school. I've been the wild side for enough men to know when that's what they're looking for. You were his, and when the ride wasn't as fun, he moved on to another ride."

"Mom…"

"I'm just being real. Don't cry any tears for him, and don't let what he did keep you from going out there and living your life how you want to now."

"We just finalized the divorce."

"So? He *just* had a baby with another woman while you were still married. Don't worry about what anyone thinks. You may not have liked the way I lived, but I hope it taught you one thing. Worrying about being what other people want you to be will only make you miserable. You've only got the one life. Go out there and figure out what you want yours to be. Have fun. Make the gossips talk. Create a scandal. At the end of the day, it'll be alright."

Brian got home after seven. They hadn't been too busy at the nursery, with just a few locals coming through looking for some items to spruce up their yards, but steady enough to make the day go by quickly. The spring rush was ending, and the closer they got to summer more people were either done with their yard projects or the weather was getting too hot for them to want to work outside.

The day may not have been bad, but he was going to feel the effects. His back was sore from pretending he was still as flexible as he'd been in his twenties when he'd tried to lift a potted shrub without help. He'd never do that again. His arms itched from the sand that had spilled out of a torn bag onto him when he'd loaded it on the back of a truck.

The minute he'd crossed his threshold, dreams of a long shower, clean clothes and a hot meal had filled his head. Shower and clothes he could handle; the hot meal on the other hand was a problem. He had nothing in the house to cook, and he did not feel like grabbing a bag of greasy fast food. He was running through his options for supper after his shower when his cell phone rang.

Smiling when he saw his mom was calling, he answered the phone. "What's up, pretty lady?"

His mom chuckled on the other end like she always did. Gretchen was a lady of grace and character. He didn't know how someone as beautiful, sweet and kind as her had ever had a kid like him. Everyone said Brian was more like his dad. Brian couldn't argue with that. Growing up he'd heard over and over again how he was the spitting image of his father. His father had been his hero, but his mom was more than that. All he ever wanted was to never disappoint her and to make her proud. He'd fallen short for a little bit after college, in his eyes at least. But his mom, saint that she was, would never agree with him.

"Are you just getting home from work?" she asked.

"I am. Just got out of the shower. Now I'm trying to figure out what I want to eat for dinner."

"I made a pot of turkey neck bones and rice today."

Brian immediately perked up. His dinner problem was solved. He didn't make it a habit to eat at his mom's house every night, but he wasn't going to turn down a perfectly good meal when she offered. "I'll be there in a few minutes."

His mom laughed. "I'll have your plate ready."

Twenty minutes later he was sitting at Gretchen's kitchen table with a plate of perfectly seasoned turkey neck bones and rice in front of him. Even though it was nearly eight, his mom was still dressed in a pair of light blue slacks and a matching top. He'd bet his business she'd changed from a housecoat to what she now wore when he said he was coming over. If he hadn't been so hungry that his mind was only focused on food, he would have told her not to make a big deal. Not that she would listen. His mom liked to be *presentable* even around friends and family.

"Mom, sit down. You don't have to hover," Brian said with a grin. She stood next to him, watching expectantly for him to take a bite.

"I want to make sure you're good before I get settled."

Brian took his mom's hand and gently pulled her into the seat next to him at the table. She gave him a *What am I going to do with you* look before sitting down. Since his older brother, DeWayne, stayed in Atlanta, she liked to spoil him.

"It's delicious as always. Now, have a seat. If I need anything I'll get it."

She gave him an approving nod before settling back. Brian had only taken two more bites before she spoke again. "Renee called today," she said politely.

The delicious food stuck in his throat. He wanted to curse but refused to do that in front of his mom. "Why is she calling you?"

"Because she wants to talk to you." His mom's tone remained sweet and calm, but he could feel the judgment just as much as he felt the fork in his hand.

His mom might not say she was disappointed, but Brian could always tell by the expression on her face and the tone of her voice. She'd used the same calm half smile in high school when the principal called because Brian had been caught making out with a girl in the bathroom or the basketball coach called because he'd skipped practice to go partying at the lake. His mom never had to say anything. That look said it all.

Unlike those times before, guilt didn't hit him. Not on this. "We're divorced. I don't have to talk to her." He took another bite of food.

"You were once married, and now she's reaching out to you. I don't think she'd do that if she didn't really need to talk to you."

"You don't know Renee like that," he mumbled. The last time he'd seen her after their divorce, she'd played with his emotions, and it was the absolute end of the phase in his life where Renee could manipulate him.

"Well, whose fault is that?" Again, his mom's voice was Southern-belle sweet, but this time the words cut like a razor.

Brian flinched. He hadn't brought Renee home to meet his mom. Their relationship had been a whirlwind that kept him from finishing his college degree. He'd met Renee at a party, and the sparks had been more than hot. They'd been explosive. They'd hooked up that first night, and their relationship had been nothing but fireworks ever since.

They eloped in Vegas the summer before his senior year of college. He'd moved to Southern California with her instead of taking an internship in Atlanta that would have set him up for a job after graduation. While his brother had been in graduate school earning an MBA, Brian was telling his parents over a video call that he was married and moving.

Brian had called home at first, but both his brother and his dad hadn't held back telling him whenever they spoke that he'd made a mistake. Brian hadn't wanted to expose Renee to their negativity, as he'd viewed it, and on the rare times he visited he didn't bring Renee with him. He'd told himself he was protecting her, but honestly, he was afraid that if he went home with her, his family would see just how toxic their relationship really was, and he hadn't been ready to face that himself.

"All I'm saying is that she doesn't know you well enough to call you," Brian argued back with a little heat.

"You may think that, but I was her mother-in-law."

Brian twisted his lips and raised a brow. His mom lifted her shoulders. "What? Just because I only talked to her over video calls doesn't mean I wasn't. Divorce broke you two up, but I'm still like a mother figure. If she needs help, I can't turn her away."

Brian dropped his fork onto his plate and placed his hands over his eyes. "She has her own mom that she can call. She's only calling you because she knows that I don't want to talk to her. What does she want? Did she call and ask for money?"

His mom placed a hand on his forearm. He dropped his hands and met her eyes. "She didn't ask for money. Just for me to ask you to call her. She and her husband are having issues. I think he may be leaving her."

"Again, not my problem. She cheated on me, Mom. Remember? I don't owe her anything."

A small frown creased his mom's delicate brow. "Who knows why people do things like that."

Because they're heartless and thrive on drama instead of stability. The bitter thought rang through his head, but he didn't vocalize it. His mom combated bitterness with Bible verses. He did not want to hear about forgiveness when it came to Renee.

"I don't care why," he said instead. "I don't owe her anything."

"She's hurting, and if she's calling us that means she knows you really cared. I'm not asking you to go back to her. I'm just asking you to be a friend."

He wanted to roll his eyes but couldn't do that with his mom. "We're not friends."

"You liked her enough to marry her, so at least answer the call." She patted his arm. "Finish eating, okay?"

That meant the conversation was over. He'd been given his

marching orders and was expected to comply. *Damn!* He cursed in his head then picked up his fork. He didn't want to deal with Renee and her problems anymore. When they'd gotten divorced her problems were no longer his. But that's what she did: found a way to manipulate a situation to her advantage. It's why he'd married her and moved to Southern California to pursue a modeling career, of all things.

"What are you doing this weekend?" Gretchen asked.

"Saturday I'm helping Tracey with a wedding. Nothing on Sunday. Maybe play basketball with Cyril and Quinton. Why, do you need me to do anything?"

She shook her head. "No," she said and sighed. "Poor Tracey. Divorced like that."

His hand froze halfway to his plate. The memory of Tracey drinking alone at the bar in Augusta drifted to his mind. He'd never wanted to ditch a date so much in his life. The need to stay there and keep her company had outweighed the lukewarm attraction he'd felt for the woman he'd been with. But he knew Tracey wouldn't have wanted or appreciated his efforts. She'd view his offer as pity, and she didn't like pity.

"Bernard didn't deserve her," he said.

His mom nodded. "I agree. He hurt her badly. After all she went through with her parents for him to do that was cruel." His mom studied him. "Be nice to her, okay?"

Brian frowned, surprised and a bit offended by the comment. "I'm always nice to Tracey. She's the one most likely to rip my head off."

His mom's lips twitched before she got serious again. "I mean…you're a little, shall we say, loose when it comes to the women you're around."

Brian blinked and sat up straight. Heat filled his cheeks. He wasn't a saint, but he'd tried to keep his devilment out of Peachtree Cove so his mom wouldn't hear. "Huh?"

She patted his arm. "I don't judge. You're getting your wings back after Renee, but be careful with Tracey. She's been through a lot. It's best if you don't go there, and let her heal."

"Mom, I don't like Tracey like that." He did. He would pursue her in a heartbeat, *if* he ever thought she would be interested. But she wasn't. Plus, she deserved better than Bernard—and better than him. He wasn't relationship material. He was one-night stand material.

His mom gave him a *Whatever* kind of smile before patting his shoulder. "If you say so. Just remember what I said." She pointed to the plate. "Finish eating."

6

Tracey raised her glass of beer and grinned at her friends, Imani and Halle, sitting across from her. "Here's to letting go of dead weight."

"Hear, hear!" her friends said together and clinked glasses.

The three of them took long sips of their drinks. Tracey had spent the entire day getting things ready at the inn for the wedding the next day. She was tired and stressed and should probably be asleep, but instead she'd opted to meet up with her friends to celebrate her divorce. They still didn't know she'd gone to Augusta to drink alone the day her divorce was finalized. She was embarrassed enough that Brian had seen her; no need for them to know just how sad and pitiful she'd been. Especially over a guy who didn't deserve her sadness.

"How are you feeling?" Imani asked, concern in her hazel eyes. She worked as an OB-GYN in town and had met them right after work. She still wore the black T-shirt and khaki slacks she usually had on underneath her doctor's coat. A few wisps of hair had escaped the ponytail holding back her long dark hair.

Tracey lifted a shoulder. "I don't know. Am I happy to be rid of him? Yes. If he was ready to go, then I wasn't going to hold on to him. Do I wish things had gone differently? Yes. I didn't marry him thinking that one day we'd break up."

Halle reached over and placed her hand on Tracey's. Halle had ditched the blazer she usually wore while working as the vice principal at the middle school, and a blue-and-white wrap dress hugged her curvy figure. Her curly hair was twisted up in a cute style. "I don't think most people get married thinking things will go bad. This isn't on you, Tracey. It's all on him."

"I know that." She sighed and stared down into her beer. "But…"

Imani groaned. "No *but*s. This isn't on you."

Tracey looked up and met Imani's gaze. "After the hearing, I asked him why."

Halle leaned forward and scowled. "What did he say? The only answer he could give is because he's a damn fool."

Tracey laughed despite herself. Her friends would always be there for her, and she appreciated them for that. "He said that I wasn't fun anymore," she admitted. "He said I wasn't fun anymore."

Imani slapped a hand on the table and sucked in a breath. "What?"

Halle cocked her head to the side and sneered. "No he didn't!"

Tracey nodded. "And then my mom said kind of the same thing. That I lost myself in the marriage and tried to be perfect."

Silence reigned over the table. Halle coughed and looked away. Imani took a long sip of her beer. Tracey's gaze flew back and forth between the two of them. "Wait a second. You aren't saying you agree with her?"

Imani shook her head. "No."

"Well…" Halle said at the same time.

Tracey zeroed in on Halle. "Well, what?"

"I don't know, you did kind of seem like you wanted to have the perfect marriage. And I thought you did."

"But he cheated on me."

She shook her head. "No. His cheating isn't what I'm talking about. *You* wanted to be perfect. Like reality-television perfect. I thought it was cool that you tried for that, but I also felt like you put a lot of pressure on yourself to be someone you thought you should be."

Tracey huffed and leaned back against her seat. "Damn, girl, tell me how you really feel."

Halle reached across the table and squeezed Tracey's hand. "That still doesn't mean what Bernard did was your fault. He messed up and chose to cheat."

"Oh, I know that. But what he said got to me." She stared at the bubbles rising in her beer before sighing. "You're right, Halle, I did want the perfect marriage. I spent the past eleven years of my life trying, and failing, to be the good wife he wanted me to be. What am I supposed to do now?"

Imani lifted a shoulder. "What do you want to do?"

Tracey sipped her beer, a tart sour that matched her mood. She had no idea what to do. She'd opened the bed and breakfast, and despite the issues with Jessica, things were going great. She'd thought she'd had it all. A successful career and a decent marriage. That was supposed to be her end game.

"And don't think small," Imani said as if reading her thoughts. "Think big, Tracey. You can do what you want without worrying about what Bernard or anyone else will think. What's something you've thought about doing but never really thought you had the time to do?"

Tracey tilted her head. "I want to market the inn better."

Halle gave her an encouraging look. "Better how? You got a lot of interest when Peachtree Cove won Best Small Town."

"I mean…really put the inn out there. Yes, business picked up with the Best Small Town label, but what happens next year when *Travel Magazine* picks a new small town? I want to increase our followers on social media and find new ways to promote the inn."

Imani nodded her head. "Yes. Do that."

Tracey chuckled. "How? I have no idea about marketing or promotion."

Halle snapped her fingers. "Mikayla Spears does."

Mikayla was a few years younger than Tracey. She'd graduated with Tracey's younger brother Devante's class, but she was one of Peachtree Cove's biggest success stories. She'd moved away from the town and made a fortune teaching financial literacy. She'd started an online school on budgeting, finance and investing that earned a partnership with a college accreditation program, and she had a best-selling book. She was the town's first self-made multimillionaire. Mikayla had come back to Peachtree Cove after her father's kidney transplant and for some reason decided to stick around and invest in her hometown.

"I know Mikayla," Tracey said. "But I don't *know* know her. Why would she help me?"

"Because she's teaching an entrepreneurship course at the local technical college," Halle said. "It'll be a six-week course, and last week at the paint class she mentioned that she was going to go over publicity and marketing as well. You should take the class."

"I don't know if I have time for a class." Tracey didn't bother to hide her skepticism. "And go back to school? I don't know if you remember, but school wasn't my strong point."

Tracey spent half of high school either in the principal's office or trying not to fall asleep in class. The only reason she'd gone to a small community college was because she knew that if she wanted to have a better life, then she needed a college degree. The business degree had helped her when she decided to open the bed and breakfast.

Halle rolled her eyes. "This isn't like high school. This is a program specifically for entrepreneurs, *and* it's being taught by Peachtree Cove's first millionaire. You better sign up and sign up quick for this. She just told me about it and registration opens on Monday. It's going to fill up fast."

"And don't come up with an excuse why you can't," Imani said, pointing at Tracey. "You said you want to do this, and this seems like fate is putting everything in front of you. Sign up before that class fills up."

Sighing, Tracey nodded. "Fine. I'll check it out when registration opens."

Halle narrowed her eyes. "Are you going to sign up for real? That didn't sound convincing at all."

Tracey put a hand over her heart. "I'm serious. I'll do it. I'm not sure about a class, but you're right. If I want to learn how to promote the inn, then I'll need to learn somewhere."

She wasn't agreeing to sign up. She was agreeing to at least check out the class. Mikayla had achieved something that seemed impossible for Tracey. She would be out of her league in a class like that, but she wasn't about to admit that to her friends. Her insecurities were hers alone.

Halle and Imani clapped. "Yay!"

Tracey laughed and rolled her eyes. "You two are a mess."

Movement at the door caught her attention, and her laughter faded. Monique, her ex-husband's mistress, came in with Mattie Bryant, the town's biggest gossip. Tracey's glass hit the table with a thud. The smiles on her friends' faces vanished, and their eyes followed Tracey's.

"What is she doing here?" Halle asked.

"This is our spot," Imani added. "She hasn't come here before."

Tracey's eyes narrowed. "She's coming to gloat."

Imani pushed up the sleeves of her shirt. "She wouldn't. Not in my fiancé's bar."

Tracey snorted. "She stole my husband from right under my nose. Why wouldn't she come to gloat at my best friend's fiancé's bar?"

Halle shook her head. "Maybe we're wrong. Let's not jump to conclusions."

Tracey turned away from Monique, but she felt the woman's eyes on her. She wished she had some of Halle's optimism, but for Monique to show up here with Mattie in tow wasn't good news. She'd avoided Tracey and her hangouts while she was pregnant and even after she'd had the baby. Why would she suddenly show up at a place Tracey came to often if she didn't have bad intentions?

Tracey tried to ignore Monique as she and Mattie went to the bar and ordered beers, but when she sat at the table right next to Tracey she knew her instinct was right. Monique had been a good worker at the inn, but she'd told Tracey enough stories about the way she treated former friends or people who slighted her to know she was petty and could be mean. After Tracey tried to slap the smile off her face when she'd first caught her and Bernard kissing at a public function at the inn, she'd known that eventually she would be on the receiving end of her pettiness.

"Girl, you know it's good to get out," Monique said to Mattie in a voice loud enough to carry to Tracey's table. "The baby is always keeping me busy, and you know Bernard can't keep his hands off me."

Tracey's hands tightened around the glass. Halle glared at them. Imani shook her head.

"Let's get out of here," Imani said.

"Why? Because the home-wrecker is here?" Tracey said in an equally loud voice. Monique was not about to make Tracey run. "This is *our* spot. I'm not leaving. I don't have anything to be ashamed of. Unlike some other people." She turned and stared pointedly at Monique.

Monique's eyes narrowed. She was six years younger than Tracey, with sandy brown skin, and she'd had the same snatched-waist, round-behind surgery Tracey's mom had undergone. In fact, Monique's experience was the reason why Loretta had gone through with hers. Even after the baby, she still had a model figure.

Monique's eyes narrowed before she flipped her long reddish-brown hair over her shoulder. "Are you talking about me?"

Tracey looked around the room. "I don't see any other home-wreckers in this bar."

Monique had the nerve to look insulted. She pressed a hand to her chest and scoffed. "I'm not a home-wrecker."

"Then, what do you want to call it? *Mistress? Side chick?* Does that make you feel better?"

"You're just jealous."

"Of what? That you ended up with Bernard? Chile, please. If he did it to me, then he'll do it to you. Good luck with that." She lifted her glass then took a sip.

"He won't do that to me because I know how to keep a man satisfied. Unlike some other people in here."

Silence fell across the bar. Tracey's cheeks heated. The words hit much too close to home. Had Bernard also told Monique that Tracey was boring? That she didn't know how to satisfy him? Why was she even asking herself that? If Bernard had said as much to Tracey, then she knew deep in her heart that he'd said as much to Monique.

Imani reached over and squeezed Tracey's hand. "Tracey, don't do this. She isn't worth it. She just wants to get a rise out of you."

Tracey knew that was exactly what she wanted. Monique wanted to act as if she'd won some kind of prize. But Bernard wasn't a prize. Tracey had once thought he was, but not anymore. For him to have broken her heart for someone as selfish and petty as Monique was the final proof she'd needed on top of the other humiliations and hurts he'd inflicted over their eleven years of marriage.

"Enjoy your sloppy seconds," Tracey said. She drained her beer and scooted to the edge of her seat. She wasn't leaving, this was *her* bar. But she wasn't going to sit there and go back and forth with Monique either. She'd move to the bar.

"Sloppy seconds?" Monique said in a mocking voice. "If that's what you have to say to make yourself feel better. I gave him what you couldn't. A family. You were too busy and didn't make time to take care of a good man. Unlike me. You always thought you were better than me. Well, look who's better now." She smirked, and Tracey saw red.

When Tracey was young she'd never held back. Her temper and the need to lash out when someone insulted her or her family had gotten her into more trouble than she cared to admit. As an adult, she'd tried really hard to do better. She hadn't let her temper fly because she didn't want to be seen as the hot-headed person she'd been as a teenager. She'd governed herself accordingly. Acted like a lady and followed all the rules. And what had that gotten her? Cheated on and humiliated at her favorite hangout spot.

Tracey jumped up. Imani and Halle hurried up as well. Before her friends could stop her, Tracey picked up the glass of beer in front of Monique and flung it in her face.

Monique shrieked and hopped up from the table. "You bit—" Before she could get the word out Tracey grabbed the other beer in front of Mattie and flung that in Monique's face, too.

She then looked at Mattie and glared. "You got anything to say?"

For once in her life, Mattie knew to keep her mouth shut. She held up her hands and shook her head. "I was just here to hang out."

That was a lie. Tracey knew Mattie had come with the hopes of getting some gossip. Well, she had it.

Monique continued to shriek. Surprisingly, the people in the bar cheered and clapped. Tracey put her hands on her hips and met Monique's furious look. She could see the rage in her eyes. She wanted to hit Tracey, and Tracey was more than ready to wipe the floor with her if she dared to try. She raised a brow and leaned forward. "Do it."

Monique glared back, but Mattie must have known better, because she got up, took Monique by the arm and pulled her out of her seat. "Come on. You've got Bernard. Forget her."

Tracey nodded. "Yes, forget me. Because if you *ever* step to me like this again, I'm going to do a lot more than throw beer in your damn face."

Monique huffed and stepped forward. Tracey grinned and balled her hands into fists. She didn't start fights, but she'd finish this one.

Mattie tugged on Monique again. "Let's go." She pulled, and Monique came to her senses and followed her out.

The rest of the patrons in the bar cheered again. Imani and Halle came up to Tracey's side and hugged her.

"Damn, girl, I thought you were going to hit her," Imani said.

Tracey pushed her braids behind her ears. "She wasn't going to get me to throw the first punch."

Halle wrapped an arm around Tracey's shoulders. "I bet she won't step to you again. Come on, let me buy you a drink."

Tracey gave her friend a smile. She looked around at everyone still cheering and wishing her well. Tracey should've felt triumphant. She'd gotten the final word in and had the support of the people in her hangout spot. Instead, embarrassment burned her cheeks. She'd be the talk of the town tomorrow. Once again, hotheaded Tracey had appeared, and all the hard work she'd put into being seen differently was thrown out the window.

7

Brian watched the wedding guests twist and turn on the dance floor. He typically dropped off the plants Tracey needed, left, and picked up his stuff the next day. When he'd dropped things off today, he'd run into the groom, Levi Moore. An old high school friend who'd insisted Brian stick around and enjoy the wedding. He'd considered saying no, but watching Tracey run around and try to get things under control while Jessica didn't offer any assistance had him nodding and saying he would come back.

He wasn't a fan of weddings. His had been at some chapel in Vegas one weekend and then he and Renee had a party on the rooftop of her apartment building with their friends. Back then he'd thought it was the best day of his life. Now he tried to avoid weddings. All that *happily ever after* and *'til death do us part* sounded good the day of but was hard to keep going once the shine wore off. He'd come back in time for the reception, and instead of enjoying the food and festivities, he searched for Tracey to see if he could help with anything.

He spotted her standing at the back of the inn watching the wedding guests on the small dance floor set up in the yard. Her arms were crossed and her brow knitted as she observed. Brian walked around the party toward her. She'd changed out of the Fresh Place Inn polo shirt and jeans she'd had on that morning while setting up and into a simple blue sundress. A gold name tag was pinned above her right breast, and her braids were pulled back in a ponytail.

"What are you doing here?" she asked when he strolled up the steps to stand next to her.

"I was invited back. Levi and I are friends," he said.

She nodded. "Oh yeah, I remember. You two did hang out sometimes in high school."

"I didn't know it was his wedding. When he saw me dropping off the plants earlier he asked me to come back. I thought I'd check and see if you needed any help."

"I'm good. It's all downhill from now. Their wedding planner has taken over, and I can sit back and hope they enjoy the facility."

Brian leaned on the porch rail opposite of her. "Then, why were you frowning?"

Her face immediately cleared. "I wasn't frowning."

"Yes, you were," he said. "You were looking out at the people dancing with a frown on your face. I thought something was wrong."

"Nah, nothing wrong. Just…"

"Weddings don't hold the same appeal after a divorce?"

Her eyes darted to his. For a second she looked like she was going to brush him off before shaking her head. "No, they don't. But they bring in good money, so here's to the happy couple." She brought two fingers to her brow and saluted toward the bride and groom chatting with guests as they sat at the head table.

"How about we grab a glass of champagne for that toast?" he offered.

She shook her head. "I don't drink with the guests during a wedding. I don't want them to think I'm trying to butt in."

Brian tapped his chest. "Well, I'm technically a guest now. And since I'm asking you to join me, it makes you my guest."

She chuckled and shook her head. "I appreciate what you're trying to do, but I'm good. For real. Go on and enjoy the wedding."

She turned to go back into the house. Brian reached out and took her hand in his. She froze then spun back to him with a surprised frown on her face.

"What are you doing?"

"Asking you to dance," he said not breaking eye contact. He didn't know why, but he didn't want Tracey to go inside and sulk about her failed marriage. He wanted her to smile. To see the spark back in her eye.

"I shouldn't hang with the guests."

He tugged on her hand. Her fingers were cold and felt delicate in his hand. The opposite of her tough-girl exterior. He considered twining his fingers with hers to warm them. He didn't like her cold, and she was far from fragile. He gave them a slight squeeze instead. "One dance won't hurt. I promise."

She looked back out at the dance floor then at him. He thought she was going to say no again, but she sighed. "Fine. I do like this song."

Smiling he helped her down the stairs toward the party. He kept her hand in his, and to his surprise, she didn't pull away. They'd just made it to the edge of the dance floor when an older woman walked over. Brian thought she looked familiar, but he wasn't sure where to place her.

"Tracey, I've been wanting to speak to you all day," the woman said pointing a finger at her.

Tracey pulled her hand from his and clasped hers together. "Ms. Simpson, I hope you're enjoying everything."

Ms. Simpson nodded. "I am. I'm really proud of what you've done with yourself. You've turned this old house into an actual bed and breakfast."

Tracey gave a polite smile. "That was always a dream of mine. I'm just happy to give people in Peachtree Cove a nice venue for weddings, birthday parties and other events."

"Yes, we do need that. Though, I never would have expected you to do it. Not when you were always such a smart mouth in my class."

Tracey's shoulders stiffened, but the polite smile remained. "We were all a little smart-mouthed in middle school."

Recognition clicked for Brian then. Ms. Simpson had taught eighth-grade history at their school. He was pretty sure she'd retired. She'd been rude to the kids and hadn't been anyone's favorite teacher.

"Ms. Simpson, it's good to see you again," Brian cut in, hoping to take the woman's attention off Tracey.

She looked at him and gave a stiff nod. "I must have taught you in school, too. I'm sorry, but with so many kids I don't remember everyone." She looked back at Tracey. "Just the ones that were troublemakers."

Brian blinked. Still rude apparently. "Well, we were just about—"

"You know, Tracey," Ms. Simpson cut him off, pointing a finger at Tracey again, "when Old Man Sullivan gave you this place we all wondered why. Of course, I didn't want to think that you were doing favors." Ms. Simpson held up a hand when Tracey started to talk. "You were a hothead but you weren't fast. I give you that much credit. When you married Bernard, well, I realized he was a good influence on you. You were very different while married to him. Got your life together and settled down. I don't condone what he did at all. Men will be men, but to betray you with your own employee..." Ms. Simpson shook her head. "That was so unlike him."

"I'd have to disagree," Tracey said. "Since he did it, I'm pretty sure that was very much like him."

Ms. Simpson lifted her chin as if affronted that Tracey would disagree. Brian hoped that was the end of the discussion, but she kept going. "Maybe so. I heard about the little scene you caused at that bar last night. I want you to know that I was very disappointed to hear that. I thought you'd turned over a new leaf. No matter how bad it gets, a lady should never show it in public. Now, the next time—"

"The next time she better hope I don't do more than throw beer in her face," Tracey said in a tight voice. "I didn't cause a scene. She antagonized me. And honestly, I don't have to be the bigger person when my ex-husband's mistress tries to embarrass me. Now, if you're done sticking your nose where it doesn't belong, I have work to do."

Tracey turned and stalked back toward the house. Brian watched her go then looked back at Ms. Simpson.

She had her hand to her chest. "Well, that was uncalled for."

Brian raised a brow then smirked. "Nah, that was called for." Ms. Simpson gasped, but he didn't wait to see what she said next. He turned and hurried to follow Tracey back into the house.

Tracey wanted a meteor to fall from the sky and squash her into a pancake. No, scratch that. She wanted the meteor to squash Ms. Simpson. Or, even better, have it squash Ms. Simpson and erase all of Brian's memories of Tracey being humiliated. Why did that man always have to have a front-row seat whenever she was embarrassed? Did the universe want to remind Brian that Tracey was from the wrong side of the tracks?

As for Ms. Simpson, Tracey had been dealing with that woman's sly remarks since setting foot in her class. Tracey didn't know exactly what had happened, but Ms. Simpson did not care for Tracey's mom at all. The rumor in school was that Tracey's mom had once "sniffed around" Ms. Simpson's beloved oldest son, but Tracey hadn't bothered to confirm the story. A lot of people had problems with her parents, and she'd been taking the brunt of that all her life.

She stormed into the inn. Thankfully, the other guests were either occupied elsewhere or sitting on the back porch observing the wedding festivities. She headed for the kitchen and then over to the fridge. She pulled out a beer, quickly twisted off the top and took a swig.

"Damn, you move fast," Brian said behind her.

Tracey spit out the beer in her mouth and swung to face him. He watched her with that bemused look he gave her whenever he saw her. As if he couldn't quite figure out what to do with her. She wiped her mouth with the back of her hand.

"Damn, Brian, can you try not to sneak up on people?"

He held up his hands in a move of surrender. "My bad. I thought you heard me behind you."

She shook her head. "Nah, I didn't."

She'd been so upset and embarrassed that she'd only focused on getting as far away from him and Ms. Simpson as possible.

"Why are you following me? You've gotten your show for the day."

A line formed between his brows. "I didn't come for a show. I came to check on you."

"I'm fine."

"No, you're not. That was uncalled for. I want to make sure you're okay."

"Why?" she tossed out, irritated.

"Because I like you," he shot back, sounding just as irritated.

Tracey blinked. Heat flooded her cheeks and prickles went

up and down her arms. She tugged on her ear and raised a brow. "You what?" She had to have heard him wrong.

He shifted back then rubbed the back of his neck. "Not like that. I mean, I like you. You're cool. Plus, we work together. Of course I'm going to check on you and make sure you're good."

"Oh." Another wave of embarrassment hit her. She should have known that's what he meant. She felt foolish for even having half a second of thinking he meant those words in a different way. She was even more upset by the flicker of disappointment in her chest. She shifted her shoulders and hoped to extinguish the flame.

"Well, seriously, I'm good. I knew the tongues were going to start wagging after what happened."

"What exactly happened?"

Sighing, she gave a brief update on her interaction with Monique the night before. Brian's face became more thunderous as she spoke.

"I can't believe she did that. What the hell is her problem?"

She shrugged, and the tension left her shoulders at his outrage on her behalf. "I have no idea. She got him. He did what lots of married man who cheat don't do. He actually left his wife. She should be the next president of Mistresses R Us."

Brian chuckled and shook his head. "I can't believe you're making a joke about this."

"I have to joke. Crying about what happened won't change anything." She took another long swig of her beer.

Brian moved cautiously as he came farther into the kitchen. Maybe he was worried she'd snap at him again. "I know how that feels. That doesn't mean you should put up with crap like that from Ms. Simpson." He stood in front of her, and he looked just as upset by Ms. Simpson's words as she felt.

"I've been putting up with crap like that for as long as I can remember. Your mom is a saint, but my parents were *the* talk of this town. My entire life I was trying to not care about one scandal or another. I stopped trying to make my own scandals once I married Bernard. I thought that if we did things right, then people would respect me in a way they didn't respect my parents."

"You don't have to make up for your parents' sins." He reached over and took the beer out of her hand. "And my mom isn't a saint." He sipped her beer.

Tracey placed a hand on her hip. "No you didn't just take my beer."

"I did," he said and held it out. "Want it back?"

She rolled her eyes and went into the fridge for another one. "Keep it. I don't know where your mouth has been."

"Nowhere it shouldn't be," he said with a grin.

Tracey's stomach flipped. Damn him for being as fine as he was. She recognized that Brian was good-looking. She wasn't stubborn enough to pretend like the man wasn't appealing, but she was smart enough to know that while he may *like* her as a colleague and friend, he would never think of her in a romantic kind of way. She'd seen the kind of women Brian dated, the ones who would look great on the covers of magazines or in designer clothes and with perfect hair. She scratched the new growth at her scalp and then dropped her hands. She was not in that category.

"Look, I know you hate me getting in your business," he said. "But I like the way you handled Ms. Simpson. You didn't let her talk to you any kind of way. Keep standing up for yourself."

She opened the other beer and leaned against the counter. "Oh, I'm going to do a lot more than that."

"What do you mean?"

"I'm tired of trying to live up to the expectations of the people in this town. First I wasn't good enough for Bernard, then when he cheated on me and I defend myself, suddenly I'm not acting ladylike. What kind of mess is that?"

"I have no idea."

"Me either. I'm damned if I do and damned if I don't. So you know what? I don't care anymore." She sipped her beer as an idea popped in her head, sprang and grew.

"What does that mean?"

"Everyone said I changed when I was with Bernard. That I wasn't me anymore. And you know what? They were right." She pushed away from the counter and started pacing. Her heart rate increased with excitement. "I wasn't me. I was who they thought I should be, and that wasn't good enough. Not anymore. To hell with what the people in this town think. To hell with trying not to create scandals like my parents did. From now on, I'm going to do whatever the hell I want to do."

Brian's eyes widened. "Oh really."

She nodded. "Really. Screw Bernard, Monique, Ms. Simpson and everyone else who thinks they can tell me how to live. From here on out, the only person I'm living for is me."

Brian stepped forward and stopped her pacing. He stood close enough for her to smell the faint scent of his cologne. She'd noticed his cologne before. The spicy scent that seemed made just for him. His dark eyes bored into hers. Eyes filled with respect. Not pity or amusement. She liked that look in his eyes. Even if it made her heart rate increase.

Brian held his beer bottle toward her. "I like the sound of that. To the New Tracey."

She grinned and clinked her bottle against his. "The New Tracey."

8

Two weeks later, Tracey arrived at Joanne's salon on Main Street at six thirty in the morning. Joanne unlocked the door and let her inside. She had a bright smile on her face as she greeted Tracey and gave her a big hug. Joanne was older than Tracey, with honey-brown skin and long blonde locs. She was also the best beautician in Peachtree Cove. She'd been doing hair in her home since she was a teenager but had opened her own salon on Main Street.

She'd been doing Tracey's hair for years. They'd been cool with each other since Tracey was in high school, and Tracey had always admired Joanne for never giving up on her dream to open a salon despite the naysayers underestimating her when she'd gotten pregnant young and her first attempt at opening a business failed. When Joanne started dating Tracey's younger brother, Devante, they'd become friends.

"You ready to do this?" Joanne said running her fingers over

Tracey's kinky hair. It had taken most of the previous day for Tracey to remove her braids.

Tracey sighed and gave Joanne a hesitant smile as she met her eye in the mirror at Joanne's station in her salon. "I think so. Otherwise, I wouldn't be here."

Joanne laughed and placed a comforting hand on Tracey's shoulder. "It's just me and you first thing this morning. The other stylists start around eight or nine, depending on their clients."

"Then, why are we here so early?" Tracey said with fake grumpiness. In truth, she was an early riser. She liked to get up early and make sure breakfast was ready when there were visitors in the inn. Then there was always some sort of maintenance work that needed to be done. The home was in decent shape, but the fact that it was over seventy years old also meant that things needing attention were constantly popping up. The success of the inn helped her handle most of the maintenance costs.

Joanne placed a hand on her hip before gently pulling and tugging on Tracey's hair. She studied Tracey's hair while talking. "Because we're going to be here all day. I like to start early when I'm installing locs." She removed the band Tracey had used to tie back her hair.

Tracey pressed a hand to her stomach. It fluttered like dozens of bees were buzzing around inside. "I can't believe I'm doing this."

Joanne gave her a knowing smile. "I'm glad you're finally doing this. I told you that you might as well loc your hair years ago. All you do is wear it in braids all the time."

Tracey placed a hand on the side of her braid-free hair. "I know, but I was just afraid to do it."

Joanne pulled out a royal blue cover that was embossed with the name and logo of her salon in gold letters and wrapped it around Tracey's front. "I don't know why you were afraid. I told you that you're going to look great."

Sighing, she met Joanne's eyes in the mirror. "Honestly, I was afraid of what Bernard would think."

Joanne scowled. "Are you for real?"

Tracey nodded. "He always said he hated locs. He thought they looked dirty and messy. He said I would look bad in them. He didn't like my hair braided, but he preferred that over locs or my natural hair out."

Tracey hadn't told anyone about the way Bernard would make her feel self-conscious over her natural hair. When she'd decided to stop getting relaxers due to the stress on her hair and scalp, he'd teased her and said she looked like Buckwheat from *The Little Rascals* whenever she'd worn her hair in its natural coils. She'd kept her hair braided or twisted to avoid him flinging any further insults disguised as jokes.

"That man is an asshole," Joanne said shaking her head. "I'd like to say I can't believe he would say that, but there are enough women who sit in my chair who've told me about the things they can and can't do to their hair because of their man."

"I hate that I let him dictate what I did for so long."

Joanne gently squeezed Tracey's shoulders. Her eyes were compassionate as they met Tracey's reflection in the mirror. "You were married to him, and he was supposed to have your best interests at heart. You're better off now and don't have to give a damn about what he has to say, okay?"

Tears pricked Tracey's eyes. She blinked them away and gave Joanne a smile. "Girl, I know that. No man is ruling me ever again."

Joanne nodded before giving Tracey's shoulders another squeeze and saying, "Good. Now, not only are we doing micro locs, but how about some color?"

Tracey's eyes widened. "Color, too. I don't know, Tracey. That might be too much. What if I look weird?"

"Heifa, if you don't get Bernard's dumb words out of your head... You are beautiful and sexy. When I'm done with you, Bernard and every other man in this town will be wishing they could curl up next to you."

Tracey burst out laughing. "The last thing I want or need is another man right now."

Joanne pursed her lips. "I am not a believer in the *every woman needs a man* philosophy, but I am a believer in getting some when you need some. All I'm saying is don't knock the next brotha because of what Bernard did. When I'm done with you and you're feeling as sexy as you look, take up one of them offers and be reminded that Bernard was a fool who didn't know how to appreciate a woman like you."

The tears pricked Tracey's eyes again. She was used to getting support from Imani and Halle. Even her mom supported her decision to leave Bernard, but she wasn't ready for the love Joanne was throwing her way. She blinked quickly to prevent the emotion swelling in her chest from showing and waved her hand. "Fine, I'll remember that. Now, stop pep-talking me, and let's do this."

After coloring Tracey's hair, Joanne took her over to the washbowl and scrubbed her hair and scalp so good Tracey couldn't help but let out a moan. She imagined all the negative things Bernard had ever said to her washing down the drain with the suds. She was doing this for her. Getting micro locs was something she'd always wanted to do. She didn't have to think about or care what Bernard or anyone else had to say. This was her head, her hair and her life.

She was back in Joanne's chair, chatting about Joanne's son and how well he was doing with his job in Chicago when the front door was unlocked and Tracey's brother, Devante, entered. He was tall and brown-skinned like her dad. But unlike her dad, his eyes weren't yellow from years of drinking, and his figure was fit from his daily workouts and job as a contractor.

Devante walked over and kissed Joanne first before bending to place a kiss on Tracey's cheek. "What's up, Tracey."

"What are you doing here?" Tracey asked.

"I always check in on Joanne before I go out for the day. Make sure she's good." He held a tray with two cups of coffee in one hand and a bag from the Books and Vibes coffee shop and bookstore in the other. "Joanne said you were coming in early today. So I brought you both some breakfast. I gotta make both of you eat."

Joanne grinned and leaned over to kiss him again. "Thank you, baby. Tracey, your brother is spoiling me."

"I'm not surprised. He's been crazy about you since he was thirteen."

Her brother shot her a look. "Stop trying to embarrass me. What are you doing with your hair?"

Joanne pointed to the small locs she'd started at the base of Tracey's neck. "I've colored it. Now we're locing it up."

She'd decided to go bold with color. She'd always wanted to have red hair, and Joanne hadn't disappointed her. The reddish-gold color complemented her brown skin and made Tracey feel as if she looked five years younger.

Devante raised a brow as he set the coffee and pastries on the small table next to Joanne's station. "You've been talking about it for a minute. It looks good."

"I was finally ready to bite the bullet. What do you have going on today?" She changed the subject. If she got into the reason why she'd delayed doing this to her hair, her brother would go looking for Bernard.

"Working on the mall renovation. Thanks to Andre making me a subcontractor on this project. Then I've got to check in on my crew working on another project in Augusta. I'll be back in Peachtree Cove later today."

The last part was more for Joanne than Tracey. She didn't keep up with her brother's schedule like that, but she appreciated the way he so casually told Joanne about his day. She'd felt like she was pulling teeth to get any information out of Bernard about what he was working on or where he had to go. More and more she realized how much he'd made her feel clingy or needy over wanting basic information.

"I'll be here late with Tracey," Joanne told him as she started working on the back of Tracey's head again.

"Alright now, getting all cute again," Devante teased.

Tracey tried to glare at her brother, but there was no heat in her gaze. "I've always been cute."

"Facts. Hey, I heard you cussed out Ms. Simpson at old boy's wedding the other day."

Tracey rolled her eyes. "Ain't nobody cuss her out. I told her to mind her own damn business. She said I was wrong and not acting ladylike when Monique tried to play me for a fool the other night at A Couple of Beers."

"No she didn't," Joanne gasped. "That woman is always in everybody's business."

"You know she's going to go and tell everyone that you cussed her out," her brother said sounding concerned. "I know you don't like people talking about you."

Tracey lifted a shoulder. "You know what? I don't care anymore. The people in this town talked about me when I acted right and when I acted up. If they're going to keep my name in their mouth no matter what I do, I might as well do what I want."

Her brother held out a fist. "That's what I've been telling you since we were kids."

She bumped his fist with hers. "I'm finally listening. No more fake-ass nice Tracey. This Tracey is ready to take over the world."

Two days later, Tracey unveiled her new hairdo to Imani and Halle. They'd agreed to go with her to Atlanta and help her pick out some new clothes. Tracey hadn't purchased new clothes in a long time. She mostly wore her Fresh Place Inn shirt and a pair of slacks every day. On her days off, she threw on a pair of jeans and a T-shirt or some other top in her closet. She couldn't remember the last time she'd gotten dressed up for anything. Not the simple dresses she occasionally wore for a wedding at the inn, but dressed up in something really nice for a night out. Bernard had been busy taking out his mistress instead of her, and outside of the occasional Peachtree Cove Business Guild meeting, she didn't have a social life.

Both Imani and Halle exclaimed with delight when they arrived at the inn to pick Tracey up.

"Oh my God, Tracey! You look amazing!" Halle said. She reached out and immediately touched Tracey's hair. "I've got to touch it, don't hate me."

"Girl, you're fine. You can touch my hair," she said to her friend.

"It does look good," Imani agreed. "I love the color!"

Tracey beamed at her friends' acceptance. She'd liked her hair when Joanne finished but had to get used to looking different. The ease of getting up and shaking out her hair each morning with the same freedom she'd had with the braids was worth the day she'd spent in Joanne's chair getting the micro locs.

"I always wanted red hair," she said. "I was just afraid to make the jump."

"Well, girl, I'm glad you jumped," Imani said. "It looks great."

"Thank you. Now to find some clothes that match my new hair."

Halle nodded. "Most definitely. I've got us covered." She pulled out her phone and opened up an app. "Last night I looked up the best clothing styles for your figure and then researched some of the best boutiques and stores with the brands perfect for you. I've already mapped out which ones to visit first and located a place to eat lunch."

Tracey blinked then laughed. "Damn, Halle, sometimes I forget you're a middle school principal, and then you do something like this."

Halle shrugged and slid her phone back in her purse. "Hey, I plan the best and most organized field trips in the district. Those skills translate."

Imani clapped her hands and grinned. "Then, let's get to it."

They piled into Tracey's car and took the two-hour drive to Atlanta. The conversation flowed easily as the three friends chatted about work, Halle's daughter Shania, and Imani's plans for her wedding. She was having it at The Fresh Place Inn late that fall. A small affair that Tracey was happy to host for her friend. Her marriage was over, and the idea of ever being in love again made her stomach twist in knots, but nothing would make her hate on her friend's happiness.

Halle's scheduling skills proved true to their word. She had them at the first store right on time. They went inside and Halle helped Tracey pick out clothes with the precision of a drill sergeant. Tracey admittedly didn't know much about fashion. Her breasts seemed to have developed overnight in middle school, garnering attention from young boys and dirty older men. Instead of being viewed like her mom, she'd always opted for clothes that were larger to hide her figure. Something she'd kept up with even during her marriage.

When Tracey came out of the dressing room in a pair of jeans she'd thought fit well, she was surprised when Halle threw up her hands and groaned.

"Tracey, if you don't stop coming out here in those big-ass pants I'm going to scream."

Tracey frowned and looked down at the jeans. They were not baggy and fit her without being constraining. "What? These are smaller than the last ones."

Imani shook her head. "They're too big for you."

"No, they aren't. I've been the same size for years. These are my size."

Halle stood up and marched over to Tracey. She jerked on the waistband of the jeans then stuck her arm inside. Tracey yelped and tried to pull back, but Halle didn't move.

"What are you doing?"

Halle looked back at Imani. "Look at this. I can fit my entire *arm* in these jeans."

Imani laughed and nodded. "That *is* your whole arm."

Halle jerked her arm back and gave Tracey a knowing look. "Now, sit here and tell me that these jeans fit."

Tracey tried to glare, but Halle didn't back down. "I don't want them too tight."

Imani walked over. "Tight and fitting are two different things. Stop hiding that ass and those boobs. Some people pay good money to have what you've got." Imani shifted her own smaller breasts.

"Exactly," Halle chimed in. She placed her hands on her ample hips. "Do you see me hiding behind big clothes? And I've got more curves than you. Your figure is perfect and sexy. Show it."

Sighing, Tracey ran a hand over her stomach and hips before looking at her friends. "I haven't felt sexy in a long time."

"Well, now is the time to start," Imani said.

Tracey cringed then admitted to her friends, "I don't know how. Like, for real. I always tried to *not* be sexy. I didn't want to be compared to my mom, so I don't know what to do. That's with my clothes and with myself. I can't even remember the last time I had an orgasm."

"What?" Halle asked, stunned.

Imani frowned. "With Bernard, or by yourself?"

"Both," Tracey said with a shrug. "I stopped masturbating because Bernard didn't like it."

"Why wouldn't he like it?" Halle asked sounding even more confused than before. "TMI alert, but Quinton loves to watch me."

Tracey glanced away, embarrassed to talk about it, but also slightly in awe that Halle would do that in front of Quinton. She'd never talked about the awkward moments in her bedroom before. She'd thought not being satisfied was better than searching for something different that would lead to her cheating on her husband.

There wasn't anyone else in the dressing room, so she spoke in a rush. "He caught me one time. Early in our marriage. He got really mad. He said he's responsible for making me come and nobody else. I felt like I'd done something wrong and stopped."

"Wait a second," Halle said and held up a finger. "He got mad about you masturbating and then didn't even make you come?"

Tracey nodded. "Basically."

Imani wrapped an arm around Tracey's shoulder. "Don't feel bad. I've heard about the same thing from patients of mine. There's nothing wrong with masturbating. In fact, doing so helps you figure out what you like so that you can orgasm with a partner. If you want, I know a sex therapist I can recommend."

Tracey pulled back. "That may be too much." She hadn't orgasmed, but she wasn't in need of sex therapy.

Imani looked at her with comforting, steady eyes. "If he's been telling you what you should and shouldn't like for years, then maybe it isn't. You might not want to start with therapy, but you have to figure out how to feel sexy again. Because you are sexy, Tracey. But until you begin to feel that way, it won't matter what we say."

"I don't know."

Halle bumped Tracey's shoulder. "Didn't you say you were going to try new things? This is your time to find out New Tracey. You can start by masturbating again."

Tracey wanted to change the subject, but not talking about

how she felt had gotten her nothing. She remembered how embarrassed she'd been when Bernard had scolded her for daring to touch herself. The way she'd denied her own pleasure and tried to always ensure he was happy. She wanted to feel sexy without being shamed or afraid that being sexy would make people think she was two steps from sleeping with any man who looked her way. Honestly, she did need to talk about and figure out what it was she liked.

Who cares what people think, remember?

Sighing, Tracey nodded and smiled at her friends. "Fine, I'll start."

Halle grabbed her cell phone. "And I'm going to update the schedule. After you try on a pair of jeans that actually fit, we're going to eat lunch and then we're going to the sex store."

Tracey's eyes widened and she laughed. "The what? Why?"

"Because if you're going to learn what you like, you're going to need some toys."

9

Brian walked in the back door right into The Fresh Place
Inn's kitchen and smiled at Shirley stirring a pot of something
that smelled a lot like her gumbo. "Hey, Ms. Shirley, how are
you doing today?"

She waved at Brian. "Can't complain. Won't change anything anyway. You here to meet Tracey?"

He nodded and walked over to the stove. The savory smell
increased, and his stomach rumbled when he got a glance of
the gumbo in the pot. "I am. She's got a wedding this weekend, and I'm bringing the shrubs over. Is she around?"

"She's out front dealing with Jessica."

Brian pulled his eyes away from the pot of food and back to
Shirley's. He lowered his voice so the two other people helping prepare the rest of the food wouldn't hear. "Is she finally
firing her?"

"Not quite, but today she's getting written up. She messed

up the reservation we had and double charged a tenant. They complained and even took it to the business bureau saying the inn tried to scam them."

"Tracey can't keep her around."

"She's already putting out an ad for a new manager. Hopefully, we'll get someone soon and can let her go."

Tracey walked into the kitchen then. Brian looked at her, blinked and straightened. Tracey looked amazing. Not that she didn't before. But her hair was different. He liked the red color and the way the tiny locs curled around her face. She was dressed not in a Fresh Place Inn polo shirt and slacks but a fitted green dress that hugged her curvy hips rather than hid them, and the V-neck brought attention to her full breasts. A short-sleeved yellow cardigan with the inn logo embroidered on the breast covered her shoulders and arms. He looked down expecting heels, but she wore a pair of green-and-yellow sneakers.

"What's wrong with you?" Tracey asked staring at him with a raised brow.

He shook his head. "Not a damn thing." He moved away from the stove and walked over to her. "This a new outfit?"

She lifted her shoulder. "Maybe. You got a problem with it?"

He held up his hand. "Not at all. You look good."

She blinked, glanced away, then her typical defiance came back and she met his gaze with a raised chin. "I know I do. You here to talk about the shrubs?"

"Yeah. You got a minute?"

She nodded. "I do. I've got the list in my office. Come on."

He turned back. "See you later, Ms. Shirley."

"Come back through before you go. I'll put aside a bowl of gumbo for you."

He grinned. "If I were a marrying man."

Shirley laughed and winked. "My husband better not hear you say that."

"Well, then he better keep treating you right," he teased then followed Tracey out of the kitchen.

His eyes followed the lines of Tracey's back as she walked. The view from the back was just as good as from the front. Her hips and ass were still as luscious as ever. His breathing quickened, and desire stirred in his groin. Blinking, he cleared his throat and looked away from Tracey's behind before his thoughts took him down the wrong path. He and Tracey were cool, but his mom was right. She was hurt, and he wasn't the guy she needed in her life right now. Tracey deserved to be cherished, treated well, and by someone who only had eyes for her. He wasn't looking for commitments or to get into any relationships.

She'd transitioned one of the downstairs parlors into her office. A desk sat next to one of the windows that overlooked the back yard. A bookshelf lined one wall and a chaise lounge was beneath another window with a view of the side yard.

Tracey went to her desk and picked up a file folder. She walked back to him as she scanned the sheet. "I've got everything they want here."

"Anything unusual?"

She shook her head and handed him the folder. "Nothing unusual. Just a few decorative shrubs around the altar and ferns along the aisles of chairs. Will you have enough?"

He scanned the list and did a quick internal inventory. "I think so. You setting up the night before?"

"I am. Can you deliver on Friday?"

"I'll get my guys on it."

She grinned, and for the first time in a long time the smile actually reached her eyes. Much different from when he'd seen her a few weeks ago at the wedding where Ms. Simpson had tried to tell her she wasn't acting ladylike.

"Is New Tracey the reason you're glowing like that?" he said, pointing to her face.

Her grin widened, and she lifted a shoulder. "Something like that. And I had a good night last night."

Her eyes darted away, and she tucked her hair behind her ears. Brian's brows drew together. A good night? Was she seeing someone? "You went out on a date?" The question came out sharper than he'd anticipated.

The smile left her face, and she gave him a pointed stare. "There you go minding my business again."

She turned to walk away, but he reached out and took her elbow in his. Her skin was soft. He had an urge to run his fingers across her arm, but he let her go when she looked back. "I'm just asking as a friend. That's all."

"That's not how you sounded with all that bass in your damn voice."

He placed a hand on his chest. "My bad. I was just surprised. I didn't think you'd be ready to date so fast."

Her shoulders and eyes softened. "Nah, it wasn't a guy. Can I only have a good night if a man is involved?"

"You can have a good time with whoever you want. As long as you're happy." He meant it and wouldn't consider why relief flowed through his veins. "It's good to see you smile again."

Tracey's shoulders relaxed, and the corners of her lips lifted. "Well, I haven't had a lot of reasons to smile, but I'm getting there."

"Good. If you need anything, just let me know."

She considered him for a second then shook her head. "Hmm… I think I'm good. What I want, you're not the person to ask."

"What do you want?"

That secretive smile came back on her face. "Don't worry. The way things go in this town, I'm sure you'll hear about it soon enough."

His cell phone rang before he could ask. He pulled it out

and cursed. He'd gotten a text from that number earlier in the day. Renee was calling him again.

Tracey leaned forward to look at his phone. "Who's calling? That your new lady?"

He sent the call to voice mail and shook his head. "More like my ex-wife."

Tracey tipped her head to the side. "You don't talk to her anymore?"

"We don't have anything to talk about."

"If she's calling you up, then she thinks you do. Look, I get it. I don't want anything to do with Bernard, but he wouldn't call me unless it's an emergency. Go ahead and answer her call."

"I'm done with her." His cell rang again.

"She's not done with you." Tracey snatched his phone, swiped the green button and handed it back before he could speak. She waved her fingers and whispered, "Use my office," before running out.

Brian watched her quick escape and scowled. "Talk about minding other people's business."

"Hello?" Renee's voice came from his phone. "Brian? You there?"

Brian let out a loud breath before putting the phone to his ear. "Yeah, I'm here."

"Good. Why haven't you called me back?" Her soft voice wasn't angry or demanding, instead she sounded sad. Years ago he would have been pulled in by the pitiful act. She'd look at him with sad, dark eyes, pout her full lips and speak in a soft voice, and he'd be ready to give her the world. Not anymore. She'd broken his heart for the last time.

"Because we don't have anything to talk about." He kept his voice neutral. If she got any hint of emotion from him she'd latch on.

"That's not true. I have something I need to tell you."

He walked over and leaned against Tracey's desk. "What is it?"

"I'm pregnant."

"Again?" he said. "That's your new husband's problem. Not mine."

"But...well... I told him about us and...what happened at Mia's party," she said in a small, apologetic voice.

Brian's body stiffened. "What?"

"I remembered what you said about honesty and stuff when we broke up. So I felt it was only right to let him know."

Brian rubbed his temples. "Renee, we've already been through this. We slept together one night before you and he eloped, but you didn't have your son until a year later. There was no need to tell him about us."

"I know, but it was a great night. I can't get you out of my mind." Her voice went breathless.

Brian clenched the phone and squeezed the bridge of his nose. A night he regretted. He'd gone to their friend Mia's engagement party knowing he might see Renee. He'd prepared himself to see her but had no intention of giving her any time. Except, just like it had always been with them, she'd come over and smiled, and common sense took off. When he'd asked if she was still with the guy she'd dumped him for, she'd said she was there alone and that should be his answer. Foolish of him not to dig. They'd slept together, and then he'd overheard her on the phone the next morning. Her new man wasn't there because he'd had to travel. Renee was planning to meet him the next day so they could elope in Vegas. Just like she'd done with him.

Brian hadn't even been heartbroken. Instead, he'd felt stupid for falling right back into her arms. He'd walked out and hadn't picked up another call from Renee since. Their friend let him know that Renee and the guy did get married the next day.

When he'd found out she was pregnant, he'd wondered if the kid was his, but the timeline didn't add up. She'd given birth more than a year after their night together. He would have done what was needed if the child had been his, but he'd also been relieved to know he was not the father. If she was pregnant again, then this most definitely wasn't his problem.

"That night between us is out of my mind and never happening again," Brian said truthfully. Anytime he thought of their last night together the memory made his stomach twist. He referred to what happened as his final humiliation.

"Well, now he thinks this baby is your baby."

Brian shot up from the desk. "Hold the hell up, Renee. That's not my baby."

"I know that, but he doesn't. He thinks our son is yours and that we're still sleeping with each other. He also thinks I'm pregnant with your kid."

Brian pulled the phone away from his face to glare at it before putting it back to his ear. "What? Nah, Renee. Again, this is your problem. Not mine."

"But I want to see you, Brian. I wish this was your baby. I miss you."

A year ago he might have believed her. He was thankful that he'd finally come to his senses and realized Renee wasn't any good for him.

"Stop playing games with me, okay? You got your man, y'all are married. Our divorce has long been finalized. Tell him that we're through and he has nothing to worry about. In fact, I'll send the DNA sample to prove I'm not the father. Don't call me with this crap again."

"But—"

"Bye, Renee." He ended the call. Cursed and stomped his foot. His heart thundered like a herd of wild elephants. She always did this to him. Stirred up drama and made him anxious. He couldn't believe he used to live off this mess. Brian navigated to her contact information and blocked the latest number she'd called him from. He hoped and prayed that Renee and her foolish husband kept him out of their relationship.

10

After going back and forth with herself and coming up with every excuse why she wasn't ready to be back in a classroom, Tracey finally had to look herself in the mirror and admit that she had to stop being afraid. New Tracey was trying new things. New Tracey was learning what she liked. New Tracey wasn't going to underestimate herself. So she'd signed up for the entrepreneurship class at the technical college before she could talk herself out of it. According to the registrar, she had gotten the last seat. She wasn't sure if she should be happy or regretful about that.

Even though Tracey had vowed never to step foot in another classroom after she'd graduated from college, her excitement had sprouted and grown like a well-watered flower as the first day drew closer. Maybe she would learn something that would help her promote the inn and drive up business. She had to find a way to make her bed and breakfast stand out enough to have travelers opt to visit hers over a hotel in a larger city.

Class started at six, but she arrived early to make sure she was in the right location and could snag a good seat. When she walked in the building she easily found the room for the class. A woman stood at the front of the classroom and used a remote in her hand to click through slides on the screen.

"Hey, is this the entrepreneur class?" Tracey asked just to be sure she was in the right place.

The woman turned around, and Tracey recognized her immediately as Mikayla. "It is." Mikayla's eyes narrowed, and she slowly crossed the room toward Tracey. A second later her eyes widened and she grinned. "Tracey, is that you?"

Tracey grinned and nodded. "In the flesh."

Mikayla laughed and opened her arms to hug her. "Oh my God, it's so good to see you."

Tracey hugged Mikayla back. She smelled good, like expensive perfume, and she looked even better. She wore a tailored green suit that fit her slim curves perfectly, and a matching green scarf was interwoven in the twists pulling her hair back in a neat bun. Her makeup was understated and flawless. Not surprising considering that Mikayla was a millionaire. Tracey had improved her clothing choices in the last few weeks. Things no longer fell off her body, and she was learning to be more confident with her own curvy figure, but she felt light-years away from looking as sexy and put-together as Mikayla.

"It's good to see you, too," Tracey said. "When Halle told me you were putting this class together she said I had to learn from the best."

"Halle is great. I'm so glad she recommended my class. I'm excited that the technical college was willing to let me do a small class here. There are so many entrepreneurs in and around Peachtree Cove, and I want to see everyone making as much money as they can."

Tracey raised a brow and nodded. "I like the sound of that."

"Girl, everyone loves the sound of making money. You've got the bed and breakfast, right?"

"I do. It's doing great thanks to the Best Small Town designation, but I really want to get better at marketing the inn. The shine from the designation won't last forever."

"I understand where you're coming from, but don't undervalue that designation. There are places still bragging about being the best something or other from 1998. That's one of the topics I want to focus on for the class. I'd like to show everyone how to leverage any recognition into even more exposure and profitability."

The words were like warm sunshine on Tracey's growing excitement. Maybe this wasn't a bad idea. "That's exactly what I need. How many people are in the class?"

"We've got fifteen, which is about all I want to handle for my first class."

Another woman walked in. Tracey waved when she recognized Carolyn Jones from Sweet Treats bakery. Tracey took the time to scope out one of the better seats in the class while Carolyn walked over to introduce herself to Mikayla. She opted for a seat on the end of the second row. She was excited, but she wasn't first-row excited.

More people filed into the classroom. Several others she recognized from around town, including Joshua who co-owned A Couple of Beers with Imani's fiancé, Cyril. Tracey tried not to roll her eyes when Mattie came into the class with one of her best friends. The two busybodies loved nothing more than to get into other people's business. Unfortunately, they chose to sit right in front of her in the first row.

"Hello, Tracey," Mattie said. Her assessing gaze roamed over Tracey's hair and the fitted black T-shirt she wore. "You're looking...well."

"Hello." Tracey didn't try to warm up her voice at all as she tried not to fidget. Mattie hadn't been one of Tracey's favorite people, but when she'd had the nerve to talk junk about Joanne and her brother when they'd started dating, followed by coming to the bar with Monique, Tracey had put the woman on her permanent Don't Fuck With list.

Maybe it was divine intervention, or maybe it was the *Don't talk to me* look Tracey was trying to convey, but Mattie turned around and started chatting with her friend. Someone pulled out the chair next to Tracey. She turned to see who her seatmate would be and froze when her eyes met Brian's warm gaze.

"What are you doing here?" she asked sharply, surprised that he was in the class. They'd worked a few weddings in the last couple of weeks, but he hadn't mentioned the class. Neither had she, but she assumed Brian didn't need any additional help. He always seemed so put-together and in control.

He slid into the seat next to her. He wasn't in the usual Henley and dirty jeans he wore when he worked but instead wore a casual dark orange V-neck shirt that clung to his shoulders and gave an enticing glimpse of his chest and a pair of fitted tan pants. "I can't learn how to make my business better?"

"Your business is good."

He turned to face her. The scent of his cologne drifted over to her. The man always smelled good. "That doesn't mean I can't make it better. Besides, if you grow, then I grow. I need to hear the secrets."

"Why are you sitting next to me?"

He chuckled as if the question were a silly one. The light in his eyes made her feel silly for asking. "I can't sit next to my friend?"

Tracey tried to ignore the flutter in her stomach. If she were foolish, she'd swear he was flirting. She sucked her teeth and shrugged. "Whatever."

Mikayla came to the front of the classroom and got everyone's attention. "Alright, it's six o'clock, and I believe in starting on time. Hello, everyone. I'm Mikayla Spears, and I'm excited to pass along some of what I've learned growing my financial planning business. I hope that the next few weeks will be beneficial to you all and that we can come up with some great ideas to help your businesses flourish."

Mikayla asked everyone to introduce themselves and their business and share what they wanted to get out of the class. Then she dove into talking about the definitions of branding and marketing, before having everyone brainstorm three words that described their business and what the core values of their business were. By the time the class ended, Tracey's head was mush. She hadn't thought about her mission or core values related to the inn before, much less distilling her work into three words.

"Between now and the next class, come back with these ideas more refined, along with a tagline or catchphrase for your business," Mikayla said at the end. "We'll present the information to the rest of the group along with why you chose that phrase. Then we'll go into how you can start using words and imagery around those phrases."

Tracey sighed as she looked down at her notes. "Okay, that was a lot."

Brian sighed next to her. "It was, but all good. Got me thinking differently about my nursery."

"Same. I never thought about values and whatnot. It'll be hard to come up with a catchphrase in a week."

"Want to get together and brainstorm later?"

Tracey's head popped up. "What, like study together?"

He grinned and lifted a shoulder. "Why not? Couldn't hurt."

"I don't need you laughing at my bad ideas."

"I promise I won't laugh if you don't laugh at mine."

She was about to immediately say no. She wasn't sure if she would come up with anything good, and she didn't want to embarrass herself. But on the other hand, Brian was smart and never gave her bad advice or tried to humiliate her. Besides, it would be better to make sure her ideas weren't too horrible before she brought them in front of the class.

"Sure, it'll be good to bounce ideas off someone who was also in the class. Give me a call, and we'll get together."

They stood and headed out of the classroom together. As they neared the front door, she heard Mattie's voice ahead of them.

"It's good for Tracey to get out. I heard she's sitting around the house looking sad while Bernard and Monique are all over town just flaunting their affair. And because it's Bernard, everyone is just accepting it. It's sad really."

Mattie's friend nodded. "It is."

"What's sad?" Tracey chimed in. "That I got rid of a bad husband? She can have him."

Mattie looked startled for a second before lifting her chin. "Good for you. Keep your head up and everything."

"I don't have to keep my head up. I'm fine."

Mattie gave her a sad look. "Well, you know what he's saying, right?"

"I don't give a damn about what he's saying." Tracey moved to walk around them.

"He's saying that you're going to just sit at home and cry. That you already begged him to come back."

Tracey spun around. "Say what?"

She hated the smug look in Mattie's eye. Mattie loved it when people took the bait, and Tracey had just latched on like a prize bass. Tracey wanted to ignore her, but if Bernard was out there talking about her as if she would even consider taking him back, then she wanted to know.

"It's true. He said you want him back because you don't know what to do without a man and you're afraid to get out there. They were laughing about it the other night when I ran into them."

Tracey saw red. Her heart twisted, and her stomach flipped.

When she thought about all the pleasure he'd denied her, Mr. I Can't Give My Wife an Orgasm but She Can't Masturbate... More like he didn't know what to do with a woman. "I know he didn't."

Mattie nodded and tried to look compassionate but failed. "Well, I just thought you should know what he's saying."

"Bernard is a liar and a cheater. And for your information, I know exactly what to do with a man. The next time you hear Bernard say that, tell him to ask the man I'm sleeping with right now if I know what to do."

Mattie's eyes widened, and she leaned forward. "Who are you sleeping with?"

"Tracey?" Brian said in a confused voice.

Tracey looked at him. Heat filled her face. She'd forgotten he was there. Once again witnessing her embarrassment and her lie. She looked back at Mattie and lifted her chin. "None of your damn business."

She turned and walked out. Brian was hot on her heels. He took her elbow and stopped her when they were in the parking lot, sending a spark of electricity up her arms.

She jerked away before crossing her arms. "What?"

"Who are you sleeping with?"

Her head jerked back. "Why do you care?"

He paused for a second before shifting his stance. "I just didn't know you were seeing anyone. And you told that to Mattie. She's nothing but a gossip."

"That's exactly why I told her that. She is a gossip, and if Bernard is talking about me, then let him hear that."

"But are you really seeing someone?" He sounded concerned.

"No, not right now, but I will."

"What's that supposed to mean?"

An idea popped into her head. New Tracey was not going to be seen as sitting around waiting for someone. What had Joanne said? Something about not letting what happened stop her from at least getting some action when she needed some. She'd played with her new toys and also given herself several glorious orgasms. Maybe the time had come to move to the next level.

She snapped her fingers and grinned. "I'm going to find me a lover."

When Brian decided to hang out with Cyril and Quinton that weekend, they opted to check out the cigar bar that had recently opened in town instead of going back to Cyril's spot. Plus, Cyril said he wanted a change in scenery since he was always at the brewery and needed to know what other places were offering in town.

The three of them purchased their cigars and ordered bourbon on the rocks before settling into large leather chairs in a corner near the front window.

"How did the first class go?" Quinton asked.

Brian nodded his head while swirling the bourbon and ice in his glass. "Pretty good. Mikayla gave us a lot to think about."

"I bet she would," Quinton said. "I heard she's a millionaire a few times over."

"She is. Made her money and then moved back to Peachtree Cove after her dad's surgery. Now she's giving back to the town. She told us that she wants everyone in Peachtree Cove to have the opportunity to be financially whole."

Cyril nodded. "Joshua said the first class was good. We spent all yesterday morning trying to figure out what the core words and our values for the brewery were. It was interesting to think about it that way."

"Yeah, I'm supposed to get together with Tracey before the next class so we can brainstorm together."

Cyril pushed back the black fedora on his head and raised a brow. "With Tracey, huh?"

Brian took a puff of his cigar before meeting his friend's eye. "Yeah. Why you say it like that?"

"You know I don't like to get into gossip."

Brian did know how much Cyril hated gossip. As someone whose life had been upended thanks to rumors and false accusations, Cyril was the one least likely to pass along gossip. "Yeah, I know."

"Well, sometimes I can't help but overhear things at the bar. I don't usually bring up what I hear, but this was about you."

"What about me?" Brian kept to himself around town. His name wasn't frequently tied to gossip.

"Apparently Mattie is going around saying that you and Tracey are hooking up."

Brian sat forward in his chair. "No the hell she isn't."

Quinton pointed his cigar in Brian's direction. "She is. I heard the same thing. I didn't believe it. I know you and Tracey aren't like that. But why would she say that?"

Brian had known Tracey's response to Mattie the other day in class might get talked about. Mattie couldn't help but spread any news she considered juicy. He hadn't expected his name to be roped into Tracey's claim.

"Because she's always in somebody's business and likes to spread lies. She was getting on Tracey about Bernard saying she wanted him back. So she said she was sleeping with someone. Then we walked out of the class together. Mattie read things wrong."

Even though Brian hadn't liked the snake of desire that wound around him when she said she was going to look for a lover, for a split second he'd considered the possibility of him being her lover. Then he'd remembered that he wasn't the relationship type, nor was he ready to sign up to be Tracey's rebound.

His friends nodded. Quinton spoke first. "All she has to do is see two people together and she's assuming something is going on. I figured you weren't sleeping with Tracey."

"Why you figure that?"

"Because you don't like drama, and you aren't looking to settle down. Tracey is fresh out of divorce. That's too much going on over there."

Cyril nodded. "Way too much. Tracey deserves better."

Brian frowned. "Better than me?"

"Nah, I didn't mean it like that," Cyril said. "Better than what she went through with Bernard. I know you're not trying to be in a serious relationship right now. You said so yourself."

"I'm not." But that was the second time someone said Tracey would be better off without him. He didn't want a relationship, but he wouldn't do anything to hurt Tracey if the two of them did happen to get together. Tracey needed someone to show her some affection, treat her right. If he were a relationship guy, he could at least do that. His divorce had soured him on long-term commitments, but he hadn't turned into a dog either.

"So Renee called me," he said thinking about his conversation with his ex.

"Man, what the hell did she want?" Quinton asked twisting his lips.

"She says her husband thinks I'm her kid's father."

Quinton's eyes bulged, then narrowed. "Are you?"

"Hell no. I haven't messed with her since that night at our friend's party. But she told her husband. Now he's jealous and thinking we're still hooking up."

"Damn, that's fucked up," Cyril said. "What did you do?"

"Told her that was her problem and blocked her number. I don't have time for that."

Quinton's assessing gaze landed on Brian. He wondered if that was the same look he gave to the players on his football team. "That woman has a hold on you."

Brian's defenses went up. She'd *had* a hold on him. He was done with Renee now. "No, she doesn't."

Both Quinton and Cyril sucked their teeth and gave him doubtful looks. Brian stared at Cyril. "Not you, too?"

"Hey, I know we've only been friends for a few years, but I've heard the way you talk about her. And I was there after you two hooked up the last time. That woman had you all the way screwed up. She's in your system, man."

"She is not in my system. That relationship is over and done with. She's having another man's baby. We are done."

Brian meant that with his whole heart. He was done playing games with Renee. He liked women who were more straight-forward with what they wanted. He didn't want to have to guess where he stood when dealing with someone.

"So if she walked in here right now, looked at you with those big brown eyes and said she missed you, what would you do?"

Brian scowled, picturing the scene in his head. Renee would expect him to trip over himself to get her what she wanted. The vision made his stomach curl.

"I'd tell her to call her husband and leave me alone with that mess." He took a sip of his bourbon.

Quinton raised a brow. "Whatever. You'd fall for it, take her right back to your place."

"Hell no," Brian said. "I am done with Renee. All the way done. I've already moved on."

"You sleeping with other women doesn't mean you've moved on," Quinton said.

Brian narrowed his eyes. "I've. Moved. On." He realized it might take time for his friends to believe him. Actions spoke louder than words, and in the past his actions proved he was Renee's plaything. Not anymore. He'd prove it to them and to his ex.

Quinton shook his head and sipped his drink. Brian looked

at Cyril, who held up a hand and shrugged. Brian accepted that they were willing to let the subject drop.

"Now, Cyril, what's up with the wedding pl…" He spotted Tracey through the window and his voice trailed off. She was on the arm of some dude and wore a dress that barely covered her ass and breasts. "What the hell?"

He watched as the two of them went to the door of the cigar bar. They came in. The man's hand on the small of Tracey's back in the too short, too tight, sexy as hell black dress. The conversation in the room lowered for a second as several sets of male eyes zeroed in on Tracey in the skimpy black dress. They made their way to the bar. Brian got a better look at the man's face and recognized him from his gym. The guy always walked around trying to hit on every woman that came in the gym and was, according to the rumor mill, sleeping with the woman who worked behind the counter.

"What is she doing with him?" Brian put his drink and cigar on the table.

"Who?" Quinton asked.

Cyril tapped Quinton on the shoulder and pointed to the bar. "Tracey, that's who."

Quinton looked at Tracey and the guy then back at Brian. "Hold up. Are you and her really hooking up?"

Brian tore his gaze away from Tracey laughing at whatever the guy had said. "We're not. I just know him. He's not right for her."

"Why?" Cyril asked.

"Because, he's sleeping with the woman that works at the gym. And he's still asking for numbers of the other women in the gym. He's not looking to settle down."

"Maybe she isn't either," Quinton said with a shrug. "I mean, she just got divorced. She might not want to get into another relationship."

"But she still needs someone decent. That guy isn't it."

He looked back at the bar. The guy's hand drifted from Tracey's lower back to the top of her behind. Brian's eyes narrowed and he stood. "I'll be right back."

He crossed the room to the bar before they could say anything. He stood behind her and spoke up. "Hey, Tracey, what's up?"

Tracey turned wide, surprised eyes on him. She'd put on makeup that enhanced the brightness of her eyes and a gloss that brought attention to the fullness of her lips. She looked damn good. Enticing. Like a woman on the lookout for that lover she mentioned. Breathing became hard.

The surprise left her eyes and was replaced with curiosity. "Oh hey, Brian. What's up?"

He didn't know what was up. He'd crossed the room ready to tell her to stay away from the player sitting next to her, but he knew Tracey. She'd say he was minding her business and push him away. He had no right to tell her who to see or date, but he hadn't been able to just sit there and not mind her business.

He racked his brain for a good reason to have approached her and said, "We still good for tomorrow?"

She nodded slowly. "Yeah, I'm still good."

He glanced at the guy, who watched him closely. Before he could interrupt and say something to Brian, he focused back on Tracey. "What time do you want me to come over?"

She raised a brow. "We already agreed that you'd come by at two. That still works."

"Just want to make sure." He looked back at the guy and lifted his chin. "Hey, don't you work out at my gym?"

The guy nodded and grinned. "Yeah, I've seen you around."

"You and the girl behind the counter. Y'all are cool, right?" Brian didn't give a damn about putting his business out there. He couldn't openly warn Tracey, but he could throw some hints.

The guy's face tightened. "Just friends."

Tracey shifted and got his attention. "Okay, Brian, have a nice night." She did two quick tilts of her head as if asking him to walk away.

She either wasn't taking the hint or was going to ignore it. He wouldn't say anything to her in front of him, but maybe if he pulled her to the side she might listen.

He pointed over his shoulder. "Can we talk for a minute?"

Tracey sighed and rolled her eyes. "No, we can't. I'm on a date. Go back to your boys, and we'll talk tomorrow."

"But—"

Tracey put her hand on his shoulder and turned him away. "Bye, Brian. See you tomorrow." She gave him a shove.

He could have resisted the movement, but that would only cause a scene. She'd dismissed him, and he had no good reason to stick around. Tracey wasn't his woman. He wasn't her man. He also wasn't the man for her. If she wanted to make a mistake, then that wasn't on him.

He glanced back at her over his shoulder. "Hey, if you need anything, give me a call, okay? Be safe out here."

Her lips pursed, and he prepared himself for her to tell him to mind his own business. But a beat later, she relaxed and nodded. "I'm good, Brian. Enjoy your night."

He looked back at the guy, who had a smug smile on his face while his eyes trailed over Tracey's body. He wanted to pull her to his side and drag her out of there. So much so, his hand clenched into a fist to stop himself from reaching for her. He wanted to tell her that she was worth more than the little bit of attention this guy would give her. But doing that meant what? That he was ready to move their relationship to something else? They were friends. He was looking out for her, had tried to give her a hint, but at the end of the day she had to make her own choices.

"Cool, but the offer still stands. If you need me, call." He looked, met the guy's eyes, and added, "Anytime." The guy frowned, and Brian cocked a brow. Then he turned and rejoined his friends.

11

Tracey got through the next morning in a daze. She helped
Shirley get breakfast together, greeted the guests, repaired the
broken hook for the curtains in the parlor and called a plumber
to check the leak in the carriage house. Things she would nor-
mally do, except her brain was only halfway there. Thoughts
of the night before kept popping into her head.

When she'd run into Craig at the grocery store in the veg-
etable aisle and he'd asked her out, she hadn't had a reason to
say no. She knew the rumors about Craig. He was a hit-it-
and-quit-it type of guy. The only thing in her future with him
would be a one-night stand, and she'd been ready and willing
to take that. After announcing to Mattie that she was sleeping
with someone, she couldn't hide out in the inn every night.
Besides, even though she was having a good time pleasuring
herself, she did miss the feel of a body against hers. The divorce

was recently finalized, but she and Bernard had been separated for a year and hadn't had sex for months before that.

She wanted to have sex, and Craig had seemed like a good enough candidate. Despite him being a serial playboy, the rumors about his abilities in the bedroom had given her hope that he would at least provide a good time.

Everything had gone great. He was a bit slick, but the appreciation and desire in his eyes was something she hadn't seen in the last few years of her marriage. She'd been on board, until Brian had to come up and kill the vibe.

Which made no sense at all. She didn't understand why he thought it was okay to interrupt her date with Craig. Then for him to try and pull her aside as if she were some female family member he needed to protect from the Big Bad Wolf was ridiculous. After sending him away, all she could focus on was his eyes staring at her and Craig in the bar. She'd practically jumped up and ran out when Craig suggested they go back to his place. Leaving the cigar lounge and going back to Craig's had seemed like the best way to get back into the Let's Get Laid game. Except, everything about Craig's setup had made her want to roll her eyes and laugh. The soft music he'd played, the way he'd supposedly accidentally spilled the wine on his shirt and had to take it off so he could flex his pecs. It was all from a played-out book of seduction. Played-out or not, she'd gone with it, and when he'd kissed her, for a moment she believed she would be able to relax and let go. His hand was beneath her shirt and her heart rate was accelerating when Brian's face popped into her mind. Her mom called at the same moment. Her mom hadn't wanted anything important, but Tracey used the interruption as an excuse to leave and help her mom with a made-up emergency.

Craig had looked disappointed, but he hadn't pushed for her to stay. He'd kissed her and invited her to come back over tonight. Tracey should go back over. Craig hadn't been overbearing or rude, he kissed well, and he'd been getting her body hot. Why not get back out there with a man who knew what he was doing?

"Ms. Tracey!"

Tracey jumped and spun around. She'd been staring out of the window in her office replaying the night before. Jessica stood at her door. "Why are you yelling?"

Jessica held up three fingers. "I called you three times. You didn't hear me."

The tone of her voice made Tracey want to ask her who she thought she was talking to. The only reason she didn't was because she had been distracted and not hearing people call her name all morning.

"My bad. What is it?"

"Brian is here. He says he had an appointment."

Tracey's heart did a nervous flip. The unexpected flutter made her want to kick the wall. Or Brian's shin. This was all his fault. Stepping in like some jealous lover and getting her brain all mixed up. They were supposed to study, but before they did anything she was going to tell Brian to stop getting in her way and minding her business.

"We do. Send him on in."

Brian stepped up behind Jessica. "I'm right here." He raised a hand. The corner of his lips lifted in a small smile.

Tracey's stomach clenched. The urge to kick returned. Time to get this over with and soon. She motioned with her finger for him to come in. "Good. Come on in."

Jessica walked away. Brian came into the office and put a book bag down in one of the chairs in the sitting area next to the window. He was dressed casually, tan T-shirt with his nursery's name that strained against muscled biceps and a pair of jeans that sagged just enough to show the top edge of his briefs. Even in casual clothes the man still looked like he could walk a runway.

Tracey walked past him and closed the office door, which he'd left open. When she turned to face him he'd come closer. She sucked in a breath as the room seemed much smaller with him there. He smelled nice, not like the earthy smell that clung to him when he was delivering the plants, but a combination of some spicy cologne and his own distinct scent.

"How was last night?" he asked.

Was she losing it, or did he sound like a jealous boyfriend? Shaking her head she pushed that thought aside and pointed at him. This was exactly why she needed to set him straight. "About last night. I don't appreciate the way you came up on me and Craig like that."

She expected him to back down. To hold up his hands in surrender and apologize like he usually did whenever she called him out for getting into her business.

Instead, he crossed his thick arms and spread his legs as if settling in to tell her a thing or two. "Since you're going there, I will, too. Craig is no good."

Tracey put her hands on her hips. "Why do you say that?"

"Because he's sleeping with half the women at the gym."

Tracey waited for something else. When he didn't give her another reason she shrugged. "And?"

Brian blinked then looked at her as if she'd sprouted horns. "And? Tracey, you deserve better than a guy like Craig."

Tracey rolled her eyes so hard she was surprised they didn't roll right out of her head. Who was he to tell her what kind of guy she deserved? She'd twisted herself into someone she didn't recognize because she'd thought she didn't deserve Bernard when they first got married. All her life she'd been told she wasn't good enough for a certain type of guy and now she was suddenly too good for another type. She wasn't living by what other people thought. She wasn't looking for a perfect guy. She was looking for someone to make her feel hot, sweaty, passionate desire after years of being frozen in a bad marriage.

"Don't tell me what I do and do not deserve. I'm not trying to marry him, damn! I'm just trying to fuck."

She used the word on purpose. She needed to be blunt. She needed him to understand that she wasn't some damsel he needed to save. She no longer cared if people thought she was being loose like her mom. She was a grown woman with needs. She was looking for a guy to sleep with, not to get tangled back up in a bad situation like she had with Bernard for years.

"Then, fuck me," he shot back without blinking an eye.

The words were so surprising and hit her with such force she stumbled back as if he'd pushed her. Her heart jumped to her throat and fell to her feet. Brian stepped forward and placed his hand on her elbow, steadying her body, but her insides still tumbled.

"Stop playing." Her voice trembled, her usual composure blown away by Brian's equally blunt words. He had to be playing. Brian was her colleague, at most a casual friend. But he wasn't interested in her. He'd never been. Had he?

"Do I look like I'm playing?" His dark gaze didn't leave hers. He took a step closer. The heat of him. The intensity of him as he stared back made her breath stutter.

"You don't like me like that." Disbelief coated her words.

Brian cocked his head to the side. "Says who?"

She sputtered for a second and waved a hand. "No one has to say it. I saw the girls you've dated since high school. The cute, pretty-girl type. Your ex-wife was a model or something."

Brian grimaced then shook his head. "No, she wasn't."

"Still, I looked her up and know what she looks like. That's not me."

She was still so surprised by the turn of the conversation that she couldn't even be embarrassed about admitting as much. The Peachtree Cove grapevine had put the word out that he'd quit college and married some model before moving to California.

Curiosity had gotten the better of her, and she'd dug through their mutual friends on social media until she'd found a picture.

"What's wrong with you?" Brian asked as if the answer wasn't obvious.

"I'm loud. I'm always messing up. I'm—"

Brian stepped even closer. Cutting off her words as his voice lowered and he said in a soft but confident voice, "The person I've wanted to fuck since I was a teenager."

White-hot desire slid through her midsection and settled heavily between her legs. Her sex clenched. The rawness of his words, the heat in his eyes and the proximity of his body made her want to believe him. She closed her eyes and held up a hand. "Okay, we can stop saying that word."

"Does it matter how I say it? *Sleep with. Make love. Have sex with.* It's all the same. I want to sleep with you, Tracey. I've wanted to sleep with you for a very long time."

Her eyes popped open. "Really?"

He nodded slowly. "Really. Why do you think I was always looking at you in high school?"

"Because I was always getting in trouble around you." Every time she got in trouble he was there. But he'd also watched her in class. In the lunch room. At school events. She'd thought he watched her because he was waiting to see her screw up again. Not because he'd been interested. He'd never looked at her with the sloppy lust some of the other guys used to throw her way.

"Why do you think I pay attention to you now?"

She poked his chest. "*You* said we were friends. That's all this was."

"We are, so let's be friends with benefits."

She sighed and held up a hand. "Men say that mess when all they want are the benefits. Not the friendship."

"I do all the friend stuff already. This way I'll also give you orgasms." His lips lifted in a half smile.

Her heart fluttered and her sex tightened. Did he know exactly how sexy he was? She wanted to sleep with someone, but a warning bell in the back of her brain said she might not be able to handle Brian. Craig, with his played-out lines and transparent attempts at seduction, made it easy to not get her emotions involved. Brian, on the other hand, was closer to her. He knew her secrets and weaknesses because he'd witnessed them throughout the years. If he wanted to embarrass or hurt her later, he could.

She shook her head. "Nah, we can't."

"Why not? You're looking for a lover. I'm a much better candidate than Craig." He tossed out Craig's name as if he was already on a list of the World's Worst Lovers.

"How would you know? You slept with him?"

"I don't have to sleep with him to know that I can make love to you much better than Craig can. He couldn't possibly crave the taste of your skin the way I do." He slid forward, erasing the final bit of distance between them. "Has he fantasized about all the ways to make you come? Thought about kissing your lips when you pull the corner of your bottom lip between your teeth? Wondered what your fingers would feel like against his body while watching you write?"

Breathing became impossible. "You do that?" Her voice was barely a whisper.

"I do. Don't sleep with Craig. If you're going to sleep with anyone, sleep with me."

Her control slipped. She was falling into the trap. Brian was also good at seduction. He was just better than Craig. "You sleep around, too."

"Not while I'm with you."

She raised a brow. "Cute girl at the bar? You're really going to stop seeing her."

"It's already over. I mean what I'm saying, Tracey. It'll just be you for the entire time we're together."

He was too close. His gaze too intense. She felt partly like a gazelle caught in the lion's gaze and partly like the lion ready to pounce on its prey. He wasn't even touching her yet, and already her skin was hot. "I don't know if this is right."

She shifted to move away. Brian shifted with her. "Why not?"

"I never thought about you like that," she lied. She'd thought about him like that more times than she could count, but it had always been a secret fantasy. Something she would let pop in her head then push away because Brian was out of her league.

"Then, let me give you something to think about."

He wrapped an arm around her waist and pressed her against him. His head lowered, his lips brushed against hers. She should push away. He would let her go if she did, but control had flown out the window like a long-caged bird. She lifted her chin and parted her lips. Brian's tongue slid across hers as his other arm wrapped around her until she was engulfed in his embrace. Had fireworks gone off, or was that just the explosion of passion in her brain? Brian's kiss blew Craig's completely out of her mind. His lips and tongue played across hers with a confidence that had her melting into him.

Maybe he sensed it, because he pushed forward, walking her back until she was pressed against the door. His hand went from her back to brush along the side of her breasts. Her nipples hardened, and she moaned. She arched her back, hoping he would touch her more. Instead, his hand moved up and gently wrapped around her neck. The slight, possessive move had her whimpering and wanting to be claimed as his.

When he pulled back his breathing was heavy, and his eyes simmered with desire. "Yes or no, Tracey?" His thumb rubbed the pulse pounding at the base of her throat.

Yes was on the tip of her tongue. She wanted to shout yes from the rooftop. But if she was anything she was stubborn. She would not let Brian think he could just come in here and get her in his bed with just a kiss. One bone-melting, heart-hammering kiss, but still it was just a kiss.

She pushed his chest. He immediately let her go and stepped back. Her fingers curled into a fist to stop herself from reaching out, grabbing his shirt and jerking him back to her. He'd proven his point. They had chemistry. Sex could be good between them. But she also knew herself. She couldn't jump into this without thinking of the consequences.

Tracey straightened her clothes and lifted her chin. "I'll think about it and let you know later this week."

Brian's lips lifted in a knowing smile. She kept her eyes on him, refusing to blink or back down. He nodded. "Later this week, then."

12

When Brian's mom asked him to install a new ceiling fan for her, he'd gone straight to her place after work. He looked at the description on the side of the box for the new ceiling fan then called down the hall. "Mom, which room did you want this in?"

"In the guest bedroom," his mom answered from the back of the house.

"The guest bedroom?" he muttered to himself. He lifted the box and headed down the hall toward the guest room. "Why do you need it in there?"

His mom came out of her bedroom and followed him into the guest room. "Your aunt is coming to visit. The last time she slept in there she said she nearly melted. Well, now she can cool off."

"You're putting a ceiling fan in here for Aunt Sharon who only stays in this room once a year." He put the fan box on the floor then kneeled to slice the tape sealing it closed with his pocketknife.

His mom sat on the edge of the quilt-covered queen bed and watched him. "It may be once a year, but I still want her to be comfortable. A fan will help."

Brian closed the pocketknife and slid it back in his pocket. "You know you can just turn the air-conditioning down?"

His mom frowned and shook her head. "Oh no. I'm not going to run the light bill up. A fan will work just fine."

Brian grinned but held back his laugh. His mom wasn't about to turn her thermostat off the recommended settings for maximum energy efficiency. Not even for one or two nights while her sister visited.

"It shouldn't take me long to put this up." He started pulling out the various parts and sorting them on the floor.

"I know. You're good at that kind of stuff."

His mom silently watched him before asking in a deceptively innocent voice, "So I heard an interesting story at the grocery store the other day."

"What kind of interesting story?" He had an idea. The rumor was already out there that he was the person sleeping with Tracey. But there was a slim chance the rumor hadn't gotten back to his mom. He kept his attention on the fan.

"One about you and Tracey."

His hand slipped, and he dropped one of the fan blades. "Huh?"

His mom gave him a small, knowing smile. "I guess it's true."

"What's true?"

She raised a brow. "Don't make me say the words. Tell me you don't know what the story is?"

He couldn't lie. "Mom, you don't have to worry."

"I can't help but worry. I don't want either of you to get hurt."

He frowned. "Get hurt? No one is going to get hurt. We aren't even doing whatever the people in the town are saying. That's just Mattie spreading rumors and getting things stirred up."

He went back to organizing the items in the box. He didn't want to look his mom directly in the face. He wasn't technically lying. Tracey hadn't given him an answer when he'd asked her to sleep with him the day before. After the kiss he'd expected her to immediately agree. The sparks between them were undeniable. But he'd seen the challenge in her gaze. She wasn't going to jump into anything with him based on sparks alone. He'd have to be patient, even though patience was killing him.

"Are you sure? There's nothing going on?"

"Tracey and I are friends and colleagues. We hang out sometimes. We'll be hanging out more because we're in the entrepreneur class together. We're working together on some of the assignments. That's all it is."

Though they hadn't worked on the assignment the day before. There was no way he'd be able to sit across from her at a table and talk about marketing ideas after that kiss. It had taken everything in him not to pull her back into his arms and kiss her again. He'd wanted to touch every part of her body. Which was why he said he'd email her his idea and then she could email him. She'd quickly agreed.

"Look at me," she said in her no-nonsense voice.

Brian turned and met his mom's gaze. Her eyes narrowed as she looked at him closer. "Are you telling the truth?"

He pulled on every ounce of self-preservation and *I don't want my mom to lecture me* he could muster and gave her a smile. "I'm telling the truth. There's nothing to worry about."

She watched him again before nodding, satisfied. Brian forced himself not to relax with relief. He'd mastered hiding his devilment from his mom when he was in high school. He loved her and didn't mind talking to her about most things, but talking about who he was and wasn't sleeping with was too much for him.

"Good. I'll go check on the pot roast while you do that."

After she left, Brian pulled out his cell phone and checked

for any missed calls. There were none. As if Tracey would call him up the next day. If anything, she'd keep him hanging while she went over all the reasons why she should or shouldn't sleep with him.

Brian couldn't believe he'd thrown the offer out there the way that he had. He hadn't gone over with the intention of doing that. He had gone with the intention of telling her Craig was no good for her before trying to convince her that she could do better. But when she'd said she wasn't looking for a relationship, that she was only looking for sex, something inside him had snapped. A decades-long crush on Tracey collided with a primitive need to be the one who touched, kissed and made love to her had him reacting before he could even think.

Now came the waiting game. Would she or wouldn't she? How could she believe he'd never been interested in her? Had she really been that oblivious to the way she affected him? Granted, in high school he'd never acted on anything because he had been immature and only interested in girls willing to fawn over him. When he'd moved back to Peachtree Cove after his divorce, he'd spent his first few years trying to forget the way Renee had broken his heart. That, and Quinton had been right: he had still been caught up on Renee. It wasn't until their last night together that he'd really and truly gotten her out of his system. If he thought about it, he understood why Tracey didn't think he was interested.

"Well, I'll have to rectify that," he said to himself.

"Rectify what?" his mom asked from the door.

Brian started and turned. "Uh, nothing. Thinking about something at work."

She nodded. "Ah, okay. The pot roast will be done soon. I'm going to watch *Wheel of Fortune*. Call me if you need anything."

"I shouldn't take too long. Just chill."

She smiled, nodded and went back to the living area. Brian got to work taking out the light fixture and putting in the ceiling fan. The entire time he thought about Tracey and how to show her that he was interested in being more than friends. He was willing to wait for her answer, but he could also work to show her that he wasn't indifferent to her. He would just have to do it in a way that wouldn't make her uncomfortable or drive her away.

He was finishing up the fan installation and had come up with the idea of visiting her tomorrow and asking her out for drinks. Maybe a casual hangout. Doing something not related to work would be a good idea before they just slept together. His cell phone chimed. He checked the text from Cyril.

Tracey is here with that Craig guy. In case you want to act like a big brother again.

Brian stared at the text and frowned. His excitement about wooing Tracey withered away. Cyril and Quinton had given him hell when he'd walked over to Tracey and Craig in the cigar bar. They'd said he was acting like an overprotective brother. They'd teased him, but his friends had known the truth: he was jealous. He guessed he had his answer. If Tracey was back out with Craig, then convincing her that he was the better choice was going to be harder than he thought.

Tracey wished she could say she'd felt disappointed when she'd received the phone call from her brother saying she needed to meet him at their mom's place immediately. It wasn't as if she enjoyed having to mediate drama between her parents. She could go the rest of her life without having to deal with their toxic relationship tendencies. But considering that she was in the middle of a date with Craig and instead of feeling a tenth of the excitement she'd had with him before when they'd kissed, she latched on any excuse to leave. She'd spent half of the date forcing herself to pay attention to what Craig was saying and the other half with her mind wandering to the kiss she'd shared with Brian.

So she'd taken her brother's call, told him she'd be there in a second and thrown a few words Craig's way about meeting up later as she'd rushed out the door. On the way to her mom's place, the home she shared with her boyfriend, Raymond, Tracey went over the events of the night. Her hands tightened on the steering wheel and her frustration and confusion grew. She'd never believed Brian was interested in her like that. When they were younger she'd refused to become like the other girls in school who'd damn near melted whenever he bothered to look their way. He'd known how good he looked and used that to his advantage. So anytime she'd sensed flirtation she'd assumed it was because that was his default when he dealt with girls. She'd thought the same when they formed a pseudo-friendship after he moved back to town. But she hadn't imagined that he would offer up a friends-with-benefits situation.

Or that he'd come on so strong.

Worse, she never would have expected that an offer from Brian would have scrambled her brain. She'd hoped putting distance between them and going on the date with Craig would minimize the effect he'd had on her. Instead, she only craved him more. And she hadn't craved a man's kiss or touch in a long time.

She was very aware that what she felt was lust. A feeling that had been dormant for too long inside of her finally coming to life. Knowing that didn't change anything. She wanted Brian, but she also liked him where he was in her life. She wasn't worried about falling for him, but she was worried about things becoming weird when they ultimately had to end. Could they really go back to working together without any awkwardness?

Thoughts of Brian fled as she pulled up to her mom's place. Her brother's truck was already in the drive. He stood out front with her dad, who looked like he was trying to get inside but

Devante held him back. Swearing under her breath, Tracey parked her car along the street and got out.

Her dad's cries for her mom to come outside and see him immediately hit her. "Loretta! Loretta, baby, I love you. Come back! I promise I won't drink no more!"

Tracey glanced up and down the street. Lights were on behind windows and curtains fluttered. The neighbors were watching. Everyone in Peachtree Cove would know this story before lunchtime tomorrow.

"Loretta! Baby, please! I swear I won't drink anymore. Not after tonight. Just come back."

Her brother pulled on her dad's arms and kept him from going up the stairs to the front door. "Dad, come on. Don't do this. Let's go home."

Tracey jogged over to her brother and father. "What's going on?"

Devante looked at her with sad, pleading eyes while he struggled to keep their dad from charging toward the front door. "Help me calm him down."

Tracey moved and stood in front of her dad. She placed a hand on his shoulder and moved her head until she caught his eye. "Daddy. Look at me."

His eyes focused on her, and he smiled. The smell of gin wafted off him. "Oh hey, Tracey girl. What are you doing here?"

Tracey looked him in the eye. "It's time to go home, Daddy."

He frowned, and it took a second for his dark eyes to focus on her face. When they did he shook his head. "No, no, no. Not until your momma comes home."

"Daddy, she won't come back if you're like this. You should go home and sober up first." She kept her voice firm. She'd learned early that pleading with her dad when he was like this didn't work.

"But that's my wife." He pointed to the house. "Up in there with another man."

"I'll get her and bring her home, okay?" Tracey lied calmly and easily. She'd say whatever she needed to say to get her dad to cooperate. "You go with Devante and calm down. You'll wake up the neighborhood like this."

Her dad looked around then back at her. His face crumpled as the shame of being seen by the neighborhood settled in. "Oh, Tracey, I'm sorry. You don't like it when I make a scene."

"I don't. So go on home, and I'll get Momma, okay?"

Her brother tugged on their dad's shoulder. "Come on, Dad. Let me get you home."

Her dad's shoulders slumped, and he nodded. "You'll bring her home?"

Tracey nodded and helped Devante turn her dad from the house. "I'll deal with Mom. You sober up. You're not supposed to be drinking anymore."

"I wasn't going to. I swear I just had one drink."

"Sure, Dad." She looked at her brother. "You got him?"

Devante sighed before giving her a quick nod. "I got him. Come on, Dad."

Tracey watched as he led their dad away from the house and to his truck. After they drove away, she walked up the steps and rang the doorbell. She doubted her mom would answer so she knocked as well.

"Ma, it's me. Come on, open the door."

The door quickly swung open. Her mom glared over Tracey's shoulder toward the street. "Is he gone?"

"He is. Devante got him and took him home."

Sighing, her mom stepped back so Tracey could enter the house. "Good. He's lucky Raymond isn't here. He would have come out and beat his ass. Bad enough half the neighborhood heard him. Now I'm going to have to deal with that and try to calm Raymond down when he hears what happened."

She'd turned and gone farther into the house. Tracey followed her to the living area. The house was large and spacious, with an open floor plan, nice furniture and modern artwork that her mom said she thought was ugly but wouldn't tell Raymond because she didn't want him to think she didn't have any culture.

"Is he going to give you any trouble?" Tracey asked concerned.

Her mom picked up a pack of cigarettes off the coffee table and gave Tracey an exasperated look. "Don't worry. I can handle anything he gives." She moved to the sliding glass doors that led out to the back deck.

Tracey quickly followed her. "What does he give? Ma, you don't have to put up with anyone treating you bad."

Loretta pulled out a cigarette and tapped it against the deck railing. "He's not treating me bad. He's just going to fuss, and I don't want to hear his mouth. That's all."

"You sure?"

Loretta lit the cigarette and took a long drag. "I'm sure. You don't have to worry about me. I can handle him. It won't be half as bad as when I had to drag your dad in the house when he passed out drunk in the front yard."

Tracey sat in one of the plush chairs on the back deck. "If you say so."

Loretta blew out smoke and raised a brow. "I do say so. Instead of worrying about me, how about you worry about yourself?"

"I don't have anything to worry about. I'm doing good."

"Oh really? Then, what's this I hear about you sleeping with Brian?"

"Would it be anyone's business if I was?" She wasn't sure what answer she wanted to give, but she wasn't about to let her mom know that she was on the fence.

Her mom lifted a shoulder. "It wouldn't be anyone's business but your own. But—"

"But what?"

"But you just got rid of Bernard."

"I'm just trying to take some time to figure out what I want. Wasn't that your advice to me?"

Her mom nodded and took another drag of her cigarette. "Since when do you listen to me?"

Tracey's cell phone rang. "I've always listened, you just never noticed." She pulled her cell out of her back pocket and frowned at the screen. "What does he want?"

"Who?"

"Bernard." Sighing, she answered the call. She wanted to ignore him, but he wouldn't call her unless he needed to. She hoped he was stranded on the side of the road and Monique had refused to get him. She'd love to leave him stranded. "What?"

"Are you messing around with Brian?" His question sounded more like an accusation.

Tracey's back straightened, and her brows drew together. "Excuse me? Why are you calling my phone with this?"

"Tell the truth, Tracey. Are you and him messing around?"

"That's none of your business. You shouldn't care about who I'm messing around with."

"I can care because you know how I feel about him."

Tracey rolled her eyes. "I don't know or care how you feel about him."

She did know exactly how he felt. Bernard didn't like Brian and hadn't for years, but when he'd started working with Tracey, he'd really started to hate on Brian. She could barely mention Brian's name without Bernard sneering and calling him a *washed-up pretty boy*. She had to admit, pissing off Bernard by making Brian the first guy she hooked up with after the divorce held a certain appeal.

"You know I don't like him. You know I always thought he

was interested in you. Have you been sleeping with him this whole time? Did you cheat on me with him?" The pitch of his voice rose with each question.

"Oh my God, I can't believe you're acting like you have any right to come at me about what I do. How's the baby, Bernard?" she asked sarcastically.

"Quit playing. You've been cheating on me, haven't you? You better not have. I knew something was going on. How could you do something like that?"

"Bye, Bernard." She hung up the phone. Tracey shoved the phone in her back pocket and swore. She pressed a hand to her temple. She couldn't believe he had the gall to call her and ask if *she'd* been cheating on *him*. The same guy who'd had a whole baby with Tracey's employee while they'd been married. Now he was calling and accusing her. She'd never once cheated on him, but for him to think he had any room to comment on her actions made her want to break something.

"Bernard mad about you and Brian?" her mom asked chuckling.

Tracey looked up at her mom. "How could he do that? What makes him think he has any right?"

"Because he's a sorry man. He can do whatever he wants, but it's probably killing him knowing you aren't sitting around every night crying about losing him. If you aren't sleeping with Brian I hope you start soon. It would serve Bernard right." Her mom's cell rang. She looked at her phone and flinched. "Damn, it's Raymond. Let me make sure he's good." She swiped across her phone and answered in a sweet voice. "Hey, baby."

Tracey watched as her mom went back into the house to finish her call. Tracey was still shocked at Bernard's audacity. She'd known he didn't like Brian. A few times she'd considered breaking up her partnership with Brian because Bernard didn't like him, but the few times she'd used another vendor to help with the plants for her weddings it had cost more and wasn't the same level of service. So she'd avoided talking about Brian in front of Bernard. Never had she considered cheating with Brian because, unlike her ex-husband, she wasn't a cheater.

But now she was single. She'd mastered having orgasms on her own thanks to her new toys and letting go of feeling guilty for masturbating. She was interested in sleeping with a person. She'd never believed Brian would be that person, but they had a spark. A spark that had started when they were younger, but neither had thought to see if that spark could be a flame. Then there was the kiss that had thrown thoughts of Craig out of her head.

She picked up her cell phone and texted Brian before she could change her mind.

My answer is yes.

13

Everything in his life conspired to make Brian late for the
next entrepreneurship class. The deliveries of new seedlings
were late, the plant installation at the new bank went wrong,
and on top of that Peachtree Cove actually had a traffic jam
when a truck carrying watermelons through town overturned
on the main road and backed everything up.

A part of him wanted to call it a day, skip the class, and go
home and chill. A bigger, more eager part of him couldn't wait
to see Tracey. He hadn't talked to her since she'd sent the text
saying her answer was yes. He'd thought she was going to say
no after Cyril texted him to say he'd seen her at the bar with
Craig. But seeing her answer had made him want to jump up
and do a two-step. Instead, he'd played it cool. Texted back
Cool. Let's talk. To which she'd responded I'll see you in class.
Talk then.

He'd been on pins and needles waiting for the day of the

next class to arrive. He hadn't felt this excited about seeing a woman in years. Not since before he'd gotten married. He didn't think too hard about how the feelings he'd had back then had ultimately led him to propose. He had no plans to ever get married again, neither did Tracey. This wasn't turning into something serious and he knew that, but he still anticipated spending time with Tracey.

The parking lot was full when he finally made it to class. "What the hell?" he mumbled to himself. "Is everyone in town here tonight?"

He found a parking space at the back of the lot, jumped out of his truck and hurried inside. He checked his watch and nodded. He wasn't that late. Just about five minutes.

He rushed down the hall. People filled each classroom. That explained the full parking lot. He entered his classroom and stopped short. His eyes scanned the crowd, which looked bigger than last time. He spotted Tracey sitting in the same spot she'd had the week before. He smiled and relaxed just seeing her. His gaze landed on the spot next to her, his spot, and he scowled.

What the hell?

His spot was taken. Carolyn sat to Tracey's left. That wasn't what made him scowl. Craig sat to Tracey's right. Why was Craig there? He didn't own a business. And what was he doing next to Tracey? Were they still a thing? She hadn't said anything about them being exclusive. Was she planning to see both of them? The idea made him want to walk in and push Craig out of his seat. He'd had his share of nonexclusive relationships. Since his divorce he hadn't had a problem with that because it was less likely for things to get serious or expectations for forever to fall on him. The sudden strike of jealousy at the idea of having to share Tracey with anyone else surprised him.

"Oh, Brian, there's a seat up front." Mikayla waved him to the front of the classroom.

Everyone turned his way. Tracey gave him her normal look.

Neither excited to see him nor indifferent. Craig, on the other hand, smirked as he watched Brian at the door.

Damn watermelons tying up the roads, Brian thought before nodding and making his way to the front.

Once he was settled, Mikayla resumed talking. "I was just getting started. We're going to go over everyone's ideas from last week before focusing on setting goals for everyone's business. As we work on updating our business plans, these goals will be your road map moving forward."

There were a few questions from some of the people in the class that Mikayla answered easily before she started on the subject for the next session. She'd asked her business partner to remote in and talk about developing a business plan and identifying short- and long-term goals.

The information was useful and interesting, but Brian couldn't focus. He wanted to look back at Tracey. He was happy every time someone behind him asked a question so he could use it as an excuse to turn around. Each time Tracey didn't make eye contact. He didn't think she was avoiding looking at him, more like she was engrossed in the subject. She was always taking lots of notes or asked her own questions. Had she changed her mind?

Brian thought he'd get a chance to talk with her during the break, but even then he didn't get the chance. During the first break, Tracey and a few other people in class went over to Mikayla to ask questions. Tracey went to the bathroom on the second break, and Carolyn caught him up in a conversation about his business plan. When Tracey came back into the room, Craig quickly moved to be by her side. By the end of the class, Brian could barely concentrate. He watched the clock incessantly and tapped his shoe as he waited for the session to end. He was going to talk to Tracey before leaving there if it was the last thing he did.

"Alright, that's it for tonight," Mikayla finally said. "We'll pick up next week. If anyone has questions in the meantime, feel free to email me. I'll try to get back to you all as soon as I can."

Brian jumped up, ready to get out. He turned toward Tracey, but Mikayla called his name. Mentally pushing aside his frustration, he faced forward again.

"What's up?"

"I want to talk to you about presenting at one of our classes," she said.

He blinked, shocked by the request. "Me? Why?"

"Because your business is doing well. You've been well-established for a long time. I was surprised you joined the class."

Brian shrugged. "It's never too late to learn new things. I want to find a way to expand on what I've been doing. You've done great things, so I couldn't turn down an opportunity to learn how you made your business grow."

"Thanks. I appreciate that."

"I really don't know what I can contribute." Compared to what Mikayla had achieved, his success was minimal.

"When we talk about budgeting, invoicing and payroll, I'd like you to talk about your process. I think it'll be good to hear from someone local who's done it. You won't have to teach or anything, but I'd like to call on you to describe your process. It may seem routine to you, but those are the basics that every small business needs to understand. I may even critique how you do things. If you're okay with that?"

He nodded, surprised and overwhelmed that she wanted to use him as an example. "That's cool with me. If you can help me find a way to make that easier, then you won't get a complaint out of me."

She grinned and held out her hand. "Great. I'll email you later in the week to talk about it more."

He shook her hand. "Sounds good."

He turned back to the classroom. Several classmates were

still there, but Tracey was nowhere to be found. His shoulders deflated.

Swearing under his breath, Brian rushed out of the class. He had his cell phone in his hand and was preparing to call Tracey when he spotted her standing by the exit door. Craig was nowhere in sight. She saw him coming her way and lifted her chin in acknowledgment.

"I thought you were gone," Brian said.

"I was waiting on you."

Those were the best words he'd heard all day. She hadn't disappeared with Craig. The level of relief and excitement he felt scared him. So he played it cool. "What for?"

She raised a brow. The look she gave made him feel like she saw straight through him. "What for? What do you think what for? To talk about what we agreed on."

"I wasn't sure if you still wanted to do that. You ignored me half the night."

Tracey scoffed and shook her head. "Hold up. How did *I* ignore you?"

"You wouldn't even look at me."

"I did look at you. What did you want me to do, jump up and down and cheer?" The corner of her mouth lifted in a half smile.

He hadn't expected her to do all that, but the image of Tracey cheering for his arrival had a certain appeal. "You could have at least looked a little bit happy to see me."

She rolled her eyes, but the smile remained on her full lips. Damn, she was sexy. "Goodness, your ego is bigger than I thought."

"My ego? Come on, Tracey, you know I was happy to see you."

She cocked her head to the side, her eyes doubtful. "Were you?"

"Yeah. You couldn't tell? I spent half the class trying to catch your eye. Or were you too busy paying attention to Craig?"

"Are you jealous because he sat beside me?" she asked, a teasing tone in her voice.

Brian nodded. "Yes. I was."

The teasing left her expression. Her lips parted, and her eyes widened. "Seriously?"

He shifted closer and lowered his voice. "Tracey, what part of the fact that I'm interested in you don't you get? I didn't offer this up just for fun."

"I didn't say you did." Her voice was defensive, but the doubt remained in her eyes. He'd work hard to remove any doubt from her mind.

"Good. Because everything I said I meant."

She stared at him for a few seconds. He wondered what she had expected from him. He didn't like that she underestimated his interest. He'd always thought his interest in her was plain to see. Bernard had noticed and never liked him. Even his mom had noticed.

Tracey's shoulders straightened, and she lifted her chin. "Let's go back to your place."

Brian blinked several times. "Now?" She couldn't be serious? He had no arguments against it, but he'd thought they'd ease into this.

She shifted her weight. For a split second something flashed in her eyes before she gave him a confident grin. "No time like the present."

She didn't have to ask him twice. "Let's go."

Tracey parked behind Brian's SUV in his driveway. She took a deep breath, but it did nothing to stop the fluttering in her stomach. Her palms sweated, and her heart vibrated like a hummingbird's wings. She hadn't felt this nervous in years—decades maybe. She was about to sleep with Brian. She hadn't slept with anyone but her ex-husband for the past eleven years. They'd gotten married young, and she'd only slept with one other person before Bernard. In the last few years of her marriage, he'd only shown a passing interest in making love to her. She'd convinced herself she was ready to jump into a sex-only relationship, but old insecurities and years of bad sex made her wonder if she was out of her depth.

Brian turned back to face her car. He raised a brow and gave her a look that asked if everything was okay. She couldn't let him know she was nervous and slightly embarrassed about not knowing how to navigate this situation. He'd give her that pity look and then say they needed to wait. Or, worse, the part of him that was attracted to her would come to its senses and move on. Tracey never let anyone see her vulnerabilities. She wasn't about to start now.

Smiling with a self-assuredness she most definitely didn't feel, she opened the door and got out of the car.

"Everything alright?" Brian asked.

She nodded and forced herself to sound relaxed, chill, a woman ready to handle a friends-with-benefits situation. She was only nervous because it was Brian. She didn't want to make a fool out of herself in front of him again.

"I'm great. I was just checking my messages to make sure everything is good back at the inn."

He nodded, and the concern left his gaze. He tilted his head toward the house. "Come on."

She followed him into his place. Brian stayed in a nice one-story house in an established subdivision. The inside was decorated in simple furniture with a few framed pictures of sports icons such as Michael Jordan scoring a basket when he played for the Chicago Bulls or Muhammad Ali standing over an opponent he'd just knocked out.

"You like sports?" she asked.

He looked at the framed photos and grinned. "I like winners. People who achieved great things and didn't worry about what the world thought of them."

"That's interesting."

He took a few steps toward her, his eyes sexy as they looked over her curves. "Interesting, huh?"

Her heart jumped into her throat. She couldn't talk. He was looking at her like a man ready to make love to a woman. That woman being her. Did that mean it was time to start? No chitchat, just dive right in?

"Are you ready to get started?" she blurted out. She tended to just say what was on her mind when she was nervous.

Brian blinked then chuckled. "How about we ease into things a bit? Talk about the rules of this."

She nodded, relieved and a little let down that he wasn't going to follow up his look and make love to her right there in his living room. Though, she'd never made love in a living room before. Would he want to have sex with her on the floor like in movies? She glanced down. When was the last time he'd vacuumed the carpet? What if he wanted to have sex on the couch? Her gaze darted to the black leather sofa. Would it be comfortable? Would he want her on top? She hoped her knees were up for that. Maybe she should have stretched first.

"Do you want something to drink?" His question broke into her rambling thoughts.

Tracey nodded quickly. "Yes. That would be good." That's exactly what she needed. Something to calm her damn nerves.

She followed him into the kitchen, where he pulled out a bottle of rum from a cabinet above his fridge. "I can mix up a rum punch. Or do you want something lighter?"

"Rum punch is perfect."

She watched as he quickly pulled out orange, pineapple and lime juice. She sat at the kitchen table while he mixed everything together.

"What kind of rules were you thinking?" she asked when he came over holding two glasses.

He handed her one glass and then sat next to her. "First rule is that we don't sleep with anyone else."

She stopped in the middle of taking a sip and quickly swallowed. "You want us to be exclusive?"

"I do. I'm not one to sleep around with multiple people at the same time."

Tracey narrowed her eyes. "Are you sure? I've heard that you be out there in them streets." She sipped the punch. It was sweet, and she could barely taste the rum. In other words, it was perfect.

"I've dated and I haven't been in a long-term relationship, but I'm not trying to get caught up in any drama either. One person at a time, and I'm also very clear if it's just a hookup or something else. Are you okay with us being exclusive?"

With the way her stomach was in knots, and feeling like an impersonator of a woman confident in her sexuality, she didn't want to even think about bringing another man into the mix. "I'm good with that." She took another sip then held up a finger. "But if we're not sleeping with other people, I don't think we need to have too much sex."

He shifted and leaned forward. "What do you mean by that?"

"I don't know how this will work out, but we both know that we don't want emotions to get involved. How about we only have sex twice a week?"

Tracey had never been in a situation like this, but she'd watched enough movies and read enough books to know that sex-only relationships could get very messy when feelings got involved. If they treated their hookups like an appointment that would keep it impersonal, Brian would be her twice-a-week fix, nothing more, nothing less.

"Twice a week?"

"Do you need it more than that?" Maybe her rules were severely cutting back what he was used to.

He shook his head. "I mean, would I like it more? Yes. But I'm cool with twice a week."

She relaxed and took another sip of her drink. That was one potential problem solved. "Good. How about...Tuesday and Thursday? That way we keep our weekends open."

He considered for a second before agreeing. "Cool with me. But we can see each other outside of those days."

"For what?"

"We still work with each other. I'd like to keep our business arrangement going."

"That makes sense. We just can't talk about our arrangement at work."

The rumors linking her to Brian were already out there, but she didn't want to feed into that by openly discussing their arrangement in front of other people.

"I wouldn't do that anyway. What's between us is between us."

"I like that. I don't want anyone else in my business."

"Neither do I."

He put his glass aside and stood. The hummingbird in Tracey's chest started up again. Now that they'd established the rules, they were getting started. She put the glass to her mouth and quickly downed the rest of the drink. She slammed it back down and popped out of her seat.

"You ready now?"

He chuckled then reached for her hand. "Anxious?"

She shook her head. "Me? No. Not at all. I'm just ready to get this started."

He pulled her closer. "Then, let's not wait any longer."

His head lowered, and Tracey squeezed her eyes shut. When his lips met hers she tried to relax and enjoy the kiss. Now they would have sex. But her mind refused to shut down. Were they going to do it in the kitchen? Would he put her on the counter or the table? In theory, that would be extremely sexy, but when was the last time he'd wiped down the counters? Did he always have sex outside of the bedroom? She couldn't ask. What if he thought she wasn't exciting enough? Bernard hadn't thought she was exciting. Maybe she really didn't know what she was doing.

Brian lifted his head and frowned down at her. "You good?"

She nodded stiffly. "Yeah. Why do you ask?"

His hands rested on her hips. "You seem a little distracted."

Damn, she was already messing this up. What was wrong with her? She needed to get out of her head. "No, just…getting in the mood. Warming up the oven." She wrapped her arms around his neck and pressed her body against his. "Kiss me some more."

His lips lifted in a sexy grin. "Gladly."

His mouth covered hers, and this time she forced thoughts from her head. She focused on the moment. His lips were soft and smooth. He tasted just as good as the rum punch he'd made. Her body relaxed, and she was losing herself in the kiss when he pressed forward and her hip bumped the table.

He really was going to put her on the table! Could the table hold her? What if he thought she was too heavy when he lifted her? What if he saw her naked and thought her body wasn't sexy anymore? What underwear had she put on? She hadn't prepared for this at all.

Brian broke the kiss. "You sure you're okay? You keep tensing up."

Double damn. She was really messing this up. Maybe Bernard was right. She pushed that aside. "I'm fine. Really. Are we doing it in here?"

He looked at her for a few seconds before shaking his head. "How about we move to the bedroom? Relax and take our time."

"Yes, the bedroom will be good."

He took her hand and led her to the bedroom. On the way she gave herself a pep talk. She was sexy. She was confident. She was not boring!

Once inside she moved to pull up her shirt. Brian stopped her with a hand on hers. "Hold up. Let's lie down. Let me rub your back and shoulders for a little bit. Help you relax."

"I'm relaxed."

He ran his hands up her arms and gently massaged her shoulders. Brian took a step closer, his eyes never leaving hers. "Let me take care of you, Tracey."

The words knocked all the random thoughts out of her head and hit on something much deeper. When had anyone ever taken care of her? She'd come over with the promise of sex and expected him to be solely interested in that. Instead, he was focused on taking care of her instead of rushing to sleep with her. The gesture warmed her insides. That and the rum seeping through her system.

The tension eased out of her shoulders, and she nodded slowly. She leaned in to the effects of the rum and the good feeling of knowing Brian didn't want to rush. He wanted her to be comfortable. "Okay."

They lay on the bed, her back to his front. Brian rubbed on her shoulders, her arms and her back. She sighed and relaxed even more. Her body sank into the mattress. It was so soft. She wondered if it was a pillow top or maybe one of those foam mattresses. The sheets smelled like Brian. Her eyes closed and she breathed in the smell of him. His big body was warm and comforting behind her. His lips drifted across her shoulder, and Tracey smiled, and she relaxed into the gentle caress of his hands on her body.

14

Tracey slowly opened her eyes and stretched. Sunlight filtered through the blinds. Not the lacy curtains in the room she slept in at the inn. Tracey froze. She rubbed her eyes, but the window coverings didn't change. She looked around: this was not her room. The night before rushed to her. Following Brian back to his place, having a drink, the awkward kiss followed by him leading her to his bedroom. They'd gotten on the bed, Brian had rubbed her back and shoulders. She'd relaxed and then...she couldn't remember.

She was going to be so pissed off if she'd finally had sex and couldn't remember any of it. Tracey lifted the covers and checked her body. She was still dressed. Her shoes were gone, but the rest of her clothes remained. Surely she wouldn't have gotten dressed after having sex. She clenched her sex, checking for any signs of soreness. Nope, everything felt perfectly normal down there. So if they hadn't had sex, what happened?

"Did I fall asleep?" she wondered out loud. Heat crept across her chest, up her neck, and through her cheeks and forehead. She closed her eyes and groaned. She had.

Not only had she not known what she was doing, she'd doubled down and fallen asleep like the tired old woman Bernard claimed her to be. Brian wasn't in bed next to her. She could only imagine what he'd thought. He was probably ready to call their deal to an end. No one wanted the person who fell asleep in the middle of their seduction.

Tracey sat up and saw a yellow sticky note affixed to the nightstand. She recognized Brian's loose, easy handwriting. *There's a new toothbrush in the bathroom. Take your time.*

She got out of bed and went into the adjoining bathroom. After cleaning up, she headed toward the front of the house. She would make this quick and easy. Get out before he could make her feel like crap for falling asleep on him. She'd deal with the fallout of this later.

Brian was in the kitchen. When she entered, he grinned and pointed toward the table. "I've only got two different kinds of cereal. I don't eat breakfast a lot, and when I do it's usually a frozen breakfast biscuit or something quick that I can eat before going to work. I hope you don't mind."

She looked from his smiling face toward the cereal and back. "You want to have breakfast?"

He nodded. "Yeah. Do you have to hurry back to the inn?"

She did need to get back. Shirley would be there handling breakfast. She wasn't even sure if Jessica had made it there on time to make sure the guests were covered. She had interviews lined up for an office manager later that afternoon. Following Brian home had been a whim and something she shouldn't have done knowing everything she needed to do today.

"I kind of do. I have a lot going on."

"Can you spare me twenty minutes before you run out? It's still early. Not even seven yet."

"You still want some of my time?" The words came out before she could think. Guess her get-out-and-deal-with-this-later plan was a waste.

"Why wouldn't I want any of your time?"

"Because I fell asleep when we were supposed to be having sex."

He nodded and crossed his arms. "Yeah, I can't say that's happened to me before."

Embarrassment made her want to turn and run out of his place. Pride kept her feet cemented to the ground. "So are you mad?"

He shook his head. "I'm not mad. Disappointed, a little. But mostly, I want to know what happened."

"I fell asleep," she said defensively. She braced herself for his anger. For him to call her a tease or say she was playing with him.

"I mean, what was up with you last night? I could tell your head was somewhere else."

"I don't know what you mean."

She didn't meet his eyes. He'd noticed that, too. She should have stuck with her vibrator. She been worried about being a bad lover. How in the world was she supposed to explain that?

Brian crossed the room and stood in front of her. "Nah, don't do that. If we're going to be together, then we need to talk. I'm not a mind reader, Tracey. You've got to tell me what's going on up there." He gently tapped her temple.

Tracey looked up and met his eyes. "I wasn't distracted."

He raised a brow, and his stare called bullshit. "Tracey, be real with me. If you can't trust me enough to tell me what's going on, then we might as well not do this."

"Is that it? You want to stop?" she asked defensively.

He shook his head. "That's not what I said. I want to do this. I *really* want to do this, but I don't want to if you're not ready. I won't force anything on you. Understand?"

She closed her eyes. She wanted to sleep with Brian. She was just nervous and afraid. She could walk away right now and he'd never bring up what happened last night again. She could say nothing and pretend she was okay and sleep with him, but he'd think she was forcing herself to have sex with him. Or she could tell him the truth.

"I don't know how to do this," she said in a rush.

"What do you mean?"

Tracey opened her eyes. He studied her face. As if he really wanted to know what was up instead of just saying pretty words to hurry and get her in bed.

Let me take care of you. His words from the night before. Even in the middle of everything he'd shown concern for her. Brian wasn't going to make her feel bad about what happened.

She took a deep breath and then blurted out everything in her head. "I was nervous. I couldn't get out of my own head. I've only had sex with one person for the past eleven years. And only another person before that. I know everyone in this town thinks I'm like my mom. That I had a dozen guys lined up outside my bedroom before Bernard lowered himself to marry me. But I didn't. I talk a good game, but I'm no hot girl or whatever the kids are saying these days."

Once the words were out she wanted to run. But if she couldn't figure this out with Brian, then who would she figure it out with? Craig? The thought of doing something similar with him made her stomach sour. As much as she hated that Brian was always there when she was embarrassed, he never made her feel bad when she was at her lowest. She didn't trust anyone easily, but he'd earned her trust enough that she would try and be open with her feelings.

"I don't expect you to be a hot girl or whatever the kids are saying these days."

"Then, what do you expect?"

"Exactly what you did just now. Be honest with me. Tell me what you want. What you like."

"I don't know if I know what I like. I mean, I'm trying to figure that out, but I'm worried about doing something wrong."

"You can't mess it up."

She put a hand on her hip then pointed back toward the bedroom. "I fell asleep."

He chuckled. "And I'm glad you felt comfortable and safe enough with me that you would fall asleep. We'll try again. You tell me what you're thinking, and don't worry about messing anything up, okay?"

"But you've been with a lot of women."

He brushed her hand on her hip aside and replaced it with his before pulling her closer. "And none of those women were you. I'm not thinking about those women. Right now, the only person I want is you."

Her bones turned to mush, and she leaned into his body. "You're good at this sweet talk stuff."

"It's not sweet talk. It's the truth."

He cupped the side of her face and stared into her eyes. He lowered his head and kissed her. Tracey relaxed into the kiss. Her mind swam not with the thoughts of how things would mess up or what she needed to do but floating on the clouds of his words about wanting to take care of her and his interest in knowing what she wanted. The kiss started slow but quickly increased to the point where her body heated and a delicious tingle started between her legs.

"Do we have time for a quickie?" she asked. "I can make up for last night."

Brian groaned and kissed her again. "No quickie. Not today."

"Why not?"

"Because, I don't want our first time to be a quickie. Just like I didn't want you overthinking like you were last night. Plus, we both have to work. Tomorrow's Thursday. We agreed on Tuesday and Thursday. Let's try again."

"Do you want me to come back here?"

"I don't think so."

"Why not?"

Brian's grin said he already had a plan forming. "Because I've got an idea for a better place."

Brian was in his office scrolling through a travel site when Natalie knocked on the door. He looked up quickly before glancing back at the computer screen.

"What's up?"

"Your brother is out here."

Brian sat back and frowned. His brother lived in Atlanta where he worked as an investor at a bank. He only came to Peachtree Cove for birthdays, holidays or when their mom insisted that she needed to see his face.

"For real? Send him in."

"I'll get him." Natalie turned away, and a few seconds later his older brother breezed through the door.

"What's up, B," DeWayne said with a grin. He was the same height as Brian with the same dark skin and low-cut hair. He was slimmer than Brian with more of a runner's physique. His tailored clothes always showed off his long legs and arms.

"Nothing much. What are you doing in town? Did Mom call you back for a visit?"

DeWayne shook his head and sat in the chair across from Brian's desk. "No, but I am going to go by and see Mom. I had a golf outing with some clients in Augusta, so I decided to swing through before going back home. I came to see if you wanted to hang out after work."

Brian grinned and nodded. "Sure, but I don't get off for a while."

DeWayne glanced around the office. "You own this place. You can get off when you want."

"I do, but I need to check in on a plant installation that went wrong yesterday. I can meet you around seven. That's not too late is it?"

DeWayne twisted his arm to check the expensive watch on his wrist. He frowned and shook his head. "I've got an early meeting tomorrow. I'd hoped to check in on Mom and have an early drink with you so I can get back to Atlanta." He slapped his hands on his crisply pressed slacks then sighed. "How about I chill with you for a few minutes and we get a rain check on drinks?"

Some time with his brother was better than none. Only three years separated Brian and DeWayne, but they hadn't hung out much when they were kids. DeWayne was always focused on two things: making money and getting girls. His brother had done everything their parents expected of him. He'd gone to college, pledged their dad's fraternity and gotten a successful nine-to-five job. Brian had tried to follow his brother's foot-steps, but their love of ladies was the only similarity. Brian couldn't imagine sitting behind a desk all day and having an early morning meeting discussing numbers.

Despite their differences, their relationship was good. They didn't have to talk every day, but Brian knew if he called De-Wayne for anything his brother would be there, and DeWayne knew the same.

"You can chill for a minute. I'm not leaving for that job just yet."

"Cool. What were you working on before I came in?" De-Wayne leaned forward and looked around at Brian's computer screen. "Hotels? Where you going?"

Brian closed the screen with the list of hotels. "I'm thinking about spending the night out of town."

His brother chuckled and leaned back in his seat. "Ah, I get it. Who's the lady? You still seeing Angelica?" DeWayne had introduced Brian to Angelica when he'd visited his brother in Atlanta.

Brian shook his head. "No. I never got to tell you that we didn't work out."

"I thought you were feeling her." DeWayne's disappointment wasn't a surprise. His brother liked to succeed in everything. Even when it came to introducing his brother to a woman he thought he'd be into.

"It just didn't work out. I wasn't ready to give her all she wanted."

DeWayne narrowed his eyes. "Renee called you." His brother said as if that was the answer. "You not starting up with her again, are you?"

"What? No! I'm not even thinking about Renee." Thankfully, she hadn't called him again since he'd last told her that her marital issues weren't his problems.

"Mom mentioned that she called. I'm just checking."

"She called, and I told her that I'm not getting in her business anymore. She'll be good."

"Then, if it's not Renee or Angelica, who is it?"

"Don't worry about all that. Just know it's not either of them."

He didn't want to tell his brother that he was looking up romantic hotels for his next night with Tracey. He wanted her to relax and enjoy their time together. He'd wondered if maybe getting her out of town would help. If he could take her mind off things and focus just on them. No distractions, just the sparks that flew when she let her mind free and got lost in their kiss.

"How was the class?" DeWayne asked.

"Huh?"

"The class?" DeWayne said in an *Earth to Brian* tone. "You had class last night, right? How did it go?"

Brian had forgotten all about going to the entrepreneurship

class the night before. Tracey and their time together had consumed his thoughts. "Oh, it went well. Mikayla wants to use my business as an example in one of the sessions."

DeWayne sat up straight. "For real? That's cool."

His brother sounded impressed, which made Brian sit up a little straighter. He didn't do much that impressed his brother. DeWayne didn't support most of Brian's boneheaded decisions. He'd cursed him out when he'd dropped out of college and eloped with Renee. He'd been frustrated when Brian decided to open a nursery instead of take the job he'd lined up for him at the bank. So for DeWayne to be impressed by Mikayla's request meant his brother might think this was a big deal.

"Yeah, but I didn't see the reason to use my business. I mean, I haven't done much."

"You've done a lot. I may not have agreed with you opening a nursery, but you've kept it in business and you're growing. I don't want to play with plants and dirt all day, but you're making this a success. Don't downplay what you've built."

Those were the most encouraging words his brother had spoken to him in a long time. Brian shifted in his seat. He didn't deserve that much credit. "But I'm in the class to learn how to keep my business successful, not to brag on what I did."

"Go ahead and brag. Hell, even I didn't think you'd make it this far."

Brian scoffed and tilted his head to the side. "Why not? Because I dropped out of college?"

DeWayne frowned before meeting his brother's eye. "Because, man, you were heartbroken when you moved back. I thought you were doing this nursery thing as a rebound before you bounced back and started doing other things."

"I wasn't heartbroken."

His brother raised a brow. "Yes, you were. I would have clowned you, but I was worried you'd break down in tears.

You were worse than one of those sad nineties brokenhearted love songs."

Brian grunted and waved a hand. "Whatever. I wasn't that bad."

"You were pretty bad. That's why I'm glad you're not dealing with Renee and whatever she's trying to bring up and that you're going to a hotel with someone new. Even if it's not Angelica. Don't get tied up in some drama like that again."

"I have no plans on getting tied up in anything. Even though I wasn't nineties brokenhearted love-song sad, I'm not trying to get back in that place. I'm good."

DeWayne nodded and leaned back in his chair. A satisfied look crossed his face. "Good. Then, don't worry about bragging on what you've done with this nursery either. Mom is proud of you. Dad would be proud to see you settled and doing something. I'm proud of you. It's time for you to be proud of yourself."

"I am proud of myself. I just…" He sighed then grinned at his brother. "I'm not as arrogant as you."

His brother glared before wiping at the shoulders of his shirt. "I'm not arrogant. I'm confident."

They both laughed, and Brian relaxed. He looked around his small office. Nowhere near as shiny and opulent as the office his brother had, but it was his. He had started something when he was at his lowest, and now it was successfully thriving. He was proud of what he'd done.

He looked back at his brother. "Thanks for dropping in today." He'd needed the pep talk from his brother. He looked up to him and his words encouraged him.

"Anytime, brother."

15

Tracey walked the last interviewee from her office to the front door. She kept her steps even and measured even though she wanted to skip. The applicant, Debra, was perfect. Not only did she have experience working in the hospitality industry at a small bed and breakfast and most recently at a hotel but she also had a lot of ideas of ways to improve the check-in process and increase their social media presence. The few minutes Debra had taken to talk about making short videos and her ideas for topics that would generate engagement and interest in staying at the inn had Tracey ready to offer her the job immediately.

When they reached the front door, Tracey held out her hand and grinned. "Debra, thanks so much for coming by. I appreciate your interest in working here."

Debra accepted Tracey's handshake with a firm grip and confident smile. "I'm excited about the opportunity. I like what you've built up here, and I would love to be a part of helping you grow even more."

"That's the kind of thing I like to hear. We'll be in touch soon."

After Debra left, Tracey turned back toward her office. She caught Jessica's curious stare. Jessica also had applied for and interviewed for the general manager position. Her interview had gone well enough, except for the fact that all of the things Jessica bragged about doing to help around the inn were things she'd only started doing after Tracey posted the manager position. If Jessica had worked that hard from the start, then Tracey might have considered her for the position. Considering that she hadn't tried to learn the registration process, hadn't bothered to help whenever they'd asked and had acted as if she didn't have any ideas of ways to make the inn better, Tracey wouldn't dare make her own role harder by giving Jessica the job. She'd already shown her true colors.

Tracey gave her a tight, noncommittal smile before hurrying back to her room. Shirley sat at the table where they'd conducted the interviews. When Tracey walked in Shirley looked up and nearly bounced in her seat. The excitement on her face matched the happy shimmy she did in her chair.

"I think that's our girl."

Tracey nodded and sat down next to her. "I think so, too. She's perfect. She has everything we're looking for."

"I know. And she let it slip that she's happily married, which means it's less likely that she'll be inserting herself in anyone's relationships."

Tracey rolled her eyes. "That doesn't concern me anymore. I won't be having any serious relationships for her to butt in to."

She thought about Brian, that kiss and the way he hadn't given her a hard time when she'd fallen asleep. Bernard used to have an entire meltdown when she was tired. Brian's understanding made her even more confident in her decision to sleep with him. But sleeping together wasn't a relationship.

"You might not, but I care. I don't need anyone trying to mess with my Otis."

Tracey laughed. "Anyone who messes with your Otis better be ready for a fight."

"Ain't that the truth," Shirley said with a laugh. "So when are you going to offer her the job?"

"I wanted to offer it the second we finished, but before I make a big decision I need to at least let it sit for a second. I think I'll call her tomorrow morning. It'll also give me time to think of what to say to Jessica."

Shirley waved her hand. "Jessica can't possibly think we'll give her the job. She's only been coming to work on time and trying to learn the system in the past two weeks. She's chasing money and a title. She's not trying to help you."

"I know that, but it doesn't mean I want to be rude when I tell her we're going with someone else. I'm trying to be professional."

"You're better than me," Shirley muttered, crossing her arms and frowning.

"Either way, I hope she understands."

Shirley shook her head. "She won't. She's going to be mad, and I bet you she'll quit."

"You think so? Maybe she'll start looking for another job, but I don't think she'd just quit."

"I hope not, but she seems like the type to have a chip on her shoulder. Don't be surprised if she ups and leaves."

"She may not be the best receptionist, but right now I need her to cover the evening shifts."

There was a knock on the office door. Jessica opened it after Tracey called out to enter.

"Your three o'clock is here. Ms. Kemp and Ms. Parker."

Tracey's eyes widened, and she looked at her watch. "Damn, I forgot about that."

Shirley picked up her paperwork and stood. "What's up with you today? You've been running two steps behind ever since you got here."

"I overslept, and it threw me off. That's all." She looked at Jessica. "I'll come up there and get them."

She ushered Shirley out of her office before she could start spouting off remedies to help her sleep better at night. Especially when the remedies weren't needed. Since she had no problem falling asleep and staying asleep.

Imani and Halle stood in the front room chatting when Tracey walked in. They were meeting to go over the logistics for Imani's wedding. Imani made everything easy. She didn't want anything elaborate for her wedding. Just a simple service where she and Cyril could exchange vows in front of their family and closest friends.

Tracey walked over to her girls. "My bad. I've been so behind today."

Imani leaned in and gave Tracey a hug. She was dressed in a pair of loose-fitting linen pants and a flowy top. "Girl, you're good."

Tracey switched from Imani and hugged Halle. "I almost forgot about our meeting today."

Halle tilted her head to the side. She wore a pair of yellow fitted pants and a cute black blouse. "Almost forgot? Was today that busy?"

"I've been running behind all day," Tracey said. "I overslept."

Imani's brows drew together. "You're not feeling sick? Is everything good?"

Tracey nodded. "Everything is good. Come on out. Let's go to the courtyard where we'll have your ceremony."

"I've already seen the courtyard. Let's just sit down with Shirley and talk about the food."

Tracey raised a brow and nodded her head toward the door. "You might need to see it again." Imani was more than famil-iar with the setup, but Tracey wanted to share about what hap-pened with Brian to them. Somewhere where they wouldn't be overheard.

Imani shook her head. "Nah, I'm good. I trust you to get it right."

"I still think you need to see it." Tracey raised her brows and looked toward Jessica watching them then back to her friend.

A line formed between Imani's brows. "I don't know why."

Halle slapped Imani's arm. "Yes, let's go look at the court-yard again."

"Why did you hit me?" Imani asked.

Tracey took one of Imani's arms, and Halle took the other. The two ushered Imani out of the main house to the side court-yard. As soon as they were outside and away from the house Halle turned to Tracey.

"What's up?"

Imani looked at Halle. "What's up is why did you hit me?"

Halle sighed and gave Imani an exasperated look. "You are so dense sometimes. Couldn't you tell Tracey wanted us to come out here so she could tell us something?"

Imani spun toward Tracey. "You did?"

"Yes. I need to tell you about what happened last night."

Imani leaned in. "Last night? With who?" she asked eagerly.

Tracey glanced toward the house making sure they weren't followed before answering. "With Brian."

Halle pushed forward and wrapped her hands around Tracey's bicep. "Hold up, you were with Brian last night?"

"I was."

"What happened? Did you finally get some? How was it?" Halle asked in rapid-fire succession.

"The night was good, but I didn't get any."

"What? Why?" Imani asked.

Tracey told them about the night before and the morning after. She was still embarrassed about falling asleep on Brian, but she also wanted to talk about the way he'd been so understanding the day before.

"It was weird," Tracey confessed.

"Weird how?" Halle asked. "It sounds sweet."

"Yeah, but I'm not used to that. God forbid if I fell asleep with Bernard. If he didn't roll me over and try to get me to wake up, then he'd give me hell the next morning for neglecting his needs."

Imani crossed her arms and scowled. "No he didn't do either of those things."

"Yes, he did. All the time. I expected Brian to be upset. To give me a hard time about giving him blue balls or something. When I first woke up, I wondered if we'd had sex and I didn't know it."

"Brian wouldn't do that."

Tracey nodded. "I know. He left me fully dressed in his bed and made me cereal the next morning. He says he wants me to be relaxed and not so in my head." She leaned forward. "He could tell I was in my head. It's kind of scary."

"Scary how?" Halle asked.

"He pays attention. I'm not used to that."

"It doesn't mean you don't deserve that," Imani said. "You shouldn't feel pressured to have sex just because your partner wants it or when you're not feeling it. You should be able to relax and enjoy. The fact that he wants you to relax and get out of your head is a good thing."

"But what if..." She trailed off.

"But what if what?" Imani asked.

"What if I'm all messed up because of my time with Bernard? What if I don't know how to be sexy or how to ride the D or how to give good head."

Imani placed a hand on Tracey's shoulder and gave her a small shake. "Girl, stop overthinking. If you think about it too much, then you won't be able to enjoy. Just be honest. Tell Brian exactly what you like and don't like. Be vocal. And if you don't like what he's doing, then tell him you don't like it. Don't lie. That's half the problem. Life is too short to have bad sex."

"Amen to that." Halle held up a hand for a high five with Imani.

Tracey sighed. "Lord knows I've gone too long having bad sex. That's why I don't know if I'm even good at it. I don't even know if I can ride the D the right way. Bernard hated me on top."

"It's all in the hips," Halle said easily.

Imani grinned and nodded. "Exactly, not just an up-and-down motion. That's okay for a while, but you need some hip action going."

Tracey tilted her head to the side. "Hip action?"

Halle put her hands on her hips, bent her knees, and then rotated her hips in a slow, circular motion. "Like this."

Tracey laughed and shook her head. "Okay, Halle! I see why Quinton is always ready to answer when you call."

Halle stopped her demonstration. She fanned her face with her fingers and batted her lashes. "What can I say? A girl got skills."

"Well, maybe I'll try the hip action with Brian." As soon as the words came out her chest constricted. What if he thought she looked foolish? "What if he doesn't like it?"

Imani placed a hand on her shoulder. "Tracey, I get it. You spent years with a guy who didn't appreciate or try to nurture you. Don't try too hard with impressing Brian, okay? Worry about what feels good to you and making sure *you're* enjoying what's happening. Tell him what you like and ask him to do the same. Brian will get his regardless. So focus on getting yours."

She let out a breath and nodded. "You're right. I know that. I'm not used to putting myself first in the bedroom."

Halle gave her a concerned look. "Are you ready to start doing that?"

Tracey thought about the last eleven years. How she'd put Bernard's pleasure before her own every time they had sex. He wasn't concerned about what she liked. Except for saying *Like that* or *Say my name*, he never checked in or made sure she was good. She wasn't going to be that passive about her own pleasure ever again. Not with Brian or anyone else.

Tracey lifted and lowered her chin with confidence. "Yes. I'm not letting the past keep me in a choke hold. I'm going to get out of my head and enjoy."

16

Shirley had been right. The moment Tracey told Jessica that she wasn't chosen for the manager position, the woman had immediately copped an attitude. First asking for the reasons why. When Tracey explained, she then deflected and made excuses. Finally, she'd resorted to tears, and when the tears didn't penetrate Tracey's resolve, she'd gotten angry and walked out.

Tracey couldn't believe the woman's audacity. Her walking out without another word only proved that Tracey had made the right decision not promoting her. Jessica leaving had saved Tracey the trouble of ultimately having to fire her, but damn if she didn't pick the worst day to quit. There were several people checking in on Thursday for the Peach Festival happening that weekend, combined with a wedding that Saturday and many people from the bridal party also checking in early.

Tracey had hoped to have Jessica's help to get through the check-ins and getting everyone settled, but without her it left a hole. Tracey was busy attending to people and showing them to their rooms while trying to answer questions about where to eat or what store was best for a quick run for some essentials.

She was in the middle of coming back from showing two women who were in town for the festival around the house before heading back to the reception when she spotted Brian's SUV in the parking lot. It was Thursday night. Their scheduled sleep-together night. She'd gotten so thrown off by Jessica quitting and the rush of guests showing up that she'd forgotten all about her grand plans to let go and dive into being her most sexy self. Further proof that she was failing at being a let-loose-and-enjoy kind of person.

"Score number two for being horrible at this friends-with-benefits thing," she muttered to herself.

When she returned, Brian was standing by the reception desk. He turned to her, and his lips lifted in a smile so bright, she turned to look and see if someone was standing behind her. Nope, no one there. That smile was seriously for her?

"Hey, you ready to head out?" he asked.

She tried to return his smile, but her lips could only muster up a sporadic twitch. "About that…"

His brows drew together as he frowned. "What's wrong?"

"I can't go anywhere tonight. Jessica quit on me today when I told her she wasn't getting the manager job. My other front desk clerk is still new, and I can't leave her by herself. I've got at least two other parties checking in tonight. I need to be here."

Even though she kept her voice even and strong, her insides wavered. Before, he'd been understanding when she'd fallen asleep on him. That was one good thing, but she couldn't expect him to be as forgiving this time. She waited for the disappointment to cover his face. Disappointment followed by anger. She could imagine the words he'd say. She'd once again be accused of putting the business before everything else. Would he already have someone else lined up to keep him company if she couldn't go? He'd said he wanted to get her away for the night: he might demand that she pay him for whatever plans he'd made. If he went that far, she'd just give him the money and tell him to never call her again.

"Jessica quit? She just walked out on you like that?" Instead of sounding upset with Tracey, he sounded pissed about Jessica quitting suddenly. "I told you to get rid of her."

"Well, she made it easy for me," Tracey said. "I was counting on her being here so I could get away. Honestly, I probably wouldn't have been able to leave anyway. There's a lot going on this weekend with the wedding and the festival. She would have needed me here. I know you made plans, if you want me to pay you."

He shook his head. "Why would I want you to pay me? You didn't make Jessica walk out."

"Well, I kind of did when I told her she wasn't getting the manager job."

"That didn't mean she had to walk out. Are you good? Do you need anything?"

Tracey shook her head, still waiting for him to get upset or throw a hissy fit because she was canceling on him. "I think I'll be—"

The door to the inn opened, and four people walked in. Tracey smiled at them. "Welcome to The Fresh Place Inn. How can I help you?"

"We're checking in," one of the men in the group said.

"Then, I can help you with that." She waved them over. She was turning to tell Brian he could leave when one of the women she'd previously checked in entered from the side.

"I'm trying to find the kitchen," she said. "You said there were snacks there."

Before Tracey could answer Brian spoke up. "I can show you. This way."

The woman gave Tracey a curious look. Tracey nodded

and pointed toward Brian. "He can show you exactly where they are."

She relaxed and nodded. "Great." She followed Brian.

Tracey worked to check in the group of four. While she did that, Brian handled another visitor's question about local restaurants and the best place to get breakfast. When she showed them to their rooms and came back, he was standing next to the other clerk and pulling together the flyers and handouts about local attractions and the rules of the inn they gave to every guest.

For the next hour Brian became the extra pair of hands she needed to get her guests checked in and settled for the night. Not only did he jump in and help where he could, but he didn't complain. With each passing minute, Tracey thanked her lucky stars that Brian was actually doing the *friend* part in their friends-with-benefits arrangement. She liked this side of Brian. The side that was the friend who helped out and didn't judge. This Brian was sexier than she'd anticipated, and if she weren't careful, this Brian could worm his way into her heart.

Tracey settled the final guest three hours after Brian arrived. The reception desk officially closed at eleven and the doors were locked to outsiders unless a guest had an active room key that could activate the lock if they needed to get into the kitchen after hours. That's where she found Brian, sitting at the kitchen table nursing a bottle of water and scrolling through his cell phone.

She leaned against the doorframe and watched him. A smile curled up the corner of her mouth. He'd really helped her out tonight. She would have survived the night: it wasn't the first time she'd had to make do being short-staffed, but he'd made getting through the night easier. Brian was a good person and friend. She'd never appreciated that before. She'd spent so much time focusing on the way he seemed to always be around when she'd been embarrassed or believing that they were somehow from two different worlds that she hadn't given herself the chance to acknowledge all the good in him.

He looked up from his phone and caught her eye. "What are you smiling at?" He put the phone faceup. Bernard had never placed his phone faceup when she was around.

"You," she said tilting her head to the side.

He cocked a brow before leaning his elbow on the table and resting his head on his fist. His biceps bulged against the short sleeve of his buttoned-up shirt. "Oh, I make you smile like that?"

She laughed lightly and shook her head. "Don't start getting a big head or anything. You're making me smile like this tonight."

"Why is that?" His casual stance made him look every bit a male model posing to have the maximum effect on a woman's equilibrium.

"Because you were nice tonight. Thank you."

A line formed between his brows. "It wasn't about being nice. You needed help, I stepped in and helped."

"Well, you didn't have to do that. You could have thrown up deuces and left to go mind your business."

"Don't you say I'm always minding your business?" He stood and crossed the room to her. His dark eyes never left hers as he neared. Another thing she'd noticed and liked about him: his gaze wasn't shifty. He didn't hide his thoughts from her. He stood just close enough to make her want to forget that her feet and shoulders hurt from the long day. Instead she wanted to end the night like they'd planned. But did he?

Tracey shifted until her back leaned against the doorjamb and she could look up into his eyes. "You do be minding my business. I guess that's why you stuck around then, huh?"

He shook his head. "That's not the only reason."

"What's the other reason?"

Brian placed one hand on the jamb above her and placed the

other at the back of her neck. His fingers gently pressed and made small circles as he massaged. The feeling was perfect, and Tracey relaxed as her lids lowered.

Brian leaned in, his lips not quite touching hers, the desire in his eyes burning hot. "Because I hoped to do this before the night was over."

He waited two agonizing heartbeats before kissing her. Tracey had been waiting for this all night. She never would have realized how sexy support could be before that night. Brian tilted her head to the side and slightly pressed his tongue along the seam of her lips. Her mouth opened, and his tongue glided across hers. Slow, sensual heat pooled between her thighs, her breasts felt heavy and the tips sensitive. He eased forward, pressing his solid chest, abs and crotch against her body. His hand roamed from her neck down her side, to cup her breast before his fingers gently pinched her nipple.

Tracey hissed. Brian lifted his head and met her eyes. A line between his brows. "Did I hurt you?"

She shook her head. "No. That...felt good."

His face cleared, and he repeated the movement. "Lighter or harder?"

Tracey's eyes narrowed, and she pushed her chest forward. She bit her lip, and when he squeezed again she gasped. "A little harder."

His lips parted, and a spark flashed in his eyes as he added more pressure. "Like that?"

Tracey moaned and twisted her hips. "Yes, like that."

He lowered his mouth and kissed her again. "Are all your rooms full?"

"My room isn't. I'm staying in one of the upstairs rooms."

"Can we finish this upstairs? I doubt everyone is asleep."

The realization was like a cold splash of water. Any one of her guests could have walked in and spotted them. Embarrassment made her want to tell him to go, claim she was too tired and finish this on another day. The slickness between her legs and the low thrum of desire still simmering after his kiss told the truth. She didn't want him to leave.

"Yes, let's go upstairs."

She took his hand and led him up the stairs and to the room in the back corner she'd moved into after her split. She crossed to turn the lamp off, but Brian came up behind her.

"Can we leave it on? I want to see you."

She swallowed. She hadn't been naked in front of anyone in a long time. She looked at herself every morning in the mirror when she got out of the shower. She'd never considered herself sexy, but she also didn't hate the way she looked naked. Her breasts were full, hips curvy and stomach relatively flat. She didn't want his thoughts on her naked body to change the way she saw herself.

He placed his hands on her shoulders and then gently ran them down her arm. "You're so damn sexy. I want to see you."

She glanced over her shoulder. "You think I'm sexy?"

Brian's lips brushed against her ear. "Tracey, you have no idea how damn sexy I think you are."

She bit her lip, then nodded. "Okay, lights on."

"Just relax. Tell me if I do something you don't like, okay?"

"Okay."

He kissed the side of her neck, gently sucking and nipping at the sensitive skin until Tracey tilted her head to the side. Opening herself up more to his tender kisses. One arm came around, and his hand slid up her shirt. He cupped her breast.

"Still good?" His breath whispered between kisses.

She nodded quickly. She wanted him to gently tug on her nipples like he'd done downstairs. She waited for him to do that, then remembered her promise to herself. If she wanted something she would say it.

"Pinch my nipples."

Brian's deep moan echoed through the room before he

obeyed her request. Tracey was lost in sensations. He listened when she asked for him to pinch harder and quickly eased up when she said he'd gone too hard. He squeezed both breasts with his hands when she asked, and Tracey became just as aroused by what he was doing to her as she was by him waiting for her direction.

"Can I take your clothes off now?" Brian asked as he kissed her shoulder.

Tracey couldn't wait to get her clothes off. "Please."

He turned her to face him, and they undressed quickly. Brian kept his eyes on her the entire time she pulled off her clothes. Heat burned across her chest, neck and cheeks. His stare was unwavering and hungry. Instead of feeling objectified, she loved the look in his eye. The yearning to touch her. Not someone else. Just Tracey.

He stepped forward and lightly ran his hands over her shoulders, down the sides of her breasts, and rested them on her hips. "I want to kiss every inch of your body."

Tracey pictured him doing that. She thought about the places she wanted him to kiss and the ones she wasn't so sure about then decided to focus on where she wanted him to kiss and touch her.

"Start here." She slid her fingertips down her neck.

Brian pulled her into his arms and placed his lips on her neck. He kissed her confidently. His tongue flicked lightly across her pulse before he gently sucked the sensitive spot.

Tracey's hands clenched Brian's waist. His skin surprisingly smooth beneath her fingertips. Her head fell farther back and to the side. Brian let out a low moan.

"You really like that spot, huh?"

The flutter of his lips against her neck sent shivers across her body. "Yes."

He lifted his head and looked into her eyes. A sexy smile

lifted the side of his mouth. "Tell me whatever you want." He kissed her. "And I'll do it."

Tracey's sex clenched. But more than that, there was a funny feeling in her chest. A tingling warmth that made her stomach quiver and knees weak.

"Let's move this to the bed."

She didn't have to say another thing. He swept her into his arms and placed her gently on the bed. They kissed each other deeply before his lips trailed back to her neck.

"My breasts. Kiss my breasts."

Brian nodded slowly. "My pleasure." His lips played across the swell of her breasts, teasing her before the warmth of his mouth finally closed over her nipples.

Tracey grasped the side of Brian's head and arched her back. When she asked for more he sucked harder until she thought she would explode from the pleasure.

His long fingers brushed across her thighs. Squeezing her legs together to increase the pleasure wasn't enough, she thought about the way she touched herself and wanted him to do the same. She parted her legs. "Touch me." She didn't care if her words sounded like a plea or a demand, she only cared about having his hands on her body.

Brian followed her instructions like a straight-A student who wanted to excel. His fingers slid between her legs and dipped into her wet folds.

"Damn, you feel good against my fingers." Brian's voice was decadent and gravelly. "Tell me what you like. This?" His fingers rubbed gentle circles across her swollen clit. "Or this?" He increased the pressure slightly and went back and forth over the hard nub before pushing two fingers inside her body.

Tracey cried out. Her legs spread farther, and her hips lifted. "That. Do that again."

He repeated the movement. Whatever she said—*faster, slower, deeper, softer*—he listened. His breathing became more ragged, his erection harder with each direction she gave him. Tracey's thoughts didn't stray to other things. Her mind remained tuned in to the delicious sensations happening to her body.

When his body covered hers, both ready, he met her eyes again. His eyes asked the question. The emotion that squeezed her heart made her bite her lip to keep from grinning. "I'm ready."

The tension around his eyes eased, and then he pushed inside her. Tracey gasped and closed her eyes.

"Oh my God, it's been too long," she moaned.

Brian pressed his lips to her forehead. "Damn, Tracey, just... damn. You feel so good."

Tracey felt like she was filled with sunshine and glitter. *She* felt good. Not just Brian. She didn't hold back her grin. She met his eyes and pulled his head down for a kiss.

"Damn right I feel good."

17

Brian woke up to a dimly lit room, the soft warmth of a woman's body pressed into his back. His lips lifted. Tracey's body. His first time with Tracey had been better than he'd expected. He immediately thought of going for another round, but a tickle in his throat had woken him up. He cleared his throat and let out a soft cough. He needed some water.

He eased toward the end of the bed. Tracey's arm was draped over his waist. He liked that she'd cuddled up to him in her sleep. A lot more that he wanted to explore. He'd find his pants, run down to grab a sip of water, and then come back up and see how she'd respond if he woke her up by kissing her body.

He felt around on the floor until he found his pants. He had one leg in when Tracey's soft voice broke the silence.

"Sneaking out?"

Brian froze and spun around to face her. "What? Nah."

The sheets rustled as she shifted from lying on her back to

sitting up. She pulled the sheet up to cover her breasts. His frown deepened. He really liked her breasts and would love to see them again.

"It looks like you're sneaking out. That's cool. I get it. We didn't sign up for cuddling and all that other stuff."

He shook his head and then pointed toward the door. "I was going down to get a bottle of water. I'm used to keeping water by the bed so if I wake up in the middle of the night I can take a sip. Believe me, I was coming back."

"Oh." She glanced away and rubbed the back of her neck.

Brian sat on the edge of the bed and reached for her hand. He squeezed it, and she met his gaze again. "I wouldn't run out on you like that. I know what we're doing, but I still respect you too much to just hit and run. Understand?"

She nodded. "I do. I just don't want to overstep any expectations to this."

"Then, let's add that to our rules. No one runs out while the other one is sleeping."

"What if it's an emergency?"

"Then we at least leave a note. That's one of the *friend* parts in the friends-with-benefits relationship we got going on here."

The corner of her lips lifted and she shrugged as if what he said was no big deal, but he'd seen the satisfaction in her eyes. "That's cool." She pointed to the corner of the room. "I've got water over there."

Brian turned in that direction. A black minifridge stood in the corner. "You've got a fridge in your room?"

She nodded. "Hell yeah. If I need water or a snack at night I'd rather grab it here than go downstairs and possibly run into a guest."

"Doesn't that go against your hostess hospitality rule?"

"Maybe…but one night I went down for a late snack and came across a couple going at it in the kitchen."

Brian let out a bark of laughter. "No you didn't."

She nodded and grinned. "Yes I did."

"What did you do?"

"Turned around and came back upstairs. The next morning I discreetly reminded them that the common areas are not for that type of activity."

"What did they say?"

"They weren't embarrassed at all. In fact, they seemed excited that I caught them. That's when I said if it happened again they'd have to leave. I think they kept it to their bedroom for the rest of the trip."

"You would have kicked them out?"

"Sure would have. No one would want to be a part of their exhibitionist show. Plus, that was a wedding weekend and we had kids staying. I had to buy a new kitchen table."

"Why did you replace the table?"

"You wanna eat where they were having sex?"

He frowned and then stood. "You should have charged them for the new table."

"I should have. Bring me one, too."

He opened the fridge. "Damn, you've got all kinds of snacks in here." He pulled out two bottles of water. There was also a meat and cheese tray, fruit, and yogurt. A tray on top of the fridge held crackers, chips and a can of roasted peanuts.

"I basically live here now," she said. "I need quick snacks for when I need a moment to recoup."

Brian grabbed a bag of nuts and came back to the bed. He handed a bottle to Tracey. She leaned against the headboard and opened her water. He sat on the bed facing her.

"You okay staying here full-time? I thought you'd look for a new place."

She looked around the room and shrugged. "I don't mind staying here. It's my dream. I fought to keep this place. Staying here feels like home."

"Fought to keep it?" Tracey's inn was doing well long before the town got a boost from being recognized as one of the best small towns in the nation.

"Bernard tried to claim a portion of it in the divorce. But that's hard to do when you blame my working here as the reason why you cheated in the first place. Honestly, he made the entire divorce more drawn out and difficult than it needed to be. I think on some level he thought that I would stick around and forgive him."

"Not after everything he did. Why would he think that?"

She lowered her eyes and picked at the wrapping on the water bottle. "I stayed the last time."

Brian froze. "Hold up. This wasn't his first time?"

She sighed then shook her head. "No. The first time was right after we got married. I found out he was sleeping with a woman at his job. I threatened to leave. He cried, said it was a mistake, that he loved me and it meant nothing. He said we belonged together and that everyone doubted we'd make it. That we couldn't break up so easily. He knew I was insecure about us being together. So I thought about how my dad stuck it out with my mom and decided to stay. I suspected something was happening again, but I didn't know for sure. I even suspected Monique but convinced myself that surely he wouldn't disrespect me like that."

She spoke quickly in an efficient tone. As if what she was saying didn't matter or wasn't a big deal. Brian said, "Why were you insecure about the two of you?"

She gave him an *Are you kidding me* look. "Because we were just...different. Bernard was the golden kid in high school. He went to college and came back to town to make Peachtree Cove better. I was the girl with the mom who slept around and the alcoholic father. I didn't go to a big college, I just got a degree from the local technical school. There were literally people who came up to Bernard when he proposed to me and said he could do better."

Brian's hand balled into a fist. "That's some bullshit."

"Well, back then I kind of believed all of that. That I was lucky to have landed such a perfect guy. That if he messed up one time that didn't mean I shouldn't forgive him. Where was I going to get someone better?"

"Tracey, I wish you knew how many guys were into you. You could have done better than Bernard."

She raised a brow. "Into me, or wanted to sleep with me? I know I'm desirable. I spent half of high school having guys try to get in my panties. It didn't stop later. He was the first person who acted like he was into *me* and not just getting between my legs. I fell hard and was stupid."

He scooted forward and met her eyes. "You weren't stupid. You fell in love, and he hurt you."

"I should have known better."

"I said the same thing when my ex-wife cheated on me."

Her head snapped back. "Why would she cheat on you?"

"I appreciate that you say it like someone cheating on me is unheard of, but she did. She cheated for the classic reason. He had more money and clout than I did."

"I'm sorry."

"I am, too."

"Can I ask what happened?"

"You kind of already did," he teased.

She rolled her eyes and pushed his shoulder. "Well, you're always minding my business. I might as well mind yours."

He hadn't talked about what happened with him and Renee in a long time. Once his friends found out she'd cheated they'd just told him to forget her ass and move on. So he had. He'd slept with other women, moved back home, slept with more women and never talked about what it felt like to have the person he loved betray him like that.

"She said I wasn't fun anymore."

"What does that even mean? Bernard said the same thing about me."

Brian shook his head. "The hell if I know what it means. When we first met we were always fighting and making up. We'd argue about the silliest things, but we couldn't get enough of each other. We were both doing some modeling and stuff then decided to move to LA and try to be famous. It didn't get better out there. We snuck or hustled our way into parties. We became part of the entourage of some reality stars. Then I came home to see my dad when he got sick. He died a little after that, and I realized I was tired of chasing a dream in LA that wasn't really my dream. A friend had given us a plant, I don't even remember why, but I wanted to make it stay alive. I think I'd been smoking something and swore the plant spoke to me."

Tracey laughed. "Hold up, you must have been really high to think a plant was talking to you."

He nodded and joined in. "I kept it alive, then I started taking care of other plants. Then I started trying to make the yard of the place we rented together nice. I thought about doing yard work with my dad and how he said that always helped him clear his mind. It worked. My head cleared up. I didn't feel like arguing with her just to get aroused to have sex. She said I was boring. Honestly, a part of me knew she was cheating. When she told me she'd found someone with more money and connections, she admitted it started when I went home to visit my dad. I filed for divorce."

"And that was it?"

He shook his head. "I wish. I went back a few times."

"You did?"

"Yeah, so I get it. You love someone. You can't imagine yourself without that person. So you forgive them and think they'll change."

"But do they?"

He sighed. "Sometimes they do, but if they don't, if they

show you who they are and stay true to that, then you've got to move on."

"Do you miss her?"

He thought about it and the last time they were together only to realize she'd lied to him again. The phone calls saying that her husband thought she was pregnant with his kid. He shook his head. "Not anymore."

"Sometimes I miss being married."

"You miss Bernard?"

"No!" she said quickly and scowled. "Leaving him was the best thing I could do. He knew that I'd been insecure, and he played that up in our marriage. He made me feel like I needed him."

"Then, what do you miss?"

"Having someone hold me at night. In the beginning, he would sit up and talk with me. It wasn't all bad. I miss the companionship." She sighed then shook her head. "But I can't imagine getting married again. I don't want to be hurt like that again."

"I understand that." He felt the same. Hadn't he declared he would never get married again?

"Which is why this is good. What we're doing. Friends with benefits. And if feelings get entangled, then we'll break it off so no one gets hurt."

He couldn't imagine having a desire to break things off anytime soon. The sex with Tracey had been amazing, but not only that—he liked her. Had liked her for a long time. As long as she was cool with this, he'd be cool to keep it going, too. But if one day she realized being with him was going to hurt her, he'd step away. He liked her too much to ever break her heart.

"No one gets hurt," he said, before nodding and sipping his water.

18

Tracey sat in the back corner of Books and Vibes. Her coffee was cold and the scone she'd ordered half-eaten. She'd spent most of the time writing out her wildest dreams for The Fresh Place Inn. The process had been fun, even exhilarating while she'd daydreamed and let her imagination take control and explore the possibilities. Now as she sat there staring down at her ideas, the euphoria from dreaming was slowly being replaced with the dread of self-doubt. Along with a healthy dose of fear.

Her dreams were too big. How could she accomplish all this when she'd barely been able to get her staff levels back where they need to be? Where would she find the money to invest in the things she wanted to do? Sure, Peachtree Cove was named Best Small Town, but once that faded who would come here just to stay at her inn? Was it even worth it to try and make the inn better than it was?

Sighing, she sat back and absently reached for her mug of

coffee. She took a sip and frowned when the tepid liquid hit her tongue.

"Need a refill?"

She looked up to find Mikayla standing next to her. Two paper cups in her hands. She held one out to Tracey.

"I do, actually. But you didn't have to get me one." Tracey took the offered cup.

"When I plan to impose myself on someone, I feel it's usually better to do it bearing gifts." She sat down opposite of Tracey.

Tracey chuckled and took a sip. "Mmm, this is good. What is it?"

"A cinnamon nutmeg latte. They made it special for me."

"That's cool. I like it. Thanks again, and if you're bringing coffee, you're not an imposition."

"Good to know." Mikayla looked at the papers on the table. "What are you working on?"

"Your homework, actually."

Mikayla's face lit up. "I hoped that's what you were doing."

"Really? Why?"

"I like seeing people I'm working with doing what I tell them to. I've taught people who think the homework is just a waste of time. They think coming and listening to me is all they'll need to make their business successful."

Tracey had thought that was all the class would be. A series of lectures that would tell her what to do to grow business at the inn. Mikayla had pushed them all to continue to think about what they wanted then make a road map to get there. The homework might give her a headache, but it had challenged her to think about things she hadn't considered before.

"That's their waste of time and money. Why pay for a class if you're not going to at least try and do what you're told?"

"It's easy to say you want something in life. Actually doing what it takes to get what you want takes effort. Not everyone is ready to put in the effort."

Tracey frowned down at her papers. "I can understand why. It's scary to dream big."

"That's the other reason I decided to sit down here with you. I saw the frown on your face, and I want to help you out."

"Help me how?" Unless Mikayla had a shot of confidence in her bag that could make Tracey's doubt about her dreams disappear.

"By talking things out. If you're struggling with something or have hit a roadblock, talking about what you're working on can help."

"You're willing to spend time helping me think this through? Right now?"

Mikayla laughed lightly and nodded. "Yeah. Why is that so hard to believe?"

Tracey shrugged. "I don't know. Because I saw your prices for one-on-one coaching, and while you're worth it I can't afford you." She couldn't imagine Mikayla helping her for free.

The smile on Mikayla's face changed into one of understanding. "Well, consider this a study session with the teacher. You've already paid for the class, and this is just a bonus. Plus, I like you, Tracey. Always have. I'm proud of what you've done, and I want to help. Simple as that."

Tracey was momentarily lost for words. In high school she and Mikayla had both worked at the Taco Bell for a short time. Tracey had quit after the assistant manager who always picked on her by giving her the worst tasks had tried to embarrass her by making her clean underneath the equipment with a rag instead of using the mop. Tracey had thrown the rag in her face and walked out. Mikayla had been there that night. They'd gotten along pretty well when they worked together, but that was the extent of their connection.

"You do?"

Mikayla nodded and laughed. "I do. Ever since you told Heather off and quit. She was such a bitch and loved to pick on you. Before that, really. You never let anyone get over on you, and I admire that about you. So tell me what's got you frowning."

Mikayla's comment dazed Tracey for a moment. She wasn't used to people admiring her, much less someone as put-together as Mikayla. Thankfully, Mikayla's invitation gave Tracey something to focus on instead of sputtering and questioning if she was sure she had the right Tracey. She'd take the compliment and savor it later.

"I've got some ideas for the inn," she said, "but they seem too big."

"Too big how?"

"Well, for one thing this is Peachtree Cove. We don't really have a lot to draw people here. If I invest heavily, it's not like it'll bring more guests to the inn."

"I'd disagree. The Best Small Town designation has gotten the interest of a lot of people. The mayor is not only working on efforts to promote what's happening in Peachtree Cove but also to play up some of the recreational resources you have. The lake can be a huge draw, the walking trails around town. There is an active fishing and boating community here. That's a part of economic development that isn't just business-related. People may not always want to stay at a hotel. Your inn could fill the gap."

She hadn't considered that. She hadn't joined the Business Guild yet, and her guest membership for being friends with Cyril was about to run out, but she remembered a talk about working with the recreational community to help promote the town. She hadn't made the connection between her inn, with its perfect setup for weddings and birthday parties, as a place for boaters and outdoor enthusiasts to stay.

"Okay, that's something to consider. But regardless of the reason people come to town, they might not automatically consider my inn as a place to stay."

"Then, you *make* the inn a place to stay. Tell me your ideas."

Tracey looked down at her papers. She did want to make The Fresh Place Inn *the* place to stay, but she'd been too afraid to say it out loud. Now that Mikayla had said it as if the dream weren't impossible, Tracey began to think about how to make her big idea come true.

"Well, I've got the land next to the inn. Not just the house."

Mikayla held up a hand. "Hold up, you also have the land?"

Tracey nodded. "Yeah, Old Man Sullivan sold me the house and the land." More like gave it to her, but she didn't make that much known. People already assumed the man had helped her because she was giving him sexual favors. Which was not the case.

"What do you want to do over there?"

"I thought about putting little cottages on the land between some of the peach trees that are still there. So that you had the main inn and carriage house but also more rooms."

Mikayla sat forward. "That's a great idea! You can market them as private little getaway spots."

That was the exact thought she'd had. Still she asked, "You don't think that's too much?"

"No. What else were you thinking?"

Tracey spent the next few minutes going over her ideas for the cottages. How to make each one provide a slightly different experience than the others. Mikayla loved the idea.

"You can also go beyond just being a place to stay. You can look at events, too."

"Events? Like bigger weddings?"

Mikayla shook her head. "Wine tastings, pumpkin patches, hay rides, that kind of stuff."

Tracey considered the options. She had enough land to do that. "Hmm, I never thought about that."

"That's how you make the inn a draw. It's not just a place for weddings and to sleep but another destination. People come to an event and have so much fun they go home talking about the event to everyone they know. So not only are they coming for, say, a wine tasting, but they fight to stay at the inn because they need somewhere to lay their heads after all the drinking."

Tracey snapped her fingers. "I could invite local food trucks or vendors if I have a tasting or something like that."

Mikayla's eyes lit up, and she tapped her hand on the table excitedly. "Ooh, I like that idea. You can start that now before you have the additional cabins."

The idea of putting something together was already forming in her brain. "I could start small. Maybe a food truck event and showcase of our local breweries and wineries."

"Bring up the idea at the Business Guild meeting, and I'll bet they'll help you pull it together."

"I'm not officially a member."

Mikayla gave her a pointed look. "Then, you better join ASAP. This is something the Guild would eat up."

"You really think so?"

"Tracey, don't doubt yourself. This is a great idea. It'll take some time and planning, but I can help with that."

"But we've only got three weeks left in the class." There was no way she'd flesh out all these ideas in three weeks.

Mikayla shrugged. "Yeah, in class but also after. I just finished working with one of my mentees. So if you're interested, I'd like to mentor you on this."

Tracey wanted to jump at the offer, but the price list on Mikayla's website flashed in her head. If she were thrifty, she might be able to afford one-on-one coaching with Mikayla.

Mikayla leaned forward and smiled. "I see your brain working. Don't worry about the fee. This is for a friend."

Tracey shook her head and held up a hand. "No. I believe in paying people what they're worth. I can't ask you to do this for free."

Mikayla studied her for a second before nodding. "Okay,

then how about a discounted rate? And before you say no to that, I realize that entrepreneurs in Peachtree Cove can't pay what my clients in larger cities offer. I do have a scale based on business size and yearly profits. We can use that sliding scale."

Tracey considered then held out her hand. "Then, consider me your newest mentee."

Mikayla shook Tracey's hand. "Great! This is going to be so much fun."

Tracey smiled. The light of euphoria from working directly with Mikayla chased away the darkness of fear and doubt that had hovered over her previously. For the first time in a long time, she was excited about her future.

19

Brian tilted his head to the side and frowned at the screen of his computer. The door to his office was open, and Natalie stopped at the threshold. Her brows lifted and a worried expression covered her face.

"Uh-oh. Don't tell me there's something wrong with the order for tomorrow." She crossed her fingers on both hands.

Brian's frown deepened, and he sat up straight. "It shouldn't be. I put everything in and got the delivery arranged."

She pressed a hand to her chest. "Good. When you're frowning like that I always worry that something has gone wrong. We don't need that order to mess up."

"Nah, we're good. Believe me, if there were a problem I'd be doing a lot more than frowning. Plus, I'm helping with the installation. We're good."

They'd gotten the contract to supply and install landscaping at one of the recently renovated office complexes in town. It was one of the largest orders they'd had this year. It was why Brian insisted on helping to install the plants after the issue they'd had on a previous job. He didn't need to hire extra help for this job, but if he landed another job around the same time he would've needed extra hands. He'd only recently offered installation, so he wanted to make sure that this expansion of services was something sustainable.

"Well, if the project tomorrow is good, then why are you frowning?"

He sighed and pointed to his screen. "I'm working on my notes for the presentation in the entrepreneurship class tomorrow. I don't know if my talking points are any good."

She walked over and stood next to his chair. "You're only talking about what we're doing here as far as payroll and stuff, right?"

"Yeah, that's it."

She scanned the notes onscreen and then nodded. "This is good. You touch on all the key things to consider. What's to worry about?"

"I don't know. I guess I'm nervous about presenting."

She sucked her teeth and put a hand on her hip. "Don't even give me that. Didn't you model or try to be an actor once? How are you nervous about presenting?"

"That was different. I was playing a part."

He didn't know how to explain the difference. When he'd chased the dream of being a model, he could get lost in what the photographer wanted him to be; he took on a role. This wasn't a role. This was him and what he'd built. Standing in front of a group and hoping he sounded like he not only knew what he was doing but that what he'd done was worth hearing. The boost of confidence he'd gotten from his brother's pep talk had worn off the closer he got to the actual presentation.

"And tomorrow you're playing the part of a successful nursery owner. How hard is that?"

"You don't understand."

"No, I don't. Because this should be a piece of cake."

"I want to make sure it's not a waste of anyone's time. This is basic stuff."

"Basic to you maybe, but not to everyone. Especially people starting their own business. HR issues are time-consuming. You've got a good system here. I bet you'll say something that will help others."

He nodded and looked back at his notes. "Maybe you're right."

"I know I'm right. Now, here." She held out the stack of papers she'd brought in. "Sign this contract for the new inventory system. I'm more than ready to get it implemented."

Brian took the contract and put it on his desk. "I'll check over it and sign. You good with it?"

She nodded. "I am, but check it out. Sometimes you see things I miss."

His cell phone rang. He didn't recognize the number, but it had a local area code. He always answered local numbers just in case it was a potential customer. "I'm going to take this."

"Go ahead. Bring me the contract when you're done."

He nodded and swiped the green button on the screen. "This is Brian. How can I help you?"

"Brian, hey, it's me."

His body tensed at the sound of Renee's voice. He closed his eyes and bit back a curse. He tried to remember his mom's words, that he should at least be cordial with Renee. After all, at one point in time they had loved each other enough to get married. But knowing she was calling him about the drama with the man she'd cheated on with him made it hard to extend her any grace.

"What is it, Renee?"

"I thought you were going to hang up on me," she said with a light laugh.

"No, but I am wondering why you called. I already told you I'm not in the fight between you and your husband."

"I know, but I… I need to see you."

He was shaking his head instantly. "No, you don't."

"Yes, I do. Brian, I've got to talk to you. About what happened last time—"

"There's no need to go into last time. It was a one-and-done mistake. Our divorce is final, and I've moved on."

"But have you, really?" Her voice dipped into the low, sultry tone that used to make him hard in an instant. Her "sexy" voice no longer had that effect.

"Listen to me when I say I'm really done, Renee," he said in a calm, confident voice. "We can be cool if we're ever both in the same place, but I'm not going to be taking your calls or trying to see you again. I've moved on."

"What if fate isn't done with us?"

Brian looked to the ceiling and laughed. "Fate? Since when do you believe in fate?"

"Since fate kept pushing me back to you."

"That isn't fate, Renee. That was just because I didn't have any willpower."

"It's not about willpower. And even if it were, you can't resist me."

The confidence in her voice made him laugh. She really didn't get it. He could only blame himself. How many times had he gone back to her when they were together? But for her to declare with her whole chest that he couldn't resist her? If he wasn't already done with her then, he would be now.

"Wow, damn, for you to come out your mouth with something like that means I really did act the fool for you."

"We love each other."

"Loved. Get it straight. Look, Renee, I'm not doing this. I'm seeing someone right now."

He and Tracey weren't officially together, but they had agreed to not sleep with other people during their friends-with-benefits arrangement. That would have to count.

Possessiveness entered Renee's voice. "Who?"

Brian sighed and pinched the bridge of his nose. Renee had a whole husband and was still thinking she could question him. "It doesn't even matter. Just know that you and me, we're done. Don't call me unless it's an emergency."

"But I want to see you."

"Why?"

She hesitated a heartbeat. "To tell you something. I want to see you when I tell you."

Brian closed his eyes and sighed. She'd said that the last time they were together. That she had to talk to him alone and in person. She said she loved and missed him. That she'd made a mistake. His heart had weakened, and he'd crawled back in her bed. He'd made that mistake once. He wasn't about to make it again.

"Anything you can tell me you can do over a text. Bye, Renee."

"But—"

He hung up before she could finish then dropped his phone on his desk. He waited to see if regret or guilt would come. Feelings he usually had whenever he put a hard line between him and Renee. But all he felt was relief. Relief and a bit of pride in himself. He'd told his friends and himself that he was done, but he really and truly was no longer under her spell.

He looked back at the notes on the screen and smiled. He'd get to see Tracey tomorrow. Part of the reason he wanted his talk to be on point. He wanted to impress her. He knew they were just doing the friends-with-benefits thing, but he was enjoying the hell out of the benefits. Renee didn't need to know he wasn't in a *relationship* with Tracey or anyone else. For the short-term, Tracey was the woman in his life.

"You did really well on your presentation the other night," Tracey told Brian. It was Thursday night, and they'd met at his place.

Tracey felt she'd redeemed herself from the last time she was there. When she'd arrived, the thoughts that had invaded her mind the last time she was there had been pushed away by her excitement to be in his arms again. She'd focused on receiving pleasure and the way Brian touched and kissed her. Brian seemed intent on making sure she enjoyed whatever he did to her. The entire experience was something so new and different that she looked forward to being with him again.

Now they were in his bed snacking on apple slices and drinking water. The television in his room was off, and his attention was on her. She liked that about him, too. After they were done he didn't just roll over, slap her on the ass and say *Good job*. He also didn't seem to want to rush her out of his space. He acted like he enjoyed her hanging around and talking.

"You think so?" he said looking bashful. "I didn't ramble on too much?"

She shook her head. "Nah, you didn't. You touched on your points and gave some good advice about managing payroll and scheduling. Stuff I hadn't considered before. You've got me thinking about switching to a new payroll system at the inn."

"Really?"

"Yeah. The one I have works okay, but it doesn't make it easy to tie to the schedule. I haven't thought about shopping around since opening the place. It's a good time to see what my options are."

"Cool. I'm glad it helped. I was hoping it wasn't just stuff people already know."

She raised a brow. "If you really thought everyone in class already knew what you were talking about, then you need to get your head checked because you obviously hit it. Only a few of us in class have businesses. The majority are thinking of starting. It's good to hear from other small business owners. Helps give ideas."

"I guess I was just nervous. My brother told me not to worry about it."

"You shouldn't have."

He ran his hand over her bare leg and squeezed her thigh. "But hearing you say I did a good job, that's all the praise I needed."

His touch sent a delicious shiver across her skin. She couldn't believe she was getting turned on again. She hadn't felt like this in years. "My praise is all you need? Really?"

"Yeah, I wanted to impress you."

She shook her head. "I don't know what for."

"Because we work together. I can't have you thinking my business is jacked up. You might switch to another nursery."

Tracey laughed. Even if Brian had stumbled through his presentation, she wasn't going to pick a different nursery. "Not happening. You deliver on time, and your rates are good. Plus, you put up with me and my last-minute scheduling. You're staying hired."

"Well, I didn't know I had your business on lock. Can I get that in writing?"

Tracey smiled and rolled her eyes. "Never that. I don't need evidence that I'm praising you." He laughed. A few seconds later she said, "I liked the way you talked about why you started the nursery. How working with plants helped ease your mind and made you think about what it was like working in the yard with your dad. It made your story resonate a lot more."

His thumb made lazy circles on her leg, but his gaze was distant. "My dad had a green thumb. He could make anything grow. Including plants in the house. He loved plants. My brother hated working in the yard or watering all the plants, but I liked helping him with that stuff. The times I helped in the yard were some of my best memories growing up. After he died, I thought about how he said if he ever needed to clear his mind and make a decision that he'd go put his hands in the soil. I started doing that, and it worked. He was right. Putting my hands in soil and growing plants made me slow down and think. It brought me solace when my brain was in chaos. I was tired of the life I was living in California. I thought about what I could do that was completely opposite and would make me happy."

"And opening a nursery back home in Peachtree Cove was at the top of the list."

He chuckled and nodded. "It was. I thought about the times I was most peaceful and happy and remembered going to the nursery and working in the yard with my dad. Plus, I wanted to be close to my mom and brother. It kind of worked out."

She nodded and took a bite of her apple. Brian tapped her knee and raised a brow. "What about you? You always wanted to own an inn?"

"Actually, no."

He leaned back and raised his brows. "You didn't?"

"Nah. Back in high school and after, I wanted to be a lawyer."

"Really?"

"Why do you sound so surprised?"

He lifted a shoulder. He looked so sexy leaning against the headboard smiling at her. He handed her another apple slice. "I don't know. You didn't seem the lawyer type."

"Do you remember Mr. Fulmer back in middle school?"

His brows drew together before he nodded slowly. "Yeah. He taught science, right?"

"He did. He told me once that I would argue a point so hard until the other side was exhausted and that I should be a lawyer. It stuck with me. Thought about how much money a lawyer can make, and my mind was made up. It was going to be my ticket out of Peachtree Cove."

The dream had also been her way to shake off the stigma of her family. That she wasn't going to one day be seen as the daughter of a drunk and a whore. That she'd make a name for herself and force everyone in town to respect her.

"What happened?"

She let out a humorless chuckle. "I looked at the cost of college and then law school. I thought about years of student loans that I wouldn't be able to pay back, and I decided law school wasn't for me."

"You could have gotten grants or scholarships," he offered.

"Maybe, but not enough. I even worked up the nerve to say I wanted to be a lawyer to the guidance counselor my senior year. She worked out so that I got to job shadow at the law firm in town. That really sealed the deal. Boring as hell."

He laughed. "For real?"

"Yeah. I may like to argue a point, but I quickly realized I didn't want to be a lawyer."

"Then, what made you decide to open an inn?"

"I majored in business. Came home, married Bernard and worked part-time as a manager at one of the hotels in Augusta. Turned out that I really liked working there. Meeting new people, learning about their lives and stuff. I had a knack for it. I started playing around with the idea that I could open my own hotel one day."

"How did you get Old Man Sullivan to give you his place?"

"That's the thing, I didn't. He reached out to me. But I think I know why." When Brian gave her an expectant look she sighed and told him the story. "Okay, so you know that me, Halle and Imani used to work for him in the peach fields back in the day, right?"

"Right."

"So he was always nice to us. When I started selling some of his peaches on the side, he let it slide. Honestly, I think he kind of felt bad for me. One day my dad came to pick me up when I was selling peaches at Mr. Sullivan's stand. Dad was drunk. God only knows how he made it there to get me. Mr. Sullivan saw that, took his keys, and drove me and my dad home. My mom only picked me up after that."

"And that's why he gave you the house?"

"Not just that." She smiled and laughed. "One time he ran into me and Bernard in the grocery store. He asked how I was doing and if I still wanted to be a lawyer. I said no and that I wanted to open my own hotel." Her smile faded, and she scowled. "Bernard laughed when I said that. Basically said it was a dream and then walked away."

"He did that in front of Mr. Sullivan?"

"Sure did. Mr. Sullivan looked at me just like he had when my dad came drunk to pick me up. Told me he hoped I opened a place one day. Before he died, he called me up and said he would sell the place to me for five thousand dollars."

Brian sat up straight. "Wait, what?"

"You heard me right. The house and the land. I thought maybe it was old age and he didn't mean it. Or that his kids would get mad, but they didn't want it. They'd moved on and really didn't have anything to do with him. But he wanted me to get it before he died so that they couldn't take it from me. When I asked why, he said he'd always thought the place would make a nice bed and breakfast. I didn't ask Bernard for a dime, went into my savings and bought it. Once the title was in my name, I started on my business plan and saving up to get a small business loan. I let Mr. Sullivan stay in the house until he passed. Then I quit my job and opened the bed and breakfast."

"Damn. What did Bernard say?"

"Oh, he was pissed. Swore that I had something going on with Mr. Sullivan and said the inn wouldn't survive. But it did. I proved him wrong." Pride filled her voice with the last sentence.

"I think you did."

She smiled. "It's funny, I wasn't afraid to open the place, but I am nervous about expanding and doing more."

"I can understand that. You've been successful, expanding is a risk. But I tell you one thing."

"What?"

"You've come this far. I wouldn't bet on you failing. I can only see you continuing to soar."

"You really think so?"

"I do. Tracey, you're way more capable than you give yourself credit for. It's about time you started to be the badass that everyone else sees in you."

20

Tracey sat with her new office manager, Debra, to go over the various upcoming activities at the inn. It was going to be a busy weekend with two couples, a family and several ladies on a trip to Peachtree Cove to check out the local winery. The last group brought home Mikayla's point that she could cross-promote with the local wineries and breweries to offer tastings at her inn.

Debra was turning out to be even more of a help than Tracey had anticipated. Within a month she'd helped streamline the check-in process, was great with guests and had taken over the social media pages. Instead of the random posts Tracey put up when she'd had time, Debra posted updated pictures and information on the inn almost daily. Which freed Tracey to focus on her plans for expansion.

"I'm inviting my brother over tomorrow to look at the peach field and see if we can add some small cottages there," Tracey said. "Can you make sure the housekeeping staff gets the rooms cleaned and turned over before the next guests arrive?"

"I've got that," Debra said. "You don't have to worry about it. I'm excited to hear what your brother says."

Debra's enthusiasm for the project was the same as Tracey's. Her face had lit up as soon as Tracey had told her about the idea. Shirley felt the same way, and so had her brother when she'd asked him to help her. The support Tracey had for the project was overwhelming. The only person who'd shown any doubt had been herself. Her doubt was eroding with each word of encouragement she received along the way. Her talks with Mikayla as she finished her business plan made the process seem challenging but not impossible to overcome.

"I am, too. I like the way you've stepped in and handled the day-to-day while I work on this. I couldn't have done nearly as much without your help."

"That's what I'm supposed to do. When do you think construction can start on the cottages?"

Tracey shrugged. "I have no idea. Tomorrow is just to talk about my vision and what would be involved. I want to get an idea of the cost of what I'm thinking so I'll know how big of a leap I'll be taking."

"I can't wait to see what you two come up with. The rest of the fields are so beautiful. I can imagine them being home to some cute little spaces we can rent out."

Tracey grinned as the image of small rentals nestled between the peach trees entered her head. The scene would be even more beautiful when the trees were filled with peach blossoms.

"Me, too. When I'm done with him, let's talk about hosting a wine tasting."

Debra nodded. "I've already pulled together a list of wineries nearby, and I've got a call in to my friend who helped plan the wine and food festival in Augusta last year. She can give us some ideas."

Tracey clasped her hands and wiggled in her seat. "Oh my

goodness, Debra, you're turning out to be even more amazing than I expected."

"When I said working at a small boutique place like this was my dream, I didn't lie. Stick with me, and we'll make this place thrive."

Tracey held out her hand. "Sounds like a deal to me."

A few minutes after their meeting ended, Tracey pulled out her cell phone as she nearly skipped to her car. Not only was she excited about her plans for the inn, but it was Thursday night. Her night with Brian. She wasn't even going to pretend she wasn't looking forward to her time with him. In the month that passed since they'd added the benefits to their friendship, she'd gotten better at saying what she wanted and learning to relax and enjoy sex.

She hadn't been this excited about sex since she and Bernard had first started dating. Their sex life hadn't been the sad, dried-up disaster that it was at the end of their marriage. She now recognized that her need to be the perfect wife had turned into an anxiety and overanalyzing that made her hyperfocus on his wants and be less focused on what she wanted. She'd let go of the pressure to be perfect with Brian. She wasn't trying to be his perfect anything. Sure, they were cool and she enjoyed his company, but she wasn't looking for a boyfriend or long-term relationship and definitely not a husband. She could just be and enjoy, knowing the only thing he expected of her was to be herself and tell him what she liked.

She got in her car and then shot him a quick text before turning on the vehicle.

Going to my dad's first.

His response was quick. Everything okay?

Yeah. It's his bday.

Do you need to cancel?

Birthdays were not a big deal in her family. Growing up in her home a birthday was just another day. They didn't do cake and ice cream or get together to celebrate. She'd be lucky if her dad was sober enough to remember his kids' birthdays, and her mom would kiss them on the forehead, hand them a card and say, "Be grateful you made it another year. Some people didn't. That's your present."

Those words stuck with Tracey. Making it another year was the best present, but she still tried to acknowledge her family's birthdays in small ways. Which was why she was going to see her dad and drop off a card.

Nah. Popping in real quick then heading over, she texted back.

Cool. See you soon.

Can't wait.

She frowned as soon as she hit Send. Damn, did she sound overly eager? She was excited about sleeping with him, but she didn't want to sound clingy.

Same. I'll be waiting.

She saw the words and relaxed. He wasn't freaking out, so neither would she. This thing with Brian was so chill, she loved it. She dropped her phone in her purse and turned on the ignition.

She got to her dad's apartment a few minutes later. He still lived in the same complex they'd moved into when Tracey started high school. The low-income units were decent enough when she was growing up; they barely brushed decent now. Multiple changes in ownership over the last decade combined with a lack of maintenance, and the buildings appeared worn down. The playground area had the same swing and play equipment it had when they'd moved, and the shrubs in front of the buildings were thin and worn from overshearing.

She trudged up the steps to the second-floor apartment they'd all shared, took a deep breath then knocked on the brown door. She braced herself for seeing her dad. The one birthday he'd always remembered when she was growing up was his. He celebrated hard. Meaning she'd never seen him ring in a birthday sober. He hadn't had any other outburst with her mom since that night several weeks ago, but she still doubted she'd find him without a drink in his hand.

The door opened, and her dad stood smiling on the other side. His hair looked freshly cut. His shirt was clean and neat along with his pants. His eyes were clear.

"Hey...Dad. Happy birthday."

"Tracey, baby, come on inside." Her dad stepped back to let her in. Once she crossed the threshold, he opened his arms and pulled her in for a hug.

Tracey breathed in as he hugged her, expecting the familiar smell of musk and alcohol. Instead, his clothes smelled like laundry detergent and his skin like soap.

She pulled back and eyed him. "You're not drunk."

The words were blunt, but that's how she was with him. She and her brother realized around the age of ten that trying to coax a drunk dad wouldn't get them anywhere. Being blunt and straightforward worked best most days.

Her dad laughed and waved her words away. "I told you I'm sober now." He walked farther into the apartment and sat on the worn gray sofa in the living area.

"But you showed up at Mom's place not sober not too long ago." Tracey sat next to him on the couch.

He frowned and nodded. "Not my best day."

"Not your worst either," she replied. No judgment, just stating facts.

He winced. "No, not my worst. But I meant what I said. I had a slipup, but I'm fine now. I haven't had a drink since that day."

"What makes this time any different to previous times?"

He shrugged. "It just is." He leaned forward and picked up the remote control. "Want to watch something?"

"Nah, I can't stay long. I came by to give you your birthday present." She reached into her purse and pulled out a yellow envelope. "Here."

"Aww, thank you. You didn't have to get me anything."

"It's your birthday. I know the present is making it another year, but I still wanted to give you something."

He opened the card. Read the words quickly before stuffing the fifty-dollar bill into his pants pocket. She always gave her dad cash on his birthday. He had no hobbies other than drinking. When she was younger, she would get him gift cards to home-repair stores or tools, hoping that he would use them to work and straighten up his life like he always promised. He never did, so she got him what he wanted instead. Money to buy the whiskey or gin he loved so much.

"I appreciate that. Your brother said he was coming by later."

"I know. I spoke with him earlier. He said he would drop in after he finished with a job."

"Maybe you can stick around, and we can all have dinner together," he said hopefully.

The offer surprised her. It was the first time he'd suggested spending his birthday with his family. When she was younger she might have said yes, but she understood this moment of clarity with him might turn out to be just another broken promise later. "I've got plans tonight."

He nodded and glanced away. "Oh, I understand."

"You never really wanted to hang out on your birthday. I thought you'd be with your friends."

"Yeah, the fellas did call, but you know, I'm not into all that now."

"Why not?" she asked, not believing him for a second.

"Because I've got to get your mom back."

Tracey sighed and shook her head. "Let it go, Dad. You two are not together. Mom's moved on."

"She won't really move on. It's all a phase. She still cares about me."

"She's happy with Raymond."

He scowled. "She's happy with his money. That's all. I realized that after going over there. Now that I'm clean, I'm going to start working again. I'm going to ask your brother to let me help on some of his jobs. Once I make some money, I'll clean this place up. Hell, maybe I'll move into a nicer place. Then she'll see and come back where she belongs."

Tracey believed her mom would come back about as much as she believed her dad was going to clean up his act for good. She'd stopped hoping that her parents would be typical, normal, loving parents. Stopped hoping her mom wouldn't sleep around and that her dad wouldn't drink anymore. She was too old to believe in fairy tales. She usually shook off when the hope tried to creep up, but now she was irritated.

"Dad, just stop, okay? You and Mom are done."

"Don't say that. Don't you want us together? A family again?"

"No, Dad, I want you two to stop with the drama. Stop pulling me and Devante back into your whirlwind, okay? If you're going to be sober, then just be sober and work for you. Let Mom do her thing, and leave well enough alone."

"Stop talking like that. We'll work things out. You just wait and see. I'm not giving up on my marriage like you did with yours."

Irritation turned to anger. This wasn't the first time he'd

accused her of not trying hard enough to make her marriage work. She hadn't given up on her marriage, and she'd long stopped caring about getting her dad's approval. Too bad his words still could kill her moods. She'd been happy before stopping by, and now he was bringing her down with his accusations, unreliable promises and delusional dreams.

"You know what? I've got to go."

His cell phone rang. They both looked at the scratched screen on the surface of an even more scratched coffee table. She saw her mom's number, and her frustration intensified.

"See, what I tell you? She can't forget me." He picked up the phone and answered. "Hey, baby." He grinned and then laughed. "Oh yeah, happy birthday to me."

Tracey rolled her eyes and stood. Her dad didn't even notice as she walked to the door. He was so wrapped up in bliss that her mom had called when Tracey knew her mom was just doing what Tracey had done. Checking in just to make sure he hadn't drunk too much and stumbled into a ditch. She was so sick of them and this game. She wished one of them would finally stop this roller-coaster ride of misery they kept putting the whole family through.

21

Brian looked around his bedroom, rubbed his hands to-
gether and grinned. Everything was just like he wanted. Candles stood on the dresser, and side tables created a soft, warm
glow. Red rose petals covered the bed. He'd put up a massage
table near the foot of the bed and a bottle of scented body oil
waited in a warmer. The pièce de résistance: he'd dressed in
a pair of black silk boxers and paired it with a matching robe.
Oh yes, everything was perfect.

He'd done this before. Set up candles and rose petals and
given a sensual massage, but he hadn't been this excited before.
Just thinking about having Tracey reclining on the table, his
hands gliding over her curves, and watching the tension release
from her body before they moved to the bed had him hard as
a rock. Not just because he wanted to sleep with her but because he wanted to make her feel special. One thing he'd realized over the past month was that Tracey didn't get the chance

to feel special often. She was always taking care of business or other people, but no one took care of her. He wanted to do that for her.

He didn't think the setup was overstepping their friends-with-benefits status. Tonight was going to be sexy and some might say romantic, but because he'd done this before he didn't think the scenario was going above and beyond. He was just being a friend. Just looking out for her in a way that benefited them both. Not doing too much.

The doorbell rang, and Brian's pulse jumped. She was there. He did one last look over the room to make sure things were perfect and took a deep breath to calm his sudden, unexpected nerves before going to answer the door. He hoped she didn't think this was too much.

He swung open the door and waited for Tracey's eyes to widen then light up with anticipation the way they usually did when they got together; the way she was just as excited about their time together was sexy as hell. Tracey had no idea how sexy she was. He'd always been attracted to her confidence, and watching her bring that same bold, confident self into the bedroom had him counting down the hours until they were together again.

Tracey's eyes did widen, and her brows rose, and there was even the flare of desire he wanted, but something else was in her gaze. Something he hadn't seen since the first time they'd tried to sleep together. A glimmer of anxiety. She'd texted about going to see her dad before coming over. A visit with her dad was the one thing he hadn't accounted for while creating this romantic, sensual night. He should have anticipated that seeing her dad might affect her mood.

He took her hand and drew her inside. "You good?"

Her gaze roamed over his bare chest, down to his boxers and legs before traveling back up. "I'm better now."

Brian's concerns eased. The heat in her gaze made him consider undressing her right there. But he wanted to run his hands over her body and drive her to the brink of pleasure more. "I've got something special planned for you."

She cocked a brow. "*Special* like what?"

"Just wait and see." He took her purse and set it on the table in the entryway. "Close your eyes."

"Close my eyes? What did you do?" A trace of nervousness entered her voice.

He walked behind her and placed his hands on her shoulders. Her muscles were tense beneath his fingertips. "Nothing bad, I promise. If you don't want to close them you don't have to. Just come with me."

She nodded before relaxing and closing her eyes. Brian led her from the front of the house to the bedroom. Once he had her standing where she'd get a perfect view of what he'd set up, he leaned in and whispered in her ear. "Okay, open them."

She opened her eyes and sucked in a breath. She took in everything: the candles, rose petals and massage table. He held his breath while he waited for her response. Would she be happy, think it was too much, jump up and down with joy? He wanted the jumping up and down.

Tracey's lower lip wobbled before a tear slipped out of her eyes. She hastily wiped it away, but another came. She bit her lip and turned away.

A vise constricted around Brian's heart. He quickly moved to stand in front of her and put his hands on her shoulders. "Tracey, what's wrong? Talk to me."

She lifted her head and swiped at her eyes. "I'm sorry. This is ludicrous. I don't even know why I'm crying. Yes, I do know why I'm crying."

"Why? Did I mess up? Does this bring back bad memories?"

She shook her head. "No, I'm mad. Like, pissed off, and I want to hit something, and we're supposed to be over here having sex. You did all of this, and I can barely think about sex right now. I'm about to ruin everything, and it's pissing me off."

Brian relaxed that he hadn't messed up, but obviously something else was on her mind. "Tracey, we don't have to have sex."

"But you've got candles, rose petals and a whole massage table."

"It's cool. Why don't I rub your back and shoulders and you tell me what's got you so pissed."

"But—"

He squeezed her shoulders. "No *buts*, Tracey. We're also friends. Tell me what's got my friend all upset."

She sighed. The way she automatically would deny that something was wrong was clear in her eyes. "You sure?"

Brian knew that for however long they did this, he would never let Tracey feel bad about telling him how she really felt. As much as he wanted this night to be perfect, he also wanted her to feel comfortable and never regret their time together.

"If you ask me one more time I'm going to change my mind," he teased.

Tracey laughed and then pulled back. "Fine. Thank you."

Instead of the massage table, they settled on the bed. Brian leaned against the headboard, and Tracey sat between his legs. He placed his hands on her shoulders, but she glanced back at him before he could massage.

"Do you need me to take my shirt off?"

"Are you okay taking it off?" He'd love nothing more than to see her bare shoulders while doing this.

"If you're going to do a good job rubbing my shoulders you'll need access," she said in a no-nonsense voice and pulled her shirt over her head.

Brian placed his hands on her shoulders and rubbed his fingers along the straps of her bra. "Can I push these down?"

She leaned her head to one side and then the other. "Just take the bra off."

Brian held back a groan as she reached back and unhooked her bra. He took a long breath. He was going to listen and give her what she needed. Not be selfish, but damn, he was going to have to focus on her words and not get distracted by her beautiful breasts.

"Hold up. Let me get the massage oil." He jumped up and grabbed it before settling back behind her. He rubbed oil into his hands and then gently kneaded the tight muscles of her shoulders.

"Now, what's going on?"

Tracey let out a long low moan. Brian shifted behind her so that his swelling dick wouldn't press into her back and distract her from talking.

"My parents," Tracey said after a few seconds. "I'm so sick of them and this toxic ride they stay on. My dad showed up at my mom's house drunk a few weeks back. He wasn't supposed to be drinking again because he was proving that he could be sober. I don't know why I had hoped this time would be different because he never stays sober. Devante called me to come get him before Mom's boyfriend found out. She said she was done with him now that she's with someone else. Devante and I had to drag him home. Then today, when I went to check on him he's back to saying he wants her back. I know Mom is done with him, but what does she do? She calls him on his birthday."

Tracey hadn't told him about having to get her dad from her mom's place. She kept conversations about her parents superficial. He didn't pry because he knew that was a sore spot. "Is your mom calling him today a bad thing?"

"It is when she knows that anytime she reaches out to him he starts spiraling again and saying that they can get back together. It's just so frustrating. I don't understand. He's a drunk, and she has cheated on him from the beginning. But they can't seem to quit each other. Even though it makes life miserable for them and their kids."

Brian continued to work the knots out of her shoulders as he thought about what she'd said. He was well aware of her parents' rocky relationship. Her mother's affairs with different men around town and her dad getting drunk in public or losing contracting jobs because he'd shown up intoxicated had kept the gossips busy for years. Even his parents had commented on it. His dad judging and his mom always saying that she would pray for the kids. Those were things he'd never tell Tracey. She didn't want the judgment or the pity. She'd always taken up for her family and gone toe-to-toe with anyone who had anything negative to say about them. Despite how much they made her mad, she loved them.

"That's a lot, huh?" she said after he was silent for a while.

"Just thinking."

"My parents are a lot."

"They are, but I get it."

She looked at him over her shoulder. "How do you get it?"

"I lived it. My marriage wasn't as much as your parents', but we were toxic in our own way."

"You're right. I'm sorry. You did tell me about the struggle with your ex-wife."

"I didn't talk about my marriage a lot because I don't like everyone in my business like that. But also because I was a little ashamed by how often I'd go back. Every time I'd say I was done and we'd break up, she'd come and bat her eyes, and I was right back where I was before. Then after the divorce," he said and sighed, not wanting to admit the truth but also not wanting to hold back and keep things from Tracey, "even after the divorce I went back a few times."

Tracey's body tightened. She leaned away from him. "You still love her?"

He gently pulled her back toward him and continued to knead her shoulders. "It took too long, but I realized I am no longer in love with her."

"It took how long?" Doubt entered her voice.

"I thought I was good, but when we ran into each other at a friend's party over a year ago, old feelings bubbled up and we slept together. But the next day she told me she was engaged to someone else. The guy she'd cheated on me with."

Tracey gasped, and her hand resting on his shin tightened. "No she didn't."

"She did, but the funny thing was I wasn't hurt. I was disappointed in myself more than anything. A part of me knew that she would do the same thing, and I was tired. I knew right then I was no longer in love with her."

Tracey was quiet for several seconds. "Do you think my dad will ever get tired of my mom? Or that she'll get tired of keeping him on a string?"

Brian's hands stilled. "I don't know. But what they do is their own mess. I'm sorry that it spills over and affects you. But you've got to understand that what they're doing is not because of you. You can't stop them if they don't want to stop. You're focusing on finding your own happiness, Tracey. Keep on doing that. Don't worry about trying to fix your parents and their relationship. Until they want to fix it, you'll be banging your head against a wall. You deserve to focus just on you."

"It's so hard," she whispered.

He ran his hands down her shoulders to her arms and worked those muscles. "What is?"

"Focusing on me. I haven't had the chance to focus on me ever. It's always been my parents. Then it was Bernard."

"But despite all that, you found ways to make your own space. You've got the business, you filed for divorce from Bernard. Don't underestimate yourself, Tracey. You know how to look out for you. Just keep doing it." He leaned forward and kissed the side of her neck.

She shifted until their eyes met. "Are you for real, or are you just being nice?"

He lifted a brow. "I don't have to just be nice. Haven't we always been honest with each other? I'm telling you the truth. You've always been strong, but you've never had the chance to trust anyone enough to take off your armor. You can take it off around me. I've got you."

Her eyes softened. He didn't know where those words came from. He understood neither of them wanted promises of forever and that both of them were not ready to handle thoughts of a long-term commitment, but he meant what he said. No matter what happened, he would be there for Tracey when she needed him.

The corner of her lips lifted. She leaned toward him and brushed her lips across his. "You're a good friend."

The kiss wasn't nearly enough. The softness of her eyes, the feel of her skin beneath his hands, and the way she looked at him as if he'd just made her day made him rock hard.

"Your friend with all the benefits," he said and kissed her gently. He'd pull back if she tensed. He'd go to bed hard and let her talk all she wanted if she needed, but right now he couldn't not kiss her again.

Tracey didn't pull back. Her sweet lips opened, and her tongue teased his lips. Desire flooded Brian's midsection, his hand gliding from her arm to wrap around her body and cup her breast. She melted into him, and even though need made him want to flip her over and push deep inside, he also knew she didn't need that. Right now she just needed to feel that she could trust him when she was vulnerable. So that's what he did. He took things slow. He let her lead the way, until the tension left her body and she moaned and twisted her body against his. Then he made love to her with everything in him until her body was limp and she curled against his chest and fell asleep.

22

Tracey's brother, Devante, unrolled the conceptual drawings for cabins and placed them on her desk, and her eyes widened and she clasped her hands to her chest. She'd asked and her brother had delivered. Once she'd told him about her plans to include cabins on the property, he'd immediately found a way to get some sketches she could review.

"Devante, this is great!" She put her hand on her brother's shoulder. "I can't believe you got someone to do this for you."

Devante's chest swelled with pride. He was younger than her, but he always seemed to puff up when he could do something for his older sister. "Andre recommended an architect he knew. He called the guy up, and he said he'd give me a few ideas. He'll also work with you if you like any of them and need full design plans because you're a small business and he likes to give back."

"Thank you and Andre," Tracey said. Andre was an old classmate who had come back to Peachtree Cove to work as the general contractor for the renovation of the old shopping mall that the mayor was turning into a mixed-use development for residential and commercial purposes.

"He's helped you out, too, right?"

"Ever since he added me as a subcontractor on the mayor's project, my contracting business has grown. He's got some good hookups, and since he's dating Tamara, he's all into growing Peachtree Cove."

Tamara was the town's planning director and was a vital member of the mayor's team working to revamp Peachtree Cove.

"I'm glad Andre feels that way. Hopefully he'll keep on wanting to help me as I grow. I'm doing good, and I can handle some of the up-front costs of building the cabins, but any help I can get would be even better."

Tracey didn't usually ask for help, but in this case her brother's connections were a godsend. Plus, one thing she'd learned in Mikayla's class was the importance of having connections and not being afraid to ask for help when needed. If she wanted to make her dream a reality, she could struggle on her own or use the expertise of people who'd been where she wanted to be. She never would have imagined she'd be in this position a year ago, but she was so glad she was here now.

"Don't worry, Tracey. Between Andre's guy helping with the construction plans and me and my guys doing the actual work, we'll get this done."

"I don't want you to do everything for free. Now, don't get me wrong, I'll take the family discount, but I still want to be able to give you something. We'll start with two or three cabins, and if things go well then we can add more."

"I think you're going to need more a lot sooner than you think. You're already doing good with the weddings. Now that Debra is planning the wine tasting, you're going to blow up even more. Just watch."

"We'll see," Tracey said, trying to keep the hope out of her voice.

She wanted everything her brother said to come true, but old habits didn't just disappear because she believed in her dream. She wasn't going to jinx anything by claiming victory too early. She was starting to worry that things were going too well. The class had helped her figure out how to expand the bed and breakfast. Mikayla had agreed to help Tracey brainstorm ideas as she worked on the expansion. Her brother was offering to build them at a reduced rate. Her friends-with-benefits situation with Brian meant he was not only turning out to be a good friend but he was also giving her multiple benefits in the form of multiple orgasms. Things had never been this easy for her. She was worried that something was going to go wrong and ruin everything.

"Just wait and see," Devante said, probably sensing that she was already starting to doubt her abilities. Her brother was good at reading her moods. "You didn't think you'd get the bed and breakfast open, and look what you've got. I know what I'm talking about. Why do you always worry?"

"Because if I plan for the worst, then I can be pleasantly surprised when things turn out okay," she said with forced optimism.

Devante shook his head. "We're long past that. I think we've both proven that we can make stuff happen. We don't have to always expect the worst."

Tracey ran her fingers through her locs. "It's hard to shake off years of bad things happening."

"Nothing bad has happened recently. In fact, this year has been nothing but good things. If you think your divorce was a bad thing, then let me tell you that you're dead wrong. Bernard was a sorry-ass dude, and you're better off without him."

Tracey grinned. She wasn't hurt by the mention of her ex-husband. She also wasn't angry anymore. She was better off without him. Life with Bernard had always been unbalanced. With her thinking she wasn't good enough and trying too hard to please him at the expense of her own self-confidence. The anxiety she'd always felt when he came home and she'd have to figure out what type of mood he'd be in, or feeling as if she were somehow a failure because the house wasn't perfectly clean or dinner wasn't on the table, was gone. She finally felt comfortable in her own place and in her own skin.

"The way I finally came to realize that I needed to leave Bernard was messed up, but believe me when I say I don't consider my divorce as a failure. The marriage was a failure, but the divorce is a win."

She looked down at the various sketches of different cabins. There were four different styles. They varied from rustic to glamping. Tracey pointed to the third picture of one that was neither too fancy nor did it look like you'd be roughing it to stay there. "I like this one."

"I figured you would."

"I don't want the cabins to be too rustic. If people are getting married or staying here after a wine tasting or just coming for a quick weekend, I want them to feel like they're still experiencing the comfort of the main house. This one looks like a cute cottage."

"Then, I'll tell him that's the one you like. See if he can draw up construction plans."

Tracey's heart raced. She placed a hand over the flutters in her stomach. "This is all happening so fast."

"It'll work out. Don't worry. Nothing will go wrong."

The sound of voices outside her office in the hallway had them both turning in that direction. Tracey recognized Debra's calming voice against the loud irritated sound of her mother.

Tracey sighed and pressed a hand to her temple. "What is she doing here?"

"Is that Mom?" Devante said at the same time.

The door to Tracey's office burst open, and her mom pushed Debra out of the way to come inside. She paused before raising a hand as if warding off unwanted words. "Hold up, your important meeting is with your brother?" She cut her eyes back at Debra. "Girl, these are my kids. Nothing they do is too important for me to interrupt," Loretta said with all the authority of the president entering the Oval Office.

"Mom, what are you doing here?" Tracey looked at the suitcase her mom pulled behind her. "With luggage."

Loretta came farther into the office. "Raymond is acting all stupid. He thinks I'm still fooling around with your daddy. I told him that he was being unreasonable, but just because I spent the night with your dad on his birthday he thinks I'm sleeping with him."

"What?" Tracey said putting her hands on her hips. "Why did you stay with him?"

"I went over there to stop him from coming to me. Then he was crying and acting a fool. So I stayed there to make sure he wouldn't start drinking. That's all that happened. But Raymond was all 'I know how you are' and accused me of sleeping with him. So I left. I need a room. I'm gonna stay here until he gets his act together."

Tracey just needed ten minutes of quiet time. Between guests, planning for the expansion, and her mom being all over the bed and breakfast in everyone's business, she hadn't had any time to relax much less think in the past week. She had a chicken salad sandwich Shirley had slid to her when she'd gone through the kitchen and a can of soda and was going to snatch a few minutes in her office just to breathe.

The tension of the day eased with each quick step she took

toward her office door. She could sense the calm she'd have from the silence. She could scroll through her phone and look at random videos of cabins and glamping sites.

She opened the door to her office and froze. "Mom? What are you doing in here? I thought you were in your room."

Her mom looked up from the sketches of the cabins on Tracey's desk. "What? I can't come in your office?"

Tracey went farther into the room and put the sandwich and soda down on her desk before crossing her arms. Irritation crawled up her spine. Her mom popping in meant she'd lose at least ten minutes of quiet time. There was no way she'd get Loretta out of her office faster than that. If she tried, her mom would be stubborn and she'd lose the entire hour of her lunch break.

"My office is my working space. And this is my place of business and not your house where you can claim that you can go wherever you want."

Loretta raised a brow and propped a hand on her hip. "Oh, so you trying to pull rank on me now?"

"It's not pulling rank. It's just asking you to try and respect my boundaries."

Loretta sighed and shrugged. "Fine, I won't come in here without you knowing. I'm not trying to make your staff disrespect you."

"Thank you."

Her mom pointed at the drawings on the table. "What's all this?"

Tracey sighed and sat down at her desk. She might as well eat. "It's drawings of cabins. I'm going to build a few in the peach field so I can rent them out."

Her mom frowned down at the drawings. "Oh, you're trying to do big things, huh?"

Tracey nodded as she swallowed the bite of the sandwich she'd taken before responding. "If you want to call it that. I thought of the idea while taking the class Mikayla taught. This is the business plan I put together. Now that I've put the plan together, I might as well do the work."

Her mom studied the drawings for a long second. "This is cool, Tracey. I mean, when you opened this place, I'll admit I wasn't sure if it was a good idea."

"I know. You told me that. Often." Tracey sipped her soda and hoped this conversation wouldn't make her wish for something stronger.

"You know why I told you that?"

"Because you wanted to kill my dream?" She softened the words with a smile.

Her mom narrowed her eyes before swatting at Tracey. "Nobody tried to kill your dream. I was just worried that Bernard wouldn't support you. That man was the real dream-killer. He only wanted you at home being his perfect little housewife."

"I was far from perfect."

"Which was good. But you opened anyway, despite him fighting you the entire time. I'm proud of you, Tracey. You won't have to ever depend on some man if you keep this up."

Tracey propped her elbow on the desk. "I didn't open the inn just to not depend on a man. It's about doing something that I wanted to do."

Her mom sighed as she trailed her fingers over the plans. "I never got the chance to do that."

Tracey cocked her head to the side. "Mom, don't go there. You always did what you wanted to do."

Her gaze jumped back to Tracey. "Why do you say that?"

Tracey shook her head. "I'm not going there." She picked up her sandwich and took another bite.

Loretta placed a hand on her hip again. "Why not? You bold enough to start something, go on and be bold enough to finish what you started."

Tracey swallowed and considered saying that she hadn't

meant anything. But she was New Tracey now. New Tracey wasn't going to be afraid to say how she felt. Even with her mom. She put the sandwich down and said, "I mean, Mom, no disrespect at all, but you kind of did what you wanted when I was growing up. Even now. You didn't let Dad stop you from doing *whatever* you wanted to do."

Loretta's eyes narrowed. "You talking about me seeing other men."

Tracey looked away and sipped her soda.

Loretta grunted before saying, "I know I was out there, but do you know why?"

Tracey held up a hand. "I don't want to know the details."

"And I'm not about to give you details, but I do want you to know that when I first got married, your dad didn't want me to work. He promised to take care of me and the kids. I didn't go to college like you and your brother. So I thought I'd hit the jackpot. A man who loved me and wanted to take care of me. I was pregnant with you and then your brother long before I realized your dad's drinking had become a full-fledged problem. He wasn't the most reliable when it came to providing for the family. I tried working, but someone had to be available when things came up with you and your brother at school. So I found another way. My *friends* helped me. Devante needed a new pair of shoes, bam, I got them. I needed someone to fix the brakes on the car, no problem, I had someone who would get it done. Yeah, I took on odd jobs here and there to pay for those field trips and new school clothes y'all needed, but when I needed someone to help *me* out, then I had that, too."

Tracey blinked, not sure what to do with that information. "Mom…"

"I don't care if you judge me. I don't regret anything I ever did. I wanted to take care of you and your brother, but I also had to take care of me."

"What about Dad? Did you ever love him?"

Her mom sighed and walked to the window. "I did. At the beginning. I knew he liked to drink, but I didn't think it was bad. That's what happens when you're eighteen and nineteen and in love. When I got pregnant and he asked me to marry him, I thought that he would slow down. Well, we know how that went. I still care about your dad because he gave me you and your brother. But eventually, I got tired of sticking around and picking up the slack. You and Devante have started your own businesses and done what you needed to do. Y'all inspired me to do that for myself."

"But is Raymond really the right person for you? You know you could get a stable job or go back to school."

Tracey didn't want to say it, but she worried about her mom. She was beautiful and had made ends meet first by marrying their dad and then through the men she'd seen in between, but that wouldn't last forever. Her mom didn't have an exit plan or a strategy to take care of herself long-term. Tracey wasn't sure how to make her see that and didn't want to get into a lecture about how her mom needed a retirement plan.

Loretta shrugged. "Raymond is who I'm with for now. And can you imagine me on someone's job? Child, I couldn't imagine me taking orders from someone half my age. I know you worry about me, but you don't have to. Believe it or not, I've got a little money saved up. I was smart about my hustle. I'm not looking for you and Devante to have to take care of me."

"I'm not saying that."

"I know you're not, but I also want you to understand that your mom isn't a fool. I've got me." She turned back and met Tracey's eyes. "You go on and build up this inn and make it great. That's what you can do for me. Seeing you and Devante be successful despite the hell me and your dad put y'all through makes me happy. I'll be okay."

Tracey's mom was stubborn and tenacious enough for her to believe what she said. She couldn't agree with all the decisions her mom had made, but she also couldn't judge her. The past was the past, and despite what happened, she and Devante had turned out alright.

She sighed and nodded. "Okay. Well then, if I don't have to take care of you, how long do you plan to stay here?"

Loretta laughed. "Just until Raymond comes to his senses, which won't be long. But even if he doesn't, don't worry. I'll find a place to stay."

Tracey didn't doubt her at all. Even though her mom told her not to worry, she wasn't about to see her have to go depend on anyone else. "You can stay here as long as you want, Mom."

23

Brian had gone out on a limb and asked Tracey to come with him to the Atlanta Botanical Garden. He'd mentioned going there when he'd first moved back to Peachtree Cove to get an idea of the types of plants and shrubs he wanted to have available in his nursery and plant designs. Tracey had mentioned she'd once asked Bernard to go with her to see the Earth Goddess exhibit, and he'd said he didn't want to go see any plants. Brian knew he wasn't in competition with her ex, and if he were, then he'd already come out on top, but something in him made him want to take her to a place Bernard had refused to go.

He'd expected her to hesitate or say no. They'd agreed to just meet up on certain days and they'd stuck with that, but to his surprise she'd agreed. The two-hour car ride from Peachtree Cove to the botanical garden was fun. They'd talked about so many random topics, like the silly things they remembered from when they were in school and their thoughts on music and television shows. He'd always liked Tracey and her personality, but the fact that they could stay in conversation during the car ride made him like her even more.

Brian watched Tracey's face as they rounded the corner of the pathway that led to the Earth Goddess exhibit. Tracey gasped when the twenty-five-foot sculpture of the goddess came into view. The goddess's hair was made up of a multitude of bright flowers and her outstretched hand spilled water into a pool below. Brian couldn't help but puff his chest a little bit at seeing the appreciation on Tracey's face. His actions had done that.

"She's beautiful," Tracey said in an excited voice. "Isn't that amazing!"

Brian nodded and took in the sculpture. "It is. The first time I saw it I thought it was great."

She walked closer to the pond separating the visitors from the sculpture. She pulled out her phone and held it toward him. "Take my picture."

He took her phone and took several pictures of her before he switched the camera around and stood next to her. "How about a selfie?"

She blinked at him. "You want to take one with me?"

He nodded. "Why not?" He wrapped an arm around her shoulder and pulled her to his side before holding up the phone. "Smile."

She relaxed against him and grinned at the camera. He snapped a few pictures, ensuring he got the sculpture in the background. Someone asked if Tracey wanted them to take their picture. She nodded, and he handed over the phone, and the lady snapped their picture. They returned the favor, taking pictures of the woman with her friends, before moving on to look at the rest of the garden.

"Thank you for bringing me here," Tracey said when they were looking at orchids in one of the greenhouses.

"You don't have to thank me."

"I do. I just mentioned this to you the one day, and then you made a trip to bring me. Even though we aren't..." she shrugged "...you know."

"We're friends, Tracey," he said. "Friends can hang out with each other. I wanted to come back down here anyway."

He'd wanted to return when she'd mentioned how much she wanted to come, but that wasn't important. They were both having a good time. They could hang out and enjoy each other's company without any pressures or expectations. That's all that mattered.

"Yeah, but that didn't mean you would want to bring me along. But still, thank you. I'm having a really good time."

"Good. I am, too."

Tracey walked up to a bright yellow orchid and studied it. She looked sexy, as always. He wasn't sure what prompted her to stop hiding her figure behind baggy clothes, but he wouldn't complain. The fitted burgundy T-shirt and jeans she wore weren't overtly sexy, but on Tracey's curvy figure they were better than lingerie. She'd pinned back the sides of her locs, and large gold hoop earrings caressed her cheeks.

"You know, I never would have thought that I'd have so much fun with you."

He moved to stand next to her. "Why not? Because you used to always hate on me?"

Tracey cut her eyes at him but grinned before slowly moving down the row to admire more flowers. "Nobody hated on you. You were always there when something embarrassing or bad was happening. I just knew you were judging me."

He followed behind her. "I wasn't judging you. I already told you that I thought you were the most confident person I knew. You never let anyone get over on you."

"It felt more like I was always fighting against what people thought I would or should be."

Another couple came down the small path. Brian put his hand on the small of Tracey's back and eased her to the side. "But you always held your own. You never backed down. That's part of the reason why I was always watching you. That, and I thought you were sexy as hell."

She looked up at him. Her eyes sparkling with humor. "I still can't get over that you were into me in high school."

"I don't know why. I was always watching you." His hand on her back slid down to her hip. The pulse at the base of her throat fluttered. Brian licked his lips, imagining the taste of her skin.

"Like I said, I didn't catch the signals." Her gaze lowered to his lips then moved to focus behind him. He turned and saw that the couple who'd passed them were watching.

Tracey turned and walked to the exit. Brian kept pace beside her. Once they were outside, he placed his hand back on the small of her back and directed her around a group trying to enter and toward a bench.

"I can't get over that you don't realize how sexy you were."

She lifted a shoulder. "I know I'm cute."

"You're more than cute, Tracey."

She was quiet for a second before her shoulders straightened. "I know that. I mean, it's been so long since I felt sexy, strong or even smart. I know I have all those qualities. But when you stop remembering that, it's easy to believe that you're not."

The wind rustled the trees, and a leaf fell in her hair. He reached over and pulled it out. "I hope you don't stop remembering all of the good things about you in the future."

"Trust and believe, I won't. I'm going to do the things I want and not be afraid to dream big." She turned to him on the bench. "I've picked out the kinds of cabins I want to build on the property, and I'm working with my brother to get the construction plans together."

He'd listened as she worked on the plan during their course at the technical college and had thought the idea was fantastic. "You're going to do it? The plan you put together in the class we took?"

She gave a sheepish smile before nodding. Something she wouldn't have done when they'd first started sleeping together. She'd always been guarded around him. He liked that she was comfortable enough to show her excitement around him.

"Yeah. I asked Devante to help me, and he came through. I can't believe everything came together so quickly. A part of me thinks everything will fall through. Or that something will ruin it."

"Why?"

"I don't know. It's just the pessimist in me. So much stuff would go wrong when I was a kid, you know. My dad wouldn't stay sober. My mom would be gossiped about. Somebody at school would try to shame me. The guy I married wasn't as perfect as I thought he would be. But you know what?"

"What?"

"I also realized all those things that went wrong helped to make me stronger and who I am today. So even if something goes wrong with the cabins, I'll be okay. I'll still find a way to make them happen. I'll still find a way to keep the inn growing and successful. No matter what, I won't be giving up on my dreams."

He'd always known she was a fighter. Her resilience and confidence was something he would always appreciate. It was the thing about her that attracted him to her the most. He loved the fight in her.

He ran his fingers across her bared forearm. "Good. I'd hate for you to give up and I lose my best client."

Her eyes narrowed, but her lips twitched. "Keep playing and I'll find a new nursery to work with."

"No, you won't."

"Oh, you're sure of yourself, huh?"

"Hell yeah. No one gives you service like me." He leaned in

and kissed the side of her mouth. Her breathing hitched, and her gaze heated. "You ready to get out of here?"

"And head back to Peachtree Cove?" She didn't pout, but there was disappointment in her voice. "This is the most quiet I've had since my mom moved in. I was looking forward to spending the day with—" She snapped her mouth shut.

He raised a brow. "The day with what?"

She turned her head away. "Just spending a day in Atlanta. That's all. I finally have help at the inn. Imani is wedding shopping with her mom, and Halle is off on a family reunion trip with Shania and Quinton."

Brian placed a finger on the side of her chin and turned her to face him. He trailed his finger down the side of her neck to where her pulse fluttered. "I was looking forward to spending the day with you, too."

She sat up straight, her mouth opened. He waited on the denial to come next, but then she sighed. "Okay, good. I'm not trying to make this thing weird. We're still just friends. Right?" Uncertainty filled her gaze.

For some reason the words settled uncomfortably around him. They were friends, but they weren't *just* anything. He wasn't ready to explore the idea of that. Not right now, maybe not ever. He pushed the unsettling feeling aside and nodded.

"I got a room. If you're good with that." He prayed she was good with that. This was not a romantic getaway or a date. It was two friends hanging out and him providing a space where they could enjoy the benefits of being together. That was all.

The uncertainty left Tracey's eyes. She relaxed and squeezed his thigh. "I'm more than good with that."

24

Tracey was surprised to see her dad's old truck parked in the inn's driveway and him sitting on her back porch when Brian brought her home the next morning. The day before in Atlanta had been great: the visit to the gardens, dinner and the night in Brian's arms. She was enjoying her time with Brian so much she was wondering if maybe he'd be open to adding another day to their agreement. Was that stretching the limits of their friends-with-benefits arrangement? Maybe, but she was willing to do that as long as she got another chance for him to put her in a few of the positions he'd introduced the night before.

She wasn't in the mood to deal with her dad and whatever drama he was bringing to her door. He never dropped by to say hello, and he hadn't called to say he was coming over. She was the one who had to make the proof-of-life calls and check in on him.

"I wonder what made him come over," she said when Brian pulled up next to his truck.

"Maybe he just wanted to see you?"

Tracey shook her head. "I doubt it. My dad doesn't look for me unless he wants something specific. Might as well see what that is."

"Do you want me to leave?"

"No. I doubt he'll stay long. Let me find out what's going on, and then we can chill."

His lips lifted in a sexy smile as his eyes traveled over her body. "We just gonna chill?"

Heat flooded her cheeks, and she swallowed a giggle. Who was she and when had she become this person? Comfortable with joking about sex? She hadn't felt this comfortable with her own sexuality in a long time. The feeling was addictive.

"Maybe we'll do some other things." She winked before opening the door to get out of the car.

Her dad stood and marched over to the car. Tracey quickly scanned him. He didn't appear hurt or drunk, which were both good things.

"Hey, Dad. What are you doing here?"

He stopped in front of her and eyed Brian coming up behind her. "I just came to check on you." His eyes narrowed. "What are you doing with him?"

Brian held out his hand. "Hi, Mr. Carl. It's good to see you."

Her dad scowled at his hand and sucked his teeth. "Where are you two coming from?"

Tracey raised a brow. She crossed her arms. "Atlanta. Why?"

"When did you go?"

"Why does it matter?"

Her dad looked at her as if she'd lost her mind. "Because you're a married woman hanging out with an unmarried man."

Tracey blinked then scoffed. Where in the world was that

coming from? "Dad, in case you forgot, Bernard and I are divorced."

"That's just a piece of paper. You need to take him back," he said adamantly.

Tracey let out an incredulous laugh. "That piece of paper took over a year and too much money in lawyer fees to get. There is no way I'm taking him back."

Carl crossed his arms. "Why not?"

She held up a finger. "One, he cheated." She lifted another. "Two, he had a baby with her." She held up a third. "He lied and cheated on me for years."

Her dad waved off her words as if they were nothing. "So what? Do you know how many times I took your mom back?"

"You and Mom aren't me and Bernard. We're done, Dad. Get used to it."

He shook his head. "No. Not if you're going to be out here in these streets like your mother. I thought you would be better than her. I heard the people talking, saying you were messing around with him," he said and flung a dirty look Brian's way. "But I didn't want to believe it. That's why I came to check on you."

"And you should mind your business. I don't get in between your and Mom's relationship, and I won't let you in mine. Bernard is good where he's at."

"No, he's not. He misses you."

Tracey snorted. "I doubt it."

"I went to him first. He messed up. He didn't mean to get that girl pregnant. But now you've up and left him, and he has no choice but to stay with her. What you should do is get back with him and y'all be a family."

If her dad had said aliens had invaded the planet and named him emperor she would have been less shocked. She couldn't believe he was trying to guilt-trip her into taking Bernard back.

That he'd even want her to have the same type of pain and suffering he'd dealt with for years with her mom.

"Dad, I don't care what Bernard wants anymore. I'm living my life for me right now. He made his choice, and so did I."

Her dad scowled. "Look at you. Sounding just like your mom. Is that what you want? To be like her? To be running around and having people call you a slut?"

Brian stepped up to Tracey's side. "Hold on. That's enough."

Tracey held up a hand to stop him. She took a deep breath then looked at her dad. "Look, I don't know what you thought you were going to achieve coming over here, but if you keep talking, the only thing that's going to happen is I'm not going to talk to you ever again. So why don't you get in your truck and go and we pretend like this never happened."

Her dad shook his head then pointed at her. "You know what I'm saying is true. I always did the right thing by your mom and kept the family together. You need to do the same."

"Me and Bernard aren't a family anymore. We don't have kids, thank God, and I don't owe him a damn thing."

"You can be a family. He can't raise that kid alone, and he doesn't want to raise it with her."

Tracey did a double take. Was he serious? She shook her head and fished her keys out of her purse. "I'm done talking to you."

She walked toward the back door of the inn. Brian followed. Her dad stayed put, but he yelled after them.

"Don't be like your mom. You can do better than her, Tracey. Fix this thing instead of running around with some man that's only going to use you and drop you."

Tracey's fingers trembled as she reached for the door. Brian's hands covered hers, and she jerked. She glared up at him expecting to see the pity in his eyes. Once again, he was there when she was being humiliated.

"I've got you," he said evenly. Nothing showed in his eyes except for the same anger bubbling inside her like spewing lava.

He opened the door. Tracey quickly went inside, ignoring her dad's insistent calls that she was just as wrong as her mother. Shirley stood by the kitchen sink. She gave Tracey a comforting look but didn't speak. There were no words that could make up for her dad's insults. Thankfully the rest of the kitchen staff continued their work.

Cheeks burning that her dad would not only embarrass her but do it at her inn, Tracey hurried to her office. She paced back and forth, the need to scream, cry or hit something all churning inside her. Why did he have to say that? Just because her dad had stuck around in a bad situation shouldn't mean he wanted her to do the same.

"I can't believe he said that," Tracey said through gritted teeth.

Brian came over and stopped her from pacing. "Don't listen to him."

"I'm not like my mom, and I'm not like him either." Her eyes burned, but she refused to shed the tears. Refused to be seen as weak or vulnerable in front of Brian. Why did she always have to have her life come apart with him front and center stage?

"You're just you, Tracey."

Her back straightened. "What's that supposed to mean?"

He shook his head and shrugged. "Exactly what I said. You're you. You're not your mom or your dad. You're not what anyone expects or can tell you to be. You're your own person, and whatever works for you is all that matters."

"I know that."

"Then, why are you letting his words get to you when you already know you're not your mom?"

"Because I wanted so bad not to be her that I was actually like him," she shot back.

Brian's brows drew together, and he leaned back. "What?"

She ran her hands through her hair. She wanted to pull on the locs and yell in frustration. Instead she dropped her hands and sighed. "I did exactly what my dad did before. I ignored the signs or pretended like it didn't matter. I stuck around when I should have let go so long ago. Each and every time I stayed because we made a commitment. We vowed for better or for worse. I couldn't let the one thing that I'd wanted so much to turn out to be a failure."

Brian shook his head before his jaw flexed. "Leaving a bad situation isn't a failure."

"I know that," she snapped then sighed. Brian wasn't the enemy. "It's just that I can't believe my dad said that. This isn't the first time he said I shouldn't have left. He's said little things here and there about me getting a divorce, but for him to do this? What could have set him off?"

Brian shook his head. "It doesn't matter what set him off. Your dad shouldn't be over here telling you to go back to Bernard. I'm your man now, and everyone better get used to that."

"Exactly!" She spoke before his words sunk in. When they did, she blinked several times as if her brain had short-circuited. "Wait. You're my what?"

Brian froze. Maybe his brain had short-circuited, too. He'd said he was her man! The words didn't send a thrill through her, they made her wary. She didn't want a man, not like that anyway. She'd just finalized her divorce. She was back out here testing the waters, not signing up to get into something serious.

"Brian?" she asked softly. Maybe he'd meant it in a different way. The man in her bed? The man she was sleeping with? The man who was also her friend?

The surprise in his eyes faded, and he closed the few inches of space in between them. "You heard me, Tracey. I'm your man."

She took a step back. Was he asking or telling? The confidence and possessiveness in his eyes both made her want to melt and run. "I thought we were just chilling. Friends with benefits and all that."

"Yeah, we were, but I'm not thinking about being with

someone else right now. I know you've got your stuff to figure out, and I've still got my own things, but we can still be
together. No promises, no expectations, but also no one else. I
won't embarrass you or mislead you. When you're ready to call
this quits, that's cool, but I want to be more than just the friend
you sleep with. I want to be the man you call when you need
something. Your plus-one when you've got somewhere to go."

"You want to be my gentleman caller?" she said trying to
lighten the mood. To tease him a little bit and take away some
of the heaviness the pressure of his words had put on her.

She wasn't sure if she was ready for or wanted what he was
asking her. Was she coming out of one bad situation and going
into another? Even though she knew the only thing Bernard
and Brian and in common was their names starting with a *B*,
she still wasn't ready to step out and start a new relationship
with him.

"I'll be whatever you want to call me," he said.

Her breathing shallowed. The air felt thin, and there wasn't
enough to fill her lungs. "I don't…"

He cupped her chin in his hand then lowered his mouth to
hers. The kiss was slow, sensual, and it set her soul on fire. She
leaned into him, immediately recalling everything single thing
they'd done to each other in that hotel room in Atlanta. But
what they had was lust. Could she do this based on the fact that
they were compatible in the bedroom?

She pulled back slowly. Brian's thumb brushed her lower lip
before he dropped his hand and took a step back.

"I know I just changed the rules. Think about what I said."

"I'm not sure if I'm ready."

He nodded. "I know. And if what we're doing now is still
all you want, then that's cool. I'm willing to take whatever you
want to give me."

25

Brian wanted to call Tracey after he got off work the next day but decided instead to give her some space. She hadn't called or texted him since he'd spilled his guts like a male lead in a romantic dramedy. He still couldn't believe he'd said all that to her. What had he been thinking?

That was the thing: he hadn't been thinking. He'd only been *feeling*. Hadn't he sworn to give up just going by his feelings? He had stopped not thinking things through and letting emotions lead him astray. *Feelings* were what had him stick to Renee for longer than he should. They clouded judgment and led to impulsive, regrettable decisions.

Except he didn't regret saying what he did. In fact, he was pretty sure that if he could go back in time he'd say the same thing. He wasn't sure when it happened, but he wanted to be the person Tracey could depend on. When he'd heard her dad say that Brian would just use her and that she needed to go back to someone like Bernard, something in him had snapped. A need to prove not just to Tracey but to everyone in her life that *he* was the best person to care for and support her. He wanted her to believe that he wouldn't embarrass or hurt her. He wanted to be the man in her life.

He ran his hands over his face and sighed. *Damn!* He'd never thought he would be in this situation again. He'd thought the terrible ending of his marriage had jaded him from ever wanting to be in another committed relationship. He'd thought that was why he could date casually without any connections or regrets. He should have known Tracey would be different. As much as he didn't want to admit it, she had always had a hook in him. Ever since they were young he'd had a crush on her. Common sense would have told him that given the chance to be with her he'd be lost forever.

He left work and headed to his mom's house. If he wasn't going to call Tracey, then he needed a distraction. He hoped spending time with his mom and whatever news she had from the church's usher board would keep him from endlessly thinking about Tracey and what she was thinking—whether she was done with him or would be down with what he'd offered.

When he got to his mom's house, he expected her eyes to widen with excitement and for her to quickly usher him in. His mom loved it when he dropped by to check on her. That's why he would pop in. This time his mom came to the door, and her eyes widened but not with excitement. Instead, she seemed shocked and not in a good way. As if he were a guest she hadn't expected and didn't want to see.

"Brian? What are you doing here?" she asked standing in the door. She was dressed as if she were going out. She wore the blue suit dress she often wore to church.

"I came to see you." He pointed to her clothes. "Did you just get home?"

She ran a hand over her shirt and shook her head. "No, I've been here."

"Well, are you going to let me in?" he asked when she continued to stand in the doorway. She should already have invited him in by now.

She immediately looked contrite. "I'm sorry. You just surprised me, that's all." She took his hand and pulled him in.

He followed her inside the house. "What's going on?"

"Nothing. Nothing at all." Her pitch rose, and she waved a hand.

Brian didn't believe her at all. "Mom, what's up? You're still dressed like you're going to church. Did the pastor ask you to check in on someone today?"

"I'm good... It's just..." She trailed off as she went into the kitchen.

Brian followed her where the smell of his favorite pot roast filled the air. He inhaled a deep breath and rubbed his stomach. "You made pot roast? Why didn't you tell me?"

"Oh, I didn't think you'd want any."

"Ma, you know I always want your pot roast."

"You've been busy lately. With Tracey and whatnot."

He stopped halfway to the stove to check out the roast cooling on the stovetop. "I'm not too busy to check in on you."

"I know. I just..."

"What is it, Mom?" He leaned against the counter and focused on her.

"Are you and Tracey getting serious? Or it is just..." she waved a hand "...fun?" She whispered the last word.

Brian would have chuckled at the way she said it if he weren't slightly insulted. They hadn't talked about his situation with Tracey, but his mom was aware that she was the person he was seeing. His mom had asked him to leave Tracey alone. He knew she didn't think he was a bad person, but after hearing Tracey's dad say she needed to stay away from him, it hurt to remember his mom had also thought he wasn't the best person for her.

"She's the only person I'm seeing. As for how serious we get, we'll see how things go."

Her brows drew together. "Oh."

"Oh, what?"

She shrugged then sighed. "Well, you know, Renee called me."

Brian's spine stiffened, and he shook his head. "Why is she calling you? Mom, we're divorced. You don't owe her anything." Renee hadn't bothered him in weeks, and he'd hoped she'd moved on. He should have known she would go another route. Hadn't he just told Tracey that manipulative people found a way to get what they wanted?

Her eyes narrowed on him, and she nailed him with the look she used to give him when she suspected him of getting into trouble as a kid. "Are you sure her baby isn't yours?"

Brian sputtered. He couldn't believe she would ask him that. "Yes, I'm sure. Renee and I are done."

"Divorced, but I know how you would sometimes still see her. And, well, she sent me a picture, and that baby looks a lot like you."

Brian felt light-headed. He pressed a hand to his temple and let out an incredulous laugh. "What?"

"She sent me a picture, and he looks like you. Brian, I need to know if that's my grandchild or not. Is that your baby?"

Brian placed a hand over his heart. "I swear to you her kid isn't mine."

"It's okay if it is. I know how you felt about her. You two don't have to be together to raise the kid."

"I know all that, but I'm telling you the truth. The kid isn't mine." He'd done the math several times since finding out Renee had a kid. The timing didn't add up. She'd gotten married the day after they'd slept together, but she'd delivered twelve months after their night together. Was the timing close? Yes, but not enough for the baby to be his.

"Brian—" The doorbell rang. His mom jumped and pressed a hand to her heart.

Brian frowned. "You expecting someone?"

"I..."

A sinking feeling came to his stomach. His mom's anxiousness, the questions about Renee's kid, and Renee calling her instead of him. Brian hurried out of the kitchen and to the front door. He prayed with each step that the fear in his heart was wrong. He opened the door, and his entire world collapsed.

Renee stood on the other end. She looked the same. Tall and curvy, golden-brown skin, huge brown eyes. She usually dressed to show off her figure, and the pink jumpsuit she wore had a low-cut V-neck and the pants stretched across her baby bump. She held a young kid on her hip. A young boy with dark brown skin and big brown eyes. He looked from the kid to her.

She tried to give him a smile, but he could see from the wariness in her eyes that she hadn't expected him to open the door. "Brian, hey!"

"What are you doing here, Renee?" He couldn't pretend to be courteous. Not when she was on his mom's doorstep, pregnant and holding a kid her husband thought was his. He looked back at the baby, blinked, then back at her.

"He kicked me out. He knows that this isn't his son."

"Whose son is it?"

"Brian..."

"Whose. Son. Is. It?" He bit out the words.

A tear ran down Renee's face before she answered. "I don't know."

26

It was a rare Wednesday night when there was no one staying in the inn. The day before, she'd texted Brian to tell him something came up, but honestly, she'd needed more time to think about what he'd said. He'd texted back that was cool and they would talk soon. She was glad he wasn't pressing her for an answer, which made her want to accept his offer even more.

Her mom called her earlier in the day to say she was back with Raymond and staying at his place. Something Tracey accepted, before reminding her mom that she would always have a room at the inn. So she took advantage of having the house to herself for a night by changing into her favorite lounge suit and watching television in the downstairs sitting room. The inn would be full of people checking in the next afternoon, but for a few hours she could relax and enjoy the silence. She'd eventually move out, but the place felt like home, so she wasn't in a hurry.

The doorbell rang just as she'd put down the bowl of grapes

and glass of wine she'd planned to enjoy while watching television. Was it Brian? He hadn't called her since asking her to upgrade their friends-with-benefits relationship. She hadn't expected him to come by so soon. Not after promising to give her some time to consider. Which she had. All she'd done was think about what he'd said and if she wanted to jump into another relationship.

She picked up her cell phone and opened the app to the doorbell camera. She scoffed when the camera feed came up. Bernard stood on the front doorstep. Rolling her eyes, she dropped her phone, plopped down on the couch and picked up her bowl of grapes. She had no reason to answer the door.

She grabbed the remote and then turned the television to her favorite show. Bernard rang the doorbell again then knocked. A few seconds later his muffled voice came through the door.

"I know you're in there, Tracey. Your car is here." He knocked again. "Come on. I need to talk to you, and I'm not leaving until you answer." He rang the bell and knocked again.

Tracey grunted before putting the bowl to the side. The last thing she needed was for Bernard to make a scene outside her place of business.

She went to the door, unlocked it and jerked it open. "What do you want?"

He had the nerve to look like she'd hurt his feelings. "Why you gotta be like that?"

"Because you're at my place unannounced."

"This used to be our place, too."

She crossed her arms and glared. "This was never ours. What do you want?"

He sighed. "You're not going to let me in?"

"Why do you need to come in?"

He pointed over his shoulder. "You want anyone who passes by to watch us talking?"

"Bernard!"

"Fine. Your dad came by my place. He told me what he said to you. We need to talk."

Tracey closed her eyes and took a long breath. "My dad is delusional."

"No, he's not. He was right."

Her eyes popped open. "About what?"

"Everything."

She moved out on the porch and closed the door behind her. "What are you talking about? I know you don't want to come back. You're the one who told me you were bored in our relationship."

He rubbed the bridge of his nose. "I know I said that."

"Yeah. You said that. The day our divorce was finalized. You also stepped out on our marriage several times before that, so don't come now saying that you're feeling different, because I know that's some bull."

"It's not some bull, Tracey."

"Then, what is it, Bernard? Because we both know we aren't getting back together. Not now, not ever."

"I'm not ready for all this," he said in a thin voice. "The baby. Being a dad. I told you I wasn't ready."

He had. Several times. That's why they'd never had kids. He always had an excuse about why the time wasn't right. Tracey had wanted kids, but she'd never wanted to force kids with someone who didn't want them. Her marriage was already imperfect; she couldn't have brought a kid into that.

"Well, you should have thought of that before you got her pregnant."

Bernard pulled off his glasses and pinched the bridge of his nose. "I didn't try to get her pregnant. She told me she was on birth control, and I believed her. Tracey, you know that I wouldn't have gotten her pregnant on purpose. I think she tricked me."

Tracey crossed her arms over her chest. "Again, not my problem. You did this. I moved on."

"But you weren't supposed to move on."

"Excuse me?"

"We always made it work, Tracey. When I messed up before, we made it work."

She shook her head. "No, Bernard, I was foolish enough to think that you still loved me, but you never really loved me if you could keep on hurting me the way you did."

He slid his glasses back on and stepped closer. "I did love you, Tracey. Hell, I still love you."

His eyes were big and pleading along with his voice. The same old tired routine he'd given her when they were married. It didn't work anymore. She held up a hand in his face. "Don't give me that."

He pushed her hand aside. "But I know that I messed up. Multiple times."

"Yes, you did. Do you know how much I wanted to believe you every time you cheated on me? How much I wanted to believe that you wouldn't do that to me again? You knew how I felt about you, Bernard. You knew how insecure I was with our relationship, and you took advantage of that."

"I wasn't trying to take advantage of you."

She pointed at him. "Don't play with me now. Not when we're finally over and you have no reason to lie to me anymore. You played on my insecurities, and I let you."

Instead of arguing he got defensive. "But you did change, Tracey. I meant everything I said when we first got together. You were exciting."

"No, I was the girl your mom didn't like, and you were trying to step out and do something different. I came to my senses, and no matter what you or my dad think, I'm not going back."

"I get it. You're not coming back. But that doesn't mean you have to do worse."

She rolled her eyes. Now they were getting to the real point of all this. He didn't want her, but he didn't want her with Brian even more. The guy he never liked and never wanted her to work with. "Don't even go there. I'm doing much better now."

"But you're with Brian?" he said as if that was the most ludicrous thing he'd ever heard.

"What I'm doing with Brian is none of your business."

"Fair enough, but, Tracey, no matter what you think, I still care about you. I don't want to see you end up hurt."

She raised a brow. "I think I've learned how to handle being hurt, Bernard."

He glanced away and rubbed the back of his head. "Look, you know my brother delivers for the postal service, right?"

"And?"

"And he told me that Brian has some pregnant woman staying at his mom's house and she's got a kid there, too. A kid that looks a lot like him."

Tracey's stomach dropped. "Your brother doesn't know what he's talking about."

"My mom is friends with his mom. She won't say anything, but there is someone there. So I'm just trying to give you a heads-up."

"Or you're trying to be messy and cause problems." Brian hadn't called her, but he wouldn't have moved on that quickly. He wasn't like that. Was that the reason he'd been okay with her canceling on Tuesday? Because he had another situation going on? She wasn't going to let Bernard make her paranoid.

"I know you won't take me back."

"No. I won't."

"But if you're going to move on from me, then at least do better than me. Brian is about to put you in the same situation I did."

Tracey didn't hear from Brian on Thursday or Friday. When he didn't call her before the wedding Saturday but instead let Natalie handle things, her anxiety went up a notch. Luckily, the wedding went smoothly. Having Debra work at the inn was proving to be more and more of a blessing every day. Tracey could finally split the duties on the day of the wedding and make sure the event went well without feeling as if she were neglecting the other guests.

She'd hoped to get a chance to talk with Brian. Not just about what he'd said to her, but about what Bernard had accused him of, but he hadn't handled the delivery of the shrubs either. Instead, his delivery guy, Pat, had shown up with the shrubs she'd ordered for the wedding saying Brian had "family stuff" he needed to handle. Pat hadn't quite met Tracey's eyes when he'd said that. Tracey did not believe in borrowing trouble, but she was starting to worry there might be a tiny bit of truth behind what Bernard had thrown at her feet.

On Sunday morning, she got up, dressed and headed downstairs to make sure everything was ready for the brunch for the wedding guests. She was surprised to find Shirley in the kitchen. She usually didn't come in on a Sunday after a wedding. She let her kitchen crew handle breakfast so she could attend church and then later rest.

"Why are you in here?"

Shirley shrugged as if it were no big deal. "My backup wasn't feeling good yesterday, and I don't need her in here coughing all over my brunch. So I came in."

"Thanks for covering."

Shirley raised a brow. "What are you doing in here? You usually let others handle Sunday, too."

"I wanted to come check on things."

Shirley glanced around the kitchen. They were alone for the moment, and she waved Tracey closer. "Have you talked to Brian?"

Tracey's heart sank. Shirley's voice was filled with *Because you need to.* "I haven't. Why?"

Shirley sighed and shook her head. She went back to whisking eggs in a large ceramic bowl. "I was worried when he wasn't here yesterday."

"Pat said he had family stuff."

Shirley gave Tracey a shrewd look. "That's what I heard, but you can never be sure with gossip in this town."

As much as Tracey didn't want to ask, she needed to know. "What have you heard?"

Shirley held up a hand. "I don't like to spread secondhand information."

Tracey twisted her lip, irritated. "Then, don't bring it up at all." She turned to leave the kitchen.

"Where are you going?"

"To get firsthand information," Tracey called over her shoulder.

She grabbed her purse and keys out of her office and got in the car. She wasn't going to listen to rumors or get information from a third party. She'd lived with half-truths and rumors for years. If Brian did have some woman and kid at his house, then she needed to know sooner rather than later. She also needed to look him in the eye when she spoke to him and see his reaction. She trusted Brian but was wary enough to want to see if he would lie to her.

She was surprised to see him sitting on his front porch when she pulled up to his house. He had his phone in his hand and rubbed the back of his head with the other. Her cell phone rang just as she reached his house. He looked up from his phone, surprised to see her. She glanced at the Bluetooth in her car and saw his name. He'd been calling her.

He stood and waited while she parked behind his car and then walked toward him on the porch.

"I was just calling you," he said. His eyes traced over her as if he hadn't seen her in years and had to drink in every bit of her.

Tracey felt the same way. He looked good in the gray T-shirt that draped his shoulders and joggers that hugged his thighs just enough to make her want to wrap her arms around him. She'd missed him, and it had only been a few days. Guess she had her answer about wanting him to be the man in her life.

"I saw. Figured I didn't need to answer since I was here." She walked up the steps and faced him.

"What made you come by?" He didn't sound upset or irritated that she'd popped in on him. She tried to believe that was a good sign. If he was hiding a woman and kid from her he wouldn't be okay with her dropping in unannounced.

"I've got my answer. To the question you asked me the other day."

His body stilled. "What's your answer?"

"It depends on if you have some pregnant woman in there with a kid or not," Tracey said quickly, her heart racing as she silently prayed that everyone was wrong. That he'd frown and give her a *Have you lost your mind?* look before asking where she had come up with something so foolish.

Brian's shoulders slumped. "She's not here. She's at my mom's house. And it's not *some woman* but my ex-wife, Renee." His tone was tired, frustrated, almost defeated.

Tracey wanted to run. To walk right off that porch and forget everything she'd had with Brian. That's what common sense said she needed to do. To forget his drama and focus on her life. They'd made no promises, and she remembered how he said he'd always gone back to his ex. She should walk away, but the defeat in his voice reminded her that she was his friend. He'd opened up to her about his tumultuous relationship with Renee, and if she was there it wasn't because Brian had invited her.

"Why is she here?"

Relief filled his eyes. Maybe he'd seen her initial thought of running and thought she would do just that. He took her hand and pulled her to the chairs on his porch. Tracey let him lead her and sat next to him on the two-seater.

"Her husband kicked her out. Their kid isn't his, and he doesn't believe the one she's pregnant with is his either."

"Whose is it?" She held her breath.

He shook his head. "It's not mine."

She let out a breath. "You sure?"

"Positive. She even admitted that. But the problem is she doesn't know whose it is."

"What? How?"

"Her husband thought it was mine, but our slipup was over a year ago. When friends told me she was pregnant, I knew it was close, but not close enough to be mine. When she showed up with this, I even insisted that we have a DNA test." He met her eyes and said with assurance, "Tracey, believe me, this is not my kid."

"Then, how doesn't she know whose kid it is?"

"Because she went to a party, met up with a guy, hooked up, and she doesn't have his name or number."

"What about the people at the party? Can't they help her find him?"

He shook his head. "That would be easy, but the week after she hooked up with someone else."

"What?" Tracey put a hand to her chest. "Look, I don't judge people for who they sleep with, but why not use protection?"

"She says she did, but it slipped up somewhere. Either way, it was during a break with her husband. Just like the breaks me and her used to have. This was what she did." He glanced at her then looked away. "What we did."

She placed her hand on his knee. "Brian, I don't care what you and Renee used to do. I just want to know why she's here now."

"She says she has nowhere else to go. And my mom," Brian said closing his eyes, sighed and shook his head, "says Renee is still family. She wants us to help her until she figures out what to do next."

"Your mom is so damn nice."

"Tell me about it," Brian said sounding exhausted. "She never really liked Renee, but she also isn't the type to be rude or mean. Renee called her crying when I stopped answering her calls. She showed up the other day, and I've been trying to figure this out. Renee is trying to track down the guy from the party. The other guy isn't American and was just in town for a weekend." He pinched the bridge of his nose. "We may never find him."

"Then what will she do?"

He shrugged. "I don't know. Now she's talking about staying in Peachtree Cove where she has a support system. Tracey, I know this is a lot. Much more than you want to deal with. I had no idea this would happen when I—"

She nodded. "When you asked me about us going from friends with benefits to, I don't know, a monogamous relationship."

"I understand if you don't want to deal with this. Hell, I don't want to deal with it."

She didn't want to deal with it. She didn't want to see Renee, the woman who'd kept Brian on a string for years. The woman who'd broken his heart and sent him back to Peachtree Cove no longer believing in love or trusting relationships. She didn't want to deal with Renee's child any more than she wanted to deal with Bernard's, and she didn't have any responsibility toward either one.

She met his eyes, saw the sadness, frustration and tiny spark of hope in their depths. Something squeezed her heart. She didn't want to give up Brian. When she saw him she'd had her answer: she wanted to be with him. Not to say that they'd get married or anything, but she didn't want to be out there trying to find something with someone else that she already had with him. Just not under these circumstances.

"I think we should keep the friends and maybe drop the benefits while you figure this out," she said. "I thought I was ready, maybe I am ready, but I'm not ready for all of this."

"I'm going to fix this."

She nodded. "I know you will, and I hope that for you, Renee and that kid that you do get it all figured out. But I can't do this right now. I'll be honest, I'm falling hard for you, Brian. Have fallen hard, and that makes me want to help you with this, but I can't. I promised myself to focus on me. I'm expanding the inn and starting my life again."

Brian swallowed hard. She saw the argument in his eyes and braced herself for him to make her feel bad or try to play on her heartstrings and beg her to help him. Instead, he nodded slowly.

"That's fair. But, Tracey, when I fix this, I'm coming back to you, and I want to hear the real answer you came to give me today."

27

Brian was sitting in his living room, the television watching him as he nursed a rum and Coke, when his doorbell rang. He sat up straight. At first hopeful that the person at the door might be Tracey. The hope died almost immediately. In the week since she'd told him they couldn't be together until things were figured out, she hadn't popped in to see him. If it didn't have something to do with work or a wedding, then she didn't interact with him.

He understood why she'd stepped back. He would have done the same thing in her shoes. But damn if knowing this was the right thing to do still didn't stop him from missing her.

He stood and went to the door. Dread slowed his steps. Tracey wouldn't be here, but that didn't mean that Renee wasn't on the other side. She was acting even more needy than usual. He understood she was lost, confused and looking for a place to turn, but he didn't want her messed-up situation to interfere with his life anymore. His mom had thankfully agreed that Renee staying at her place was better than her moving in with him. Renee would only wreak more havoc if she was under his roof.

He opened the door, and his eyes widened. Cyril and Quinton stood on his porch.

"What are y'all doing here?" Brian asked.

"Hey, man, we knew you weren't going to come out, so we decided to come check on you," Cyril said.

Brian stepped back and let them in. "I don't feel like dealing with the gossips right now."

"I get it," Cyril said. "I try not to let any foolishness go down in my bar, but that doesn't mean I can stop people from asking you questions."

Quinton nodded his head. "And they will ask. I thought I had the biggest *Surprise, you're the daddy!* drama this town had ever seen."

Brian snorted and led his friends into his living area. "Except I'm not the dad." Brian picked up his drink and took a sip. "You want something to drink?"

"You sure you're not the dad?" Quinton asked.

Brian shook his head. He was sick of answering that question, but he understood why people kept asking. "No. I'm not. She doesn't know who the dad is. And I haven't touched her since that night over a year ago, so the one she's pregnant with also isn't mine."

"Damn," Quinton said and ran a hand over his face. "I'm gonna need that drink."

Cyril nodded. "Same."

Brian filled them in on Renee's problems while he mixed up a rum and Coke for each of them. By the time he finished the story, they'd all drained their glasses and were ready for the next round.

"How long is she going to stay?" Cyril asked.

"She's talking about moving here. I think she wants me to help her."

"And do you want to help her?" Quinton asked. "You said before that she was the one who always got under your skin."

"Yeah, well, now she's under my skin but not in a good way. I don't blame the kid. He didn't ask to be born into this, but I can't let that push me back with Renee. And then there's Tracey."

"You and Tracey still hooking up?" Cyril asked.

"She said she didn't want to keep seeing me with all of this going on. I can't blame her."

"So that's why Craig was sniffing around her the other day," Quinton said.

Brian's back straightened. "What do you mean?"

"She was in Books and Vibes meeting with her brother and Mikayla. He saw her and went over and asked her out."

"What did she say?"

Quinton shrugged. "I didn't get to stick around and hear the answer. I was in there with Shania, and she was ready to go. Plus, I know you two weren't real serious, so I didn't think it was any of my business."

"It was getting serious. But then Renee came." Brian's hands clenched into fists.

Cyril held up a hand. "Hold up. When did you two get serious? I thought you weren't doing serious relationships anymore."

"Hell, I thought so, too. I didn't expect this to happen."

"How serious we talking?" Cyril asked.

"I didn't ask her to marry me or anything. I just told her I wanted to be the man in her life."

"You may want to, but so does Craig."

Brian stood up. "Nah. That ain't happening." He'd go to Tracey now and beg her to wait for him.

Quinton grabbed his elbow and pulled. "Sit down. No need

to go running over there tonight and demanding anything. Not until you get this situation worked out."

Brian wanted to pull away. But Quinton was right. Demanding anything of Tracey was the best way to push her away. He let out a frustrated sigh and sat. He needed this situation with Renee to be over.

"I don't have time to get this worked out. Renee doesn't know who the dad is, and I don't think she's trying to figure it out."

Quinton sipped his drink then shrugged. "She doesn't have to know as long as you know he's not yours. She's a grown woman with the ability to make grown-up decisions. Let her figure this out."

"I need her out of my mom's house." Maybe getting her out of his mom's place would be enough to get Tracey back.

"Then, help her find a place of her own," Cyril said. "You've been nice enough to her already. You don't owe her anything."

The next day Brian went to his mom's house after work. She had Bible study, but he'd guessed Renee hadn't gone with her. He'd guessed right. Renee was home alone, draped in her loungewear, eating her mom's favorite key lime pie from the bakery while her kid's toys were scattered over the floor. The baby slept in the playpen in the corner of the living room.

Brian pointed to the mess. "You're going to clean this up?"

Renee looked around as if she were just noticing the toys and clothes all over the floor. "Yes, of course."

"You're trashing my mom's place." It had only been a week, but the house looked like Renee had been there a month. His mom liked a clean house. She wouldn't say anything to guests who were messy to avoid conflict. She must be biting through her tongue with Renee there.

"No, the baby was playing earlier that's all," Renee said. "Your mom did tell me to make myself comfortable."

Brian picked up some of the clothes and threw them in the basket next to the couch where he assumed they'd come from in the first place. "That doesn't mean that you make a mess. Look, Renee, you've got to figure out your next steps."

"What's that supposed to mean?" Her voice wobbled.

"You can't live here forever. You're going to have to go somewhere else."

Her eyes lit up, and she moved closer to him. "Do you want me to move in with you?"

He stepped back before she could touch him. "No. That's not what I mean."

She pouted. "Why not, Brian? We're so good together."

"No, we weren't, and we're not. My mom agreed to help you because we were married for so long, but that doesn't mean you can stay here forever. What's your plan?"

She shrugged. "I don't know."

"Have you tracked down the guys?" Was she even trying?

She shook her head. "Do you know how hard it's going to be, and embarrassing? To say that I don't know who my kid's father is. Why can't I just...say he's yours?"

"Because he's not mine, Renee," he said frustrated. He took a breath and lowered his voice before continuing. "This isn't your chance to try and get me to play daddy. You either work this out with your husband or find the real father. I'm not playing either role."

"You just want to kick me out?"

"I didn't ask you to come here. You showed up. If you want to stay in Peachtree Cove, cool, but it won't be with my mom or with me. You've got two weeks to find a new place."

She jerked back and scowled. "Two weeks?"

"That's it. Find a place, and stop taking advantage of my mom."

28

Tracey rounded the corner in the grocery store on a mission to get eggs. For reasons yet unknown to her, no eggs had been included in the delivery to the inn that morning. They needed at least four dozen for Shirley to make the casserole needed for the morning-after brunch for the wedding happening at the inn that night. She would arm-wrestle anyone in the dairy section who dared to try and stop her from getting eggs.

Though she hoped she wouldn't have to. She was just determined not to have anything go wrong for this wedding. She needed everything to be perfect. She also wasn't going to think about how she spent a lot more of her time focusing on the minutiae at the inn instead of thinking about the hole left in her life after walking away from Brian.

She didn't regret her decision. She knew without a shadow of a doubt that she didn't want anything to do with the drama he was dealing with, but that didn't stop her from missing him.

She'd never thought she would ever be back in this place. Falling hard for a guy again. But there she was, intent on having a cage match over eggs to stop herself from calling him.

A woman was in Tracey's way when she reached the egg display. She slowly took out a carton, opened it, and checked the contents before putting it back and picking up another carton. Tracey stepped forward to stand next to the woman when recognition hit.

"Mrs. Nelson?"

Brian's mom turned away from her egg inspection and focused on Tracey. She smiled broadly. "Tracey! How are you doing?"

"I'm good. Gotta get some eggs for brunch at the inn tomorrow."

Mrs. Nelson cringed and pointed to the eggs. "Well, you'll have a hard time finding some good ones. Every carton I've checked has cracked eggs in it."

Tracey frowned. "Really?"

"Yeah, I've been searching for some good ones. Gotta make a quiche."

"Sounds good."

They stood there for a few awkward seconds. Tracey hadn't had a lot of interaction with Brian's mom. Mrs. Nelson was the complete opposite of Tracey's mom. Heavily involved in the church, nice to everyone she met and apparently still faithful to her husband who'd died years ago. Knowing the Peachtree Cove rumor mill, she doubted Mrs. Nelson was unaware of Tracey and Brian seeing each other. She wasn't sure if the woman was happy or upset about that.

"So how have you been?" Mrs. Nelson asked finally.

"I've been good."

She nodded. "Good, good. Have you talked to Brian any?"

Tracey shook her head. "No, I haven't talked to him recently."

Her lips pressed together in a sad smile, and she nodded. "You know, I think he misses you."

Tracey blinked. "Ma'am?"

"He misses you. He was happy when you two were spending time together. I hadn't seen him that happy in a while. Not even when he was married."

"Oh… I didn't know…" Tracey didn't know what to say. She missed Brian, too, but never would have expected his mom to bring up how much he missed her.

Mrs. Nelson nodded. "He talked about you. I noticed he would bring up your name a lot. At first I was worried. You've been through a lot, and I know Brian can be… Well, he wasn't big on commitment. But when he was with you, he seemed happy. I started to hope that you two would work things out." She put a carton of eggs in her buggy. "I don't try to get into Brian's business, but I'll admit I've had an influence on him. I like to help people when I can, and when I help people he feels the need to help them, too. But even when he's helping, he still knows his own mind. And, Tracey, Brian's mind is on you."

Tracey was once again struck speechless. The conversation had gone completely differently from how she might have imagined. A part of her expected Mrs. Nelson to want Brian to stay far away from her. She'd even wondered if that was the reason why she'd let his ex-wife and her kid move in with her—because she'd rather see her with Brian than Tracey.

"He's on my mind, too," Tracey admitted. "But he's got a lot going on."

"He does. But we're getting that worked out. I can't tell you what to do. I won't ask you to wait for him to get this mess sorted out. But I do want you to know that he's thinking about you. That's all."

After staying away from Brian, refusing to call or talk to him about anything other than work, this little bit of information eased her tattered nerves. He wasn't spending time falling back in love with Renee. He really was trying to find a way to fix the situation.

"Thank you for that," Tracey said.

Mrs. Nelson patted Tracey's arm. "Good. Now, go on and check the eggs. Maybe you'll find some that aren't cracked that can work for you."

"I hope so."

Tracey put the bag of eggs on the counter when her cell phone rang. She saw her mom's number on the screen. "Mom, what's up?"

"It's your dad."

Rolling her eyes, Tracey took the eggs out of the bag. "Mom, I don't want to get in whatever you and Dad have going on."

"He's in the hospital."

Tracey dropped the carton of eggs on the floor. "He's what?"

"I'm at the emergency room now. I just called your brother, and now I'm calling you."

Tracey hadn't talked to her dad since he'd shown his ass at her place. She was still angry with him, but she didn't want him to get hurt. "Is he okay?"

"I don't know. He was screaming and bent over on the floor like he was about to die. I just called 9-1-1." Her mom's voice wobbled. "Tracey, can you get down here?"

"Yes, I'm on my way."

29

Everything at the hospital was chaos by the time Tracey arrived. Peachtree Cove's hospital was more a glorified emergency room than a full hospital. Because her dad had been in so much pain they'd taken him to the hospital in Augusta instead of the Peachtree Cove ER. When she got there her mom was berating a poor nurse about the ice machine not working. Her boyfriend, Raymond, stood to the side looking annoyed that he had to deal with this. Tracey was surprised to find him there.

Tracey hurried over to calm her mom and pull her away from the nurse, and got her settled in the waiting room with a cold soda. "Mom, what's going on? Start from the beginning and tell me what's happening with Dad."

Her mom took a deep breath before taking a sip of her soda. "Your dad called me today. He was on his usual nonsense. Begging me to come back and asking if we could talk. I went over there to tell him once and for all he needed to stop calling me.

But when I got there he was laid out on the floor, yelling and saying he was in pain. At first I thought he was fooling me, but he didn't look good."

"Had he been drinking?"

"It wasn't drinking this time. He seemed...different. So I called an ambulance. I thought he was..." She ran a hand over her face. "I thought he was dying, Tracey."

"How long before the ambulance came?" She could tell her mom was about to spiral again so she asked a question to keep her focused on telling the story instead.

"It felt like forever. The nice girl from 9-1-1 told me what to do until the ambulance came. They transferred him here and ran a bunch of tests. That's when they said that your dad hasn't been taking his medicine."

Tracey frowned. "What medicine?"

"He was on blood thinners."

Tracey gasped. "For what? And since when?"

Her mom shook her head. "I don't know. There's a blood clot or something in his legs or lungs or somewhere. So they're checking to make sure that isn't it. I thought he was about to die, Tracey."

Tracey wrapped her arm around her mom's shoulder. "He's not gone, Mom. He's going to be okay."

"But what if he's not?"

"He will be," she said firmly. "We can't think any other way."

Her brother arrived then. Her mom gave him the same update. She became calmer with him around. Not surprising. Devante was always the calming presence in the family. The one person who didn't let the drama and the hyper personalities in the household get to him. He wasn't alone. Joanne was also with him, and she helped Tracey keep their mom calm.

Not long after Devante got there, a doctor came out and asked for her mom. The three of them followed her over to get the update.

"He's going to be okay. It looks like he's trying to pass a kidney stone."

Her mom scowled. "A kidney stone?"

The doctor nodded. "Yes, and looking at the ultrasound, it's a big one. I wouldn't recommend he pass this at home. I'm going to suggest we remove it surgically."

"Surgery?" Loretta placed a hand to her throat. "When can he come home?"

"If he does well, then he'll be able to come home within twenty-four to forty-eight hours. He's being prepped for surgery now. I know it sounds like a lot, but there's no need to worry. It's a routine surgery that won't have him down for long."

Devante held out a hand. "Thank you, Doctor."

The doctor shook his hand. "You're welcome. We'll keep you informed as things proceed."

The doctor left, and they all breathed a sigh of relief. "I'll stay with him tonight," Loretta said.

Tracey shook her head. "Mom, you don't have to stay the night."

"I need to. There's no one else who can be here with him."

Raymond stepped forward. "You've done what you needed to do. You don't have to stay here with him."

Loretta placed her hands on her hips. "He doesn't have anyone to be with him."

Raymond scowled. "He's got two kids here. All this over a damn kidney stone. He'll be okay. You need to come home with me."

"You don't tell me what I need to do."

"I brought you here because you said he was dying. Now you know he's not and he's going to be okay. Your job is done."

Devante held up a hand. "I can stay with him."

Joanne placed a hand on his arm. "You have that meeting tomorrow with the mayor."

"See?" Loretta said. "I need to stay with him."

Tracey noticed the fight on Raymond's face. She was not about to let her family embarrass her up in that hospital. "I'll stay. Debra can handle the inn for me in the morning. Mom, you go and deal with...your stuff. Devante, you get to your meeting, and I'll deal with Dad."

"See? A plan has worked out," Raymond said before anyone else could chip in. He put his hand on her mom's elbow. "We need to go."

Loretta jerked her arm out of his grasp. "I'll at least wait until he's out of surgery."

Devante nodded. "We'll all stay."

Raymond didn't argue. They all sat and waited. Eventually their dad came out of surgery, and the doctor returned to tell them he was doing well, but they were going to watch him since he wasn't taking his other medicines. Once that was settled, Raymond hurried to take his wife home. Devante and Joanne left shortly after that. Tracey was alone while she waited for her dad to be put in his own room.

By the time he was finally settled and she was allowed to see him, she was exhausted. He looked tired and frail lying in the bed. She thought about their last conversation. The argument about her need to go back to Bernard. She still couldn't forgive him for wanting her to stay in a bad relationship. She'd always wanted her dad to want better for her. But now that he was sick, she couldn't muster up the same anger she'd felt before. He infuriated her, but despite everything she still loved him.

Tracey's dad slept through the night even with the nurses coming in and out to check his vitals; she barely got any sleep. She had a hard enough time getting comfortable in strange places. Being in a hospital room in a chair that folded out into a small bed didn't make that problem go away. When she finally dozed off after the nurse came in around six in the morning, the sound of her dad's voice woke her.

She sat up and glanced at him in the bed. His eyes were open, and he looked at her with both surprise and, she'd swear, disappointment.

"Dad, you're awake. Let me call the nurse." Tracey stood and crossed to his bed.

"I don't need the nurse. She was just in here."

Tracey frowned. "Did I miss her coming through?" She hadn't thought she'd slept for that long.

"You did. That's why I was calling your name. It took three times to wake you up."

"What's wrong?"

"You been here all night?"

She nodded. "I have. What did the nurse say? How are you feeling?"

"Your mom didn't stay here with me?"

Tracey frowned. That explained the disappointment. "No. She brought you to the hospital, but she didn't stay."

"Why not?"

Tracey didn't want to get into all of that, but there was no need to drag out the truth. She decided to give part of the story.

"She left with Raymond and asked me to stay here with you."

"He didn't let her stay, did he?"

"Does it matter? You and Mom aren't important right now. You getting better and going home is what's important."

He slapped his hand on his thigh. "I knew he wouldn't let her stay. He's just jealous, and your mom is playing games again."

"Mom isn't playing games. She's moved on, and you need to do the same. Focus on your health. That's what you need to do. Why didn't you come to the hospital if you were having pains and feeling bad?"

"What do you mean she's moved on? You're making excuses, but that figures. You're busy acting like her instead of going back to Bernard like you should."

"I'm not doing this with you, Dad. Not when you're healthy, and for sure not when you're sick."

"You always were hardheaded. You know that man loves you. Why are you leaving him with that girl? And you know Brian's ex-wife is back in town. He got her pregnant when she was married to someone else, and now she's with him where she belongs."

Tracey's head started to hurt. She had no idea how a conversation about his health and her mom swiveled back to her, but she wasn't in the mood for this. "I'm going to get some coffee." She turned toward the door.

"Don't run away from me."

"When I get back maybe you'll be ready to move to a better topic." She went to the door.

"Call Bernard and tell him to come check on me."

Tracey didn't turn around. She pulled her cell phone from her back pocket and went down the hall. She was going to call her brother and find out when he could take over. She wasn't going to stay there all day and listen to her dad talk nonsense.

She pulled out her phone and pulled up her brother's number when she heard someone call her name. She looked up, startled at the sound of Brian's voice. He stood at the end of the hall holding a bag in one hand and a cup of coffee in the other.

"What are you doing here?" she asked.

"I heard about your dad, so I came to check on you." Brian stepped forward and held out the bag. "I know staying in the hospital can be draining so I brought you some things to help the time go by."

Tracey took the bag and opened it. Inside were crackers, a coloring book, colored pencils, a crossword puzzle, chocolates and candy, along with a few toiletries like tissues. Her eyes burned as a swell of emotion filled her chest, and she looked back up at Brian. "You didn't have to do this."

"I know I didn't have to do this," he said. "But I couldn't help thinking and worrying about you being here by yourself."

Tracey couldn't stop herself. Before she could even think she stepped forward and wrapped her arms around his neck. His strong arms wrapped around her waist, and he pulled her tight against his body. She buried her face in the crook of his neck and breathed in the soothing scent of him. All the emotions from the day before hitting her like a Mack truck. The anxiety from finding out her father was in the hospital, the frustration of all the chaos when she'd arrived, the anger at her dad for comparing her to her mom and asking her to, once again, go back to Bernard... The tears in her eyes spilled over, and she silently cried.

Brian leaned back and placed a hand on her chin. "Why are you crying?"

"I have absolutely no idea why I'm crying," she said. "Everything is just so much, and you're still being nice to me after everything that happened."

"Tracey, we agreed to stop with the *benefits* part of the friends with benefits, but that won't stop me from being your friend. I care about you. You may not want me to be your man while I have all this stuff going on in my life, but it's not gonna stop the way I feel about you."

"I don't know what to say."

"You don't have to say anything. Just let me be your friend. Let me take care of you. Let me still be a part of your life, Tracey."

He released her and held up the cup of coffee. "I got your favorite, hazelnut. Drink this and take a break. I'll go sit with your dad."

Tracey shook her head. "No, my dad is being ridiculous this morning. He's still saying the same things he said when he was at my house the other day. There's no telling what he'll say to you."

"I don't care what he'll say to me. I'm here to support *you*, and if that means I have to put up with your dad while I do that, so be it."

Tracey's heart squeezed. How had she walked away from him before? How would she be able to walk away from him again? He still had to figure out his situation with Renee. But for now she wanted to lean into the support he was offering her today. No one had offered to take care of her in such a long time. She took the coffee and nodded. For now, she was going to go ahead and let Brian be the person that she leaned on.

30

Brian tried to be good at minding his business and not get-
ting involved in things that didn't concern him. Yet he was
growing tired of biting his tongue while he watched Tracey's
dad talk junk and criticize everything she did while getting him
checked out of the hospital and taken back home. He doubted
the man could muster up a compliment if Tracey were able to
get all the angels in heaven to come down and serenade him.
The man was determined to find something wrong with everything she did.

He didn't ride in the car with them when they left the hospital. Instead he followed them back to her dad's apartment.
Every part of him rebelled at the idea of leaving Tracey alone
in the car with her dad. The man wouldn't hurt her physically,
but he had enough bad opinions to do some mental damage.
He had told Brian to not even bother to follow them and go

home, but Brian refused. He wasn't going to sit still and watch
her suffer in silence. He was still her friend.

Brian could hear her dad complaining as soon as they pulled
into the parking lot of his apartment and Tracey opened the car
door. Brian quickly moved to help her get him out of the car.

"Didn't I tell you to go home?" Carl said sounding frustrated.
"We don't need your help."

"You telling me you want Tracey to struggle getting you up
the stairs to your apartment?" Brian asked with a raised brow.

Carl glanced at Tracey, doubt hovering in his gaze when he
glared back at Brian. "She can handle me."

"Maybe she can, but she doesn't have to handle you alone
while I'm here." Brian looked to Tracey. "I've got him."

He saw the argument in her eyes, the instinctual need she
felt to say she could handle this on her own, but a second later
the tension left from around her lips and she nodded. "Thanks."

He wasn't sure what changed, but she'd been doing just that
since he'd shown up at the hospital. She would look like she
was going to say no but change her mind and say yes. He wasn't
going to read too much into the reasons. Whatever made Tracey
feel okay with letting him help her, he was good with that.

Brian took the man's arm and wrapped it around his shoulder. "Come on, Mr. Carl, let's get up these stairs."

"I don't need any help. I can manage on my own." He
tried to pull away but wobbled. Brian grabbed him tighter and
headed to the stairs.

"I don't know why you're here or why you both are acting
like I can't take care of myself," Carl grumbled but didn't fight
further to get out of Brian's grip.

Several minutes later, they had him settled on the couch in
his living room. Tracey went into the kitchen and opened the
fridge. "Dad, you don't have anything to eat in here."

"I can find food."

Tracey sighed and shook her head. "I'll go to the grocery

store and pick up some stuff. Devante said he'll be over when he's done with his project, and he'll need to eat, too."

"When's your mom coming over?" he asked.

"I don't know, Dad."

"Ain't she staying with you?"

"She went back to Raymond's house a while ago, so she's not staying with me anymore."

Her dad grunted. "You would be okay with that. You were better when you were with Bernard. Did you call him? He should be here with you." He gave Brian a pointed stare.

Tracey closed the door to the fridge. "I'm going to the store. Brian, you coming with me?"

He glanced at Tracey. She wanted him to come, he could see that written all over her face, but he wasn't going. He had a few things he needed to straighten out over here.

"Go ahead, I'll stay and look after your dad."

Her brows drew together. "You sure?"

He nodded. "Positive."

Tracey gave him another unsure look. He lifted and lowered his head, giving her a reassuring nod. This had to be handled and he was going to do it today.

"Well, I guess I'll go to the store, then," she said.

Her dad pointed to her. "Be sure you bring back some crushed ice."

Tracey rolled her eyes but nodded. She grabbed her purse, went to the door and walked out. After she was gone Brian turned back to her dad.

Carl raised his brow and glared at him. "So what do you have to say to me? I know that's the only reason why you stuck behind."

Brian crossed his arms and eyed the man. "Yeah, I do want to talk to you. I don't like the way you're talking to Tracey."

"You can't tell me how to talk to my daughter. Who do you think you are?"

"I'm her friend and someone who cares about her. That's who I am."

"You see, that's part of the problem," Carl said, glaring at Brian. "Bernard knew his place—he didn't say anything. He knew how to keep his mouth shut."

"That's because Bernard didn't give a damn about Tracey. Do you know why he's not here? Because he told Tracey that he was too busy to check in on you."

"She texted him or called him and asked him to come back?"

"No. Tracey doesn't talk to him unless she has to. But I was there when Bernard texted her to say he heard you were in the hospital and that he would've come by but he was too busy. Tracey didn't even respond to his text because that's just like him. Always leaving her hanging. Bernard never cared about or appreciated her. And as her father, I can't understand why you would even push her to go back to a man like that."

Carl looked away then grumbled, "Bernard loves her."

"If he loved her he wouldn't have cheated on her for so many years."

"Cheating doesn't mean they don't love you."

For the first time Brian actually felt sorry for Carl. He saw in the man's eyes that he wanted to believe those words. He'd stuck with Loretta after all those years that she cheated and embarrassed him around town. He was urging Tracey to do what he had done for years: sit back, wait and hope that the person you were with realized they should treasure you instead of trample all over you.

"Cheating may not mean that they don't love you, but it sure as hell means they don't respect you," Brian said. "Everyone makes mistakes, but the way Bernard disrespected Tracey on the regular to the point that he actually got her employee pregnant proves he might have loved her but he never respected or cared about her. I care about Tracey. I want what's best for her, and Bernard is not what's best for Tracey. If you keep pushing her and belittling her the way you're doing, you won't be what's best for Tracey either."

"Are you saying you gonna try to keep my daughter away from me?"

"I won't have to try to keep your daughter away from you. She'll stay away from you on her own."

Tracey's dad crossed his arms and glared at Brian. Brian just stared back. He wasn't going to back down from this. He meant what he said. Even though he and Tracey might not be together right now, he was still going to be her friend. He might be out of line, but he couldn't sit back and watch someone belittle her. Even if it was her father.

"Well, are you gonna turn on the TV, or you just gonna stand there and stare at me?" Carl finally muttered.

Brian nodded, accepting the peace offering. He might not ever be her dad's favorite person, but he'd earned a little bit of respect with him today. Carl could have whatever fight he needed to have with her mom and whatever messed-up relationship they had going on, but while Brian was in her life, he was going to respect the fact that Brian was there for Tracey.

"Yeah, I'll turn on the TV. Just tell me what you wanna watch."

"What did you do to my dad?" Tracey said later when she and Brian were finally in her office at the inn.

Brian gave her an innocent look that she did not believe for one second as he shrugged. "What do you mean? I didn't do anything to your dad."

Tracey placed her hands on her hips and raised a brow. "Don't even play that with me, sir. I left to go to the store and my dad was being a complete jerk. I come back and the two of you are watching *Law & Order* and acting as if you're best friends."

"First of all, *Law & Order* is a good show. Second, me and your dad will never be best friends."

Tracey chuckled: he was right on both of those points. "Seriously, tell me what you did. He was so much better when I got back. Was it one of those man-to-man talks?"

Brian walked closer to her. She expected him to reach out and pull her into his arms, but he didn't. He kept just enough distance between them to still be respectful of the fact that they were just friends right now.

"Yes, it was one of those man-to-man talks. I had to let him know that as your friend I wasn't gonna sit around while he talked to you any kind of way."

Tracey grinned and chuckled. "I can't believe you said that to him."

"Did I overstep my bounds?"

Tracey considered his words. She supposed a part of her could be mad at him for telling her dad that. But all she could think about was the fact that, besides her brother, no one had defended her whenever her dad criticized her. Bernard would sit in a corner and listen but never say a word. When she would complain about the way her dad would talk to her, he would just tell her to get over it. Sometimes she'd even catch him nodding or chuckling to himself whenever Carl went off on a rant about how uncaring his kids were. Brian had showed her again that he cared. He had his own stuff he was dealing with, yet there he was helping her all day.

"Is everything all good at the nursery? I know you were with me all day. I kept you from work. I'm sorry about that."

Brian shook his head. "You don't have to be sorry. Are you sorry that you weren't at work today?"

"I'm not, but that's different. It was my dad who was sick. You didn't have to miss work because of me."

"Maybe I didn't have to, but I wanted to. That's what friends are for," he said.

The words were meant to be comforting, but they scratched

over Tracey's heart like a rusted Brillo pad. She didn't want to just be his friend anymore.

"How are things going with your ex and the baby?"

Brian shook his head. "Being handled. She's got a deadline to leave, and my brother has sent over a list of places she can afford in Atlanta near her own family. I'll tell you whatever you want to know about that situation, but I know what you're doing right now."

"What am I doing?" She crossed her arms.

He took a step closer, eliminating the space between them. "I see exactly what you're doing, Tracey. You didn't ask just to ask, you asked to try to put distance between us because I helped you today. But I need you to understand one thing. I respect that you want to put distance between us. I'm not pushing you for more right now because I understand that I got some stuff I need to take care of on my end. But all of that doesn't change the way I feel about you. I'm still gonna be there for you. I'm still going to wait for you."

Tracey's breathing stuttered. Her heart raced as heat spread through her midsection, chest and cheeks. The way this man could do this to her with just a few words should be a crime. But it wasn't just the words, it was the sincerity and determination reflected in his dark eyes as he spoke them. Not just a statement but an oath.

"Brian," she whispered, but she didn't know what she was going to say. She didn't want to tell him not to wait on her. She also didn't want to tell him there was no need to wait because she was ready right now. Fear still made her hesitate. The fear that this was too good to be true and that she'd wake up and the longing in his eyes would be just a dream and the fire between them had all been imagined.

Brian cupped the back of her head and pressed his lips against hers. His tongue glided over her lower lip begging for entrance. Tracey's lips parted. She couldn't deny herself. His tongue slid across hers as his chest and thighs were a solid weight holding her up when she would have crumbled. The growing length of his erection as the kiss went on pushed into her belly. She moaned low in her throat. She wanted this man so bad. She wanted him to pick her up and take her upstairs. She wanted him between her legs. But even more she wanted him to stay in her life just like this forever.

Brian pulled back as if he could sense the way she was wavering. His eyes were hot as they stared into hers. Slowly, and with visible effort, he took a step back. "Call me if you need anything, Tracey. I mean that."

Tracey couldn't do anything but nod. If she spoke she'd ask him to stay. She'd say forget about him getting things straight with Renee, that she'd help him with this. But his problem was one he had to settle. She would wait until he did. With one last heated look at her, he turned and walked out of her office.

31

Brian went to his mother's home after he helped Tracey.
He'd gotten the list of places Renee could move into from his
brother, and he'd reached out to her parents. If she felt comfortable enough calling his mom, then he'd felt justified in
reaching out to her parents. He already knew Renee wouldn't
come up with her own plan despite his two-week deadline.
He'd taken matters into his own hands and found a solution.
He couldn't have the situation with Renee hanging over his
shoulder much longer. He could see in Tracey's eyes today that
she was torn, but he didn't want to push her. If she came back
to him, it would have to be her decision.

He went in the house and found his mom in the kitchen
making breakfast. She was dressed as if she were going to church
in one of her nicest dresses. Renee sat at the kitchen table, her
son in a high chair next to her eating Cheerios.

His mom turned to him and smiled. "Brian, what are you

doing here? I didn't expect to see you this morning. How is Tracey and her dad?"

"She's doing okay. Her dad's back home now. I stayed with him while she went and got some groceries for him." He looked to Renee. "How's the house-hunting going?"

Renee gave him an incredulous look, as if she couldn't believe he was asking her that question. "I haven't had the chance to start looking for a place. There's a lot going on. And who is Tracey?"

"We talked about you finding a place to stay. Your two weeks is up this week."

Renee huffed and patted her son's head. "I've been trying to find day care for him. It's harder than it looks. There aren't that many day cares around here."

His mom turned off the stove and came over toward Renee. She picked up the baby and put him on her hip. "I'm just going to take him to get cleaned up before church," she said. "You two go ahead and finish your conversation."

She gave Brian a *Be nice* look before leaving the kitchen. Brian didn't plan to be mean, but he also wasn't about to be overly nice with Renee. She'd worn out her welcome, and she was doing this on purpose. If he hadn't already worked this out, she would stay longer and eventually try to move in permanently.

Brian placed his hand on the back of one of the chairs and stared into Renee's eyes. "Renee, quit playing. It's time for you to leave."

Renee crossed her arms. "Does this have something to do with this Tracey person?"

"Even if there weren't a Tracey, I would still be asking you to leave."

"Who is she?"

"Why don't you focus on getting back with your husband

or figuring out who the father of your child is instead of worrying about who Tracey is?"

Renee uncrossed her arms and jumped up from the chair. "You're intentionally trying to be mean to me."

"I'm not being mean, I'm just telling the truth. I'm not playing this game with you anymore, Renee. We are done. My mom is being nice to you, but she doesn't want you to live here permanently. I am not letting you move into my house. You have real problems that you need to figure out. We've offered you help. But you are not trying to help yourself."

She walked toward him and tried to put her hand on his chest. Brian threw up his hands and stepped back. "Don't do that."

She scoffed and looked at him as if his quick step back was an insult. "What, you don't want me to touch you now?"

"No, I don't want you to touch me, Renee. We don't have that kind of relationship anymore."

Renee tapped her toe on the floor. She eyed him for several long seconds. "Is it serious with her?"

Brian only answered because he knew she would keep going if he didn't. "Yes, it is serious."

There wasn't pain or anger in her eyes. Instead, there was disappointment. "When did it become serious?"

Brian shrugged. "I really don't know. I think it became serious before I even realized how serious it was."

"I always thought that you and I would get back together."

He didn't respond to that. He'd once felt the same way, but he was so glad that he'd finally moved on. He couldn't imagine playing games and dealing with this his entire life. He related to Tracey's dad way more than he wanted to admit.

"It was our last time together," Renee asked. "That's what changed your mind, wasn't it?"

"Yeah, that was it for me," he said. "That's when I realized

I was on a hamster wheel with you. I was ready to get off, and I knew I never wanted to get back on again."

"I still love you, Brian," she said almost sincerely enough that he believed she believed it. But he knew she didn't. Not in a way that was good for either of them.

"I want what's best for you, Renee." He shook his head and pressed a hand to his chest. "But being with me is not what's best for you."

She let out a rueful laugh and rubbed her brow. "Then, is what is best for me going back to my husband? He doesn't want me anymore."

"Start by getting yourself settled. You've got a kid now. Right now he's dependent on you for everything. The best thing you can do is provide stability for him."

"That's the thing—I don't know how to be stable. I've only been stable when I was with you, and now I don't have you and it's scary. That's why I'm still here. I'm trying to figure it all out."

"I'm no expert on parenting. But there's a ton of resources out there that can tell you what you need. Do you want to stay in Peachtree Cove or do you want to go somewhere else?"

Renee pursed her lips. "To tell the truth, I don't want to stay in Peachtree Cove. It's kind of boring, and I don't know how you live here."

Her words weren't surprising. Small-town life was never something Renee was interested in. "No problem. I talked to my brother, and he sent me a list of decent places in Atlanta near your parents."

"My parents?" She shook her head and waved a hand. "I don't want to hear what they have to say."

"I've already called them and told them you're here."

Her eyes widened before she scowled. "You called them?"

Brian shrugged, uncaring about the disbelief in her voice.

"You called my mom and showed up on her doorstep. Yes, I did call them and told them you're here."

She pressed a hand to her temple. "I can already imagine how disappointed my dad was when you told him I don't know who my kid's father is and it's not my husband."

Brian walked over to the table and picked up Renee's cell phone. He turned and held it out to her. "I know how you feel about your parents, so I didn't tell them the details. I only said you were having problems and came here. They love you, Renee, and they're willing to help. Will they judge you when you tell them? Maybe, but Atlanta is a lot more fun and interesting than Peachtree Cove. Call them."

She looked up, sadness finally reaching her eyes. "We're really done, huh?"

"Yeah, Renee, we're really done."

She stared at the phone and finally took it from him.

32

Tracey exchanged a look with Halle before they both turned to look at Imani pacing back and forth in Tracey's office. With so much going on Tracey couldn't believe the time for Imani and Cyril's wedding had finally arrived. Six weeks had passed since Tracey's dad went to the hospital, but Tracey had only seen Brian related to work. She'd been consumed with working with her brother and the architect on the drawings for the cabins and the final details of helping Halle throw a small bridal shower for Imani. Whenever someone tried to give her any gossip on Brian, she'd cut them off. Until he was ready to tell her everything, she wasn't going to listen to what the rumor mill had to say.

This weekend would be the most time they'd spent together since the hospital. He was not only supplying shrubs for the wedding but he was also a groomsman. Because Imani's wedding was small, things were going smoothly with the final preparations. Or they had been.

They were getting ready for the rehearsal at the bed and breakfast when Imani pulled Tracey and Halle aside. At first Tracey thought Imani only wanted to talk to them about the wedding, but the moment they'd gotten behind Tracey's closed office door, Imani began to pace and wring her hands.

"Imani, girl, what's going on?" Tracey asked.

"I can't believe I'm getting married. Can you believe I'm getting married? Am I doing the right thing by getting married?" Imani tossed out the questions while she continued to pace back and forth.

Tracey took a deep breath. This wasn't the first time she'd seen someone get cold feet before a wedding. But she hadn't expected it from Imani.

Halle stepped forward first and spoke in her calm and re-assuring principal's voice. "Yes, I can believe you're getting married. And yes, I do believe you're doing the right thing by getting married."

Imani stopped pacing and faced both of them. "I never thought that I would get married. What if it doesn't work out? What if I'm making a huge mistake?" Imani looked dead at Tracey as she asked that question.

Tracey blinked, and her heart lurched. Of course the question was directed at her. Of the three of them, Tracey was the only one recently divorced. When Imani first came back to town she'd praised Tracey for making things work for so long with Bernard. She originally hadn't believed Tracey was making the right decision when she married Bernard, but their long marriage had somehow convinced Imani that marriages could make it, something she hadn't believed in after the disastrous end to her parents' marriage.

Tracey wished she had the perfect answer to give her friend. But there was none. Some marriages ended, and others were successful. Many things could result in a marriage failure. Making a marriage successful took work. Work by all parties involved. If someone didn't want to do the work by not communicating, cheating or being an asshole, then the marriage might not be successful.

"So what if you don't make it?" Tracey said.

Imani placed her hands on her hips, and her eyes got wide. "What do you mean by that?"

"I mean exactly what I'm saying. So what if your marriage doesn't make it? Do you love Cyril today? Right now, do you believe Cyril loves you? Do you believe that Cyril will hurt you, wants to take advantage of you or doesn't have your best interests at heart? Because if you believe any of that today, then no, you shouldn't marry him, and you need to walk away."

"I don't know if you're helping," Halle said skeptically.

Imani nodded, and her lips lifted in a small smile. "Yes, she is helping actually."

Tracey raised her brow. "Well, do you believe any of that?"

"No, I don't. He loves me. I never thought I would end up in a place like this with someone who loves me this much, but he does."

"Then, don't let your old fears and insecurities make you doubt your decision today."

The tension making Imani's shoulders rigid disappeared, and her friend visibly relaxed. "Do you have to do this for most of the brides who get married here?" Imani asked ruefully.

"Not every bride. If I see one of them getting cold feet, I usually walk away and go get their wedding planner. I can't have any of them coming back and blaming me for them making a good or bad decision."

Imani laughed. "So I'm the only one to get a pep talk from the innkeeper, huh?"

"Yes, because you're my girl." She looked at Halle then at Imani. "You're both my best friends. And I will always be there for you no matter what. Just like you were both there for me when I married Bernard and when I divorced him."

Halle walked over and took Tracey's hand in hers then reached out and took Imani's hand in her other. "Did you ask yourself these same questions the day that you married Bernard?"

Tracey grunted and rolled her eyes. "I wish that I had. Back then I just knew that I loved Bernard and that I felt lucky someone like him wanted to marry me. I never stopped to think about what his intentions were. If I had, I would have seen it then." She kept hold of their hands so the three of them formed a circle. "No matter what happens in the future, we'll always have each other's backs."

There was a knock on the door. Imani's mom poked her head in. She gave the three of them a curious look. "Is everything good in here, girls?"

Tracey looked at Imani. "I think so. Everything good?"

Imani smiled and nodded. "Yeah, we're all good. I just needed a second with my girls, that's all."

"Well then, come on, let's get a move on," Mrs. Kemp said. "The faster we get through with this rehearsal, the faster we can eat the rehearsal dinner. Because whatever Shirley is cooking sure smells good, and I am ready to eat."

The three of them all laughed. They unclasped their hands and went to the door. "Well then, let's go ahead and do this, because I know that Shirley has made some delicious oxtails for this rehearsal dinner."

Although Tracey had hosted many weddings at her bed and breakfast, this was the first one she had also participated in. It was interesting and fun to have a wedding at her inn and view it as a member of the wedding party. She couldn't be happier for her friend.

Debra handled everything from the business side. Tracey

was so glad she'd hired her. She picked up so much of the slack while Tracey dealt with her dad then worked with her brother to finalize the plans for the cabins followed by helping Imani with the final wedding prep. Debra's help allowed Tracey to enjoy everything about the wedding and not worry so much about the behind the scenes.

She cried as she watched Imani and Cyril make their vows. She laughed as she listened to Quinton and Brian give their toast during the dinner. She even drank some champagne and danced a little bit during the reception afterward. By the time Imani and Cyril were getting in their car to drive away for their honeymoon, Tracey's heart was full. She went back to the rest of the guests who were enjoying the winding down reception and scanned the crowd. She finally spotted Brian sitting at a table talking to Imani's doctor friend from Tampa.

The woman had spent most of the day chatting up Brian. Tracey didn't even pretend she hadn't noticed, and she wasn't going to pretend she didn't care. The woman was a doctor and gorgeous. She may not have had time to talk to or see Brian since he'd kissed her after her dad was released from the hospital, but that hadn't stopped her from thinking about that kiss every day. Not just the kiss. She'd thought about him. The way he always seemed to be there when her life was falling apart, but he never once made fun of her, ridiculed her or made her feel less-than. In fact, he always offered to help or, in some cases, cheered her on. Even when they were younger and he'd seen her in the middle of something, he'd tried to help her. She'd viewed it as pity, but now she realized that was far from what he'd offered. Outside of her brother, Imani and Halle, Brian had been the most consistent and loyal person in her life.

She was tired of being afraid of what would happen in the future. How could she tell her friend not to be afraid of the future and just focus on the way she felt now if she wasn't willing to do the same herself? She been afraid to tell Bernard whenever he'd hurt her feelings out of fear that he would realize she wasn't worth it and would walk away. Her silence hadn't stopped him from making her feel small nor had it stopped him from hurting her. Ever since she'd started speaking up for what she wanted, her life started getting better. She had gotten out of her bad marriage. She learned to tap into her sexuality and speak up for what she wanted. She learned to say how successful she wanted her business to be and found people willing to help her achieve that. So why was she afraid to say that she wanted Brian?

She had no clue what was going on with his ex-wife. But she did believe him when he said that he was not in love with the woman anymore. She believed his mom when she said she'd hope Brian would be with her and that she had never seen him that happy. So why was she stepping back when the truth was right in front of her?

As if sensing her gaze on him, Brian looked up. Their eyes met, and his lips tilted up in the smallest of smiles. Tracey lifted her hand and gestured to him to come over. Brian didn't hesitate: he stood and immediately crossed the room coming her way. The doctor looked confused, and then when she noticed him coming to Tracey she just shook her head. Tracey did not care. She was not about to let anybody else move in on her man.

"Everything good?" Brian asked when he stood in front of her.

"It's good now that you're standing in front of me. I didn't get to talk to you all day."

"Yeah, we had to do a lot today. Let's just say the ring bearer almost lost the ring down the toilet, and there was a lot of panicking involved, but luckily things worked out."

Tracey gasped and placed her hand over her mouth. "Oh my God. Are you serious?"

"I am, but again, we got Cyril married. That was the goal."

"And here I thought the big drama was when the makeup

artists nearly botched Imani's brows. I am so glad we did not hear the story about the ring."

"Yes, let's just be happy we got this wedding taken care of. What are you going to do now? Do you have something to do for the bed and breakfast?"

"No, Debra is handling everything. I'm just like any other guest tonight."

"I told you that you needed good help at this inn."

Tracey cocked a brow. "There you go minding my business again."

Brian grinned then shrugged. He looked every bit the model he'd once been in the classic black tux Cyril had picked for the wedding attire. The doctor wasn't the only person looking his way that night. "I can't help it, Tracey. Minding your business and seeing you get that cute little line between your brows makes my day."

"I bet it does," she said teasing, even though the words made her heart flutter.

"Are you going back up to your room now?"

She shook her head. "I could, but honestly I'd prefer to go back to your place. If that's cool with you?"

His eyes darkened and his voice lowered. "You know that's good with me, Tracey. But what I said before and the way I feel hasn't changed. I don't want to just keep doing this as a casual thing between us. If it's because of the wedding—"

"It's not because of the wedding. Well, not completely. I was talking to Imani and trying to convince her to go ahead and get married—"

Brian did a double take. "Hold on. What do you mean *convince her to get married*?"

Tracey waved a hand. "Again, that's irrelevant. It's a story for another day. They got married, so that's the important thing. But when I was talking to her and telling her not to worry about what might happen in the future and focus on how you feel right now, it made me think about the way I feel about you right now. I know you've got some stuff you're working through with your ex-wife, but I also know that you don't want to be with her anymore. I'm tired of being afraid to trust that we'll make this work between us. I do want you to be my man."

"She's gone," he said quickly.

"What do you mean she's gone?"

"I mean she's gone. I reached out to her parents in Atlanta. They asked me to help her look for a place to stay. So that's what me and my brother have been doing. We all finally got her settled in an apartment near them. She is no longer my problem."

Tracey put a hand on her hip. "When were you gonna tell me that?"

"I was going to tell you tonight after the wedding. I didn't want our relationship to be a distraction on Cyril and Imani's big day."

"She's gone for good?"

"I think she got the picture that she wasn't welcome when she caught my mom doing a little happy dance after she said she'd finally picked a place she liked."

Tracey laughed. "No your mom didn't."

"She did. My mom is all about helping others, but I think even her Christian charity was running low. Renee is out of our lives." He took a step forward. "Which means, Tracey, that I no longer have a situation that I need to deal with. So I'm asking my question again. Can I be your man?"

Tracey did not have to consider his words; she already knew her answer. She took his hand in hers and placed it against her heart. "That depends on one thing."

"What one thing is that?" Brian's voice dropped to a low tone that made her insides tremble.

"Take me back to your place and make love to me."

His eyes widened slightly before his lips tilted upward. It was the first time she'd ever made that request so directly. She'd never wanted to refer to what they did as *making love* before, and it was a far cry from the way she'd referred to what she wanted when they'd started their friends-with-benefits situation. Despite what they'd said, making love was what he'd always done to her. If she'd had any foresight she would have known just sex wouldn't have worked between her and Brian. There'd always been something between them. An underlying current that surrounded their awkward friendship over the years. If she'd had any sense before, she would have realized that they were already too connected to just have sex and not feel anything.

Brian pulled her closer and lightly placed his hand around her neck. His thumb caressed her pulse before he tilted her head and kissed her softly. Tracey forgot about everyone else at the reception. She didn't care who saw them, she didn't care what people would say, all she cared about was that she was in Brian's arms and that he was kissing her as if she was the sweetest thing he'd ever tasted.

When he pulled back, he smiled at her and said, "Tracey, I'll be more than happy to take you back to my place and make love to you all night long."

33

Tracey grinned from ear to ear as she looked at the crowd of people standing in front of one of the two newly constructed cabins on her property. She had officially joined the Peachtree Cove Business Guild, and as a member they'd agreed to hold a ribbon-cutting ceremony for the opening of her first cabins. Tracey had expected maybe a few Guild members to show up and of course her friends and family, but she had not expected so many Guild members to be there. Sometimes she still couldn't believe that she was a part of this community. Growing up she'd always felt like an outcast, someone who never quite fit in, but she realized now that that was just the thoughts of a teenager who was afraid, lonely and unsure how to accept help when it was offered. Now she was neither afraid nor lonely nor unsure. She spoke up for what she wanted, she had the love and acceptance of her friends, her brother and Brian, and she knew exactly what she wanted for her life. She wasn't going to let anyone stop her from getting just that.

As she took the oversized scissors from Emily, the head of the Peachtree Cove Business Guild, she held her head up high and her shoulders back and proudly stood behind the red ribbon held by those who'd helped her get to this day. Her brother and his architect friend. Mikayla, who'd first given her the idea and helped walk her through the steps of financing and funding. Debra, who made everything run so much more smoothly at the bed and breakfast. And of course, the mayor was there, because she loved to support expanding businesses in Peachtree Cove.

The photographer from the local paper held up a hand to get everyone's attention. "Alright, everybody, it is time to take the picture. On the count of three, Tracey, I want you to cut the ribbon, but everyone, don't look down at the ribbon. Keep your eyes on the camera. Is everyone ready?"

Tracey nodded. "More than ready!"

The photographer gave a thumbs-up before holding up his camera. "Alright, one...two...three!"

The rest of the crowd clapped and cheered as Tracey cut the red ribbon and her cabins officially opened. After the pictures and cheers, everyone took turns walking through the inside to see the layout. Shirley had made finger foods and set them up on one of the tables outside for everyone to enjoy. Tracey answered questions and accepted the congratulations of fellow Guild members and some other business owners who'd attended the ceremony.

Her mom and dad came over to her. Her mom's boyfriend wasn't there. Tracey didn't ask about him when her parents arrived together. They were spending more time together since her dad's hospital stay. Tracey was staying out of whatever toxic connection they kept going. Her dad was sober, and her mom was making sure he was taking his medicine. That's all she cared about.

"Good job, Tracey," her mom said.

"Thanks, Mom."

Her dad looked around before nodding. "You did good."

"I appreciate that, Dad." She did. Whatever man-to-man talk he'd had with Brian had worked. He no longer bugged her about ending her marriage. She would take that.

Her mom glanced down before speaking. "I know me and your dad didn't give you the best example, but you turned out alright."

"I did, but I'm still grateful to you and Dad. Good or bad, you all helped shape me into who I am today. I do love you."

Her mom blinked. Her dad rubbed the back of his head. They didn't utter those three words a lot in her family, if ever. But Tracey did love them. They were far from perfect, but they were her parents, and they'd done what they could.

Her dad cleared his throat. "Love you, too." He patted her shoulder and walked away.

Her mom rolled her eyes at his retreating back before she hugged Tracey. "I love you, too, baby girl."

Tracey smiled as she watched her mom follow her dad. No, they weren't perfect and probably never would be, but she had turned out alright and done well. She glanced at her brother, standing with Joanne at the food table. He tilted his head up and grinned. Tracey grinned back. They'd both turned out okay.

Two hours later, Tracey sat on the porch of the cabin with Imani on one side and Halle on the other. "Ladies, thank you for coming today."

Halle elbowed Tracey. "As if we wouldn't be here. Girl, you knew we were gonna come out and celebrate you." She placed her hand on her rounded belly and rubbed.

Tracey reached over and patted Halle's belly, too. She'd waited until after Imani's wedding to let them know the reason she'd stayed away from the champagne was because she was pregnant. "You and my new niece or nephew came, which I appreciate. I know standing for a long time couldn't have been easy on you."

"I can stand for a little bit of time. Despite what people may want to say about me being a geriatric pregnant person." Halle cut her eyes at Imani.

Imani held up her hand. "That is just the medical term. I was not calling you *old*."

"You're the one who said it, so therefore you're the one who's going to get the side-eye every time I have to repeat it," Halle said shrugging.

Tracey laughed and decided to cut in before her friends started that debate all over again. "Well, despite whatever the medical term is, I'm still happy that both of you came. Because not only is today the day that I'm doing a ribbon cutting, but I also have something else for you two."

Imani's eyes got big. "What do you have for us?"

Tracey pointed to the box on the porch next to Imani. "Can you hand me that?"

Her friend handed her the box with a skeptical look. "This looks old. What is it?"

Halle gasped and sat up straight. "Is that what I think it is? Is that the time capsule we buried out here in the peach fields when we were teenagers?"

Tracey nodded and patted the top of the box. "Yeah. I didn't think this thing was still out here, but when they dug the footings for the cabin they found it. The contractor brought it to me in case it was something important or historical. They were worried that we'd have to shut down the whole project, but I immediately recognized it."

"I can't believe that it survived all this time," Imani said. "When I first moved back to town, I didn't want to see what was in this box."

Halle frowned. "Why not?"

"Because I thought it would just be a reminder of how I failed at all the good things I thought I'd accomplish in life."

Tracey raised an eyebrow. "What about now? Do you still not want to open it?"

Imani shook her head. "No, I kind of want to see if I remembered what I wrote."

Tracey looked at Halle. "What about you?"

Halle nodded quickly. "Girl, if you don't open that thing, I'm going to snatch it from you."

"No need to snatch anything," Tracey said laughing as she unlatched the box. The top was rusted, but it opened after a few tugs. Inside the box lay the plastic bag they'd put their wishes in.

Tracey pulled each folded sheet of paper with their names written on them out of the bag. She handed Imani her paper, then Halle's, and then took hers. The three exchanged a look before they each unfolded their papers. It was quiet as they read what they'd written.

Tracey's paper had three lines written:

1. I want to be successful.
2. I want to leave Peachtree Cove forever!
3. I don't want to be like my parents!!

Tears pricked her eyes, and she blinked rapidly. She'd accomplished two out of the three. With the success she'd found in Peachtree Cove, she no longer wished to leave the town forever.

"Wow," Halle breathed.

Tracey glanced at her friend. "What?"

"I said I wanted to be a teacher, help people and have a big family." Halle looked up; her eyes were also watery. "I remember wishing I'd had siblings after my mom passed away. Then when my dad died… I always wanted a family. Now Shania has her dad, Quinton's family is great, and I'm having another kid. I did it."

"Girl, you exceeded," Tracey said. "You're about to work for the district next year, too. That's big."

Halle grinned and looked back at her letter before looking at the sky. She'd been offered the job as the assistant superintendent, and despite being surprised and a little nervous, she'd accepted the offer. "It is."

She looked at Imani. "What about your letter?"

Imani lifted a shoulder. "Be a doctor, and not be afraid to fall in love. I still can't believe I wrote that back then. I was so sure I'd never fall in love after what happened between my parents."

"And another one exceeding expectations."

Imani wiped her eyes. "I did. I love Cyril and even his dad so much. Life is pretty good."

Tracey held up her paper. She read her three items to her friends. "Y'all, we did this. Can you believe it?"

Imani shook her head. "I never would have imagined we'd be here when I first wrote this."

"Me either," Tracey said.

"Well, I knew I'd at least be a teacher," Halle said. "I had been accepted to college by then."

Tracey rolled her eyes, but there was no malice. "Of course the overachiever of the group would say that."

The three of them laughed. Tracey put an arm around Halle and then around Imani. Life was good.

Tracey was still sitting outside staring at the stars when Brian found her later. She wasn't ready to go inside; she wanted to spend more time enjoying the result of her hard work.

"Can your gentleman caller join you?"

Tracey grinned and waved him over. "He can."

Brian wrapped a blanket around her shoulders before sitting next to her. "Shirley told me you were still out here. You're not ready to come in?"

She shook her head. "Not yet. The cabin is real. The bed and breakfast is real. This life I'm living is real."

He wrapped an arm around her. "It is."

"And you know what's funny?" She leaned her head on his shoulder.

"What, you keep waiting for something bad to happen?"

She shook her head. "The opposite of that. I'm thankful for what I have, and I want to enjoy every minute instead of worrying about how things will mess up."

"You did this, Tracey. I know you had help, but the idea and the success was because of your hard work. I always knew you'd be great."

She raised a brow. "No, you didn't."

"Yes, I did. Even in high school when you wouldn't let anyone treat you any kind of way, I knew you'd do the damn thing. You keep proving me right."

She sighed and entwined her arm with his. "I wish I'd had that confidence then, but I'm so glad that I have it now."

Brian was quiet for a moment before he turned to face her. "I love you, Tracey."

His words didn't surprise or shock her. She'd felt his love a long time ago in the way he'd stood up for her, supported her and cared for her. She'd recognized the signs of love but had been too insecure to acknowledge his feelings. She wasn't going to pretend she didn't see the good things happening in her life.

"I love you, too."

Brian sucked in a breath. "I didn't expect you to say it back."

"I didn't expect to ever say those words to anyone again, but here we are."

"I just want you to know how I feel. I'm not saying this to pressure you into anything."

"I know you aren't. That's one of the reasons why I love you."

They hadn't moved in together or talked about getting married one day. They both were content with just being there for each other. For the first time she didn't feel unsettled or unsure where she stood with another person. If, one day, they were ready for something else, then that would be okay, but for now she was happy with what they'd built.

"What are the other reasons?" he asked.

She leaned forward, kissed him then tilted her head toward the cabin. "Take me inside, and I can list them while you demonstrate." She didn't hesitate to say what she wanted. That's the other thing she loved: the freedom to express her needs without worrying that she'd be judged, ridiculed or rejected.

"You want to break in the cabin?" Heat filled his eyes.

"Oh, most definitely."

Brian took her hand and helped her stand. "Your gentleman caller is at your service."

Laughing, and full of joy, Tracey followed him inside.

★ ★ ★ ★ ★

Please turn the page for a sneak peek at the first book in
Synithia Williams's charming
and witty Peachtree Cove series,
The Secret to a Southern Wedding,
to see how it all began!

Enjoy this excerpt from
The Secret to a Southern Wedding!

1

Imani licked her lips and reached out, flexing her fingers open and closed in a "gimme" fashion toward her lunchtime savior. Loretta worked behind the counter in the hospital's busy lunch line. Her black hair was covered by a hairnet and laugh lines creased the dark brown skin around her nose and mouth.

Loretta shook her head and smiled, but Imani didn't care. She was starving and Loretta had exactly what she needed.

"I made sure to put one to the side for you today," Loretta said handing over the red-and-white-checkered food boat with a golden brown fried corn dog in the middle.

"I owe you big-time, Loretta." Imani grinned as she snagged the corn dog and placed it on her tray. "I just knew I was going to miss getting one."

"You're the only person I know who gets so excited when we have corn dogs for lunch," Loretta said. "Most of the doctors prefer the fancy stuff."

Imani shook her head. "Give me a corn dog and mustard any day over fancy. How's your daughter and the baby?"

Loretta's smile broadened, revealing one gold tooth. "They're doing great. I'm so glad I told her to come see you instead of that other doctor. Thanks again for fitting her into your schedule. I don't know if she would have made it without you."

Imani's cheeks warmed and so did her heart. "Of course I'm going to fit her in. You always save the best corn dogs for me." They both laughed before Imani sobered. "Seriously, I'm glad they're okay. Tell her to call the office if she needs anything."

"Will do, Dr. Kemp," Loretta said with a bright, grateful smile.

The man next to Imani in line cleared his throat. Loretta threw him an annoyed look. Imani shrugged and waved a hand. "I'll see you tomorrow."

She moved on down the line and grabbed a handful of mustard packets and a bag of baked potato chips before scanning the crowded seating area for her lunch partner. She spotted Towanda Brown, a doctor from the hospital's orthopedic practice, sitting in a corner near one of the windows.

Maneuvering through the filled tables, Imani kept her eyes down to avoid eye contact as she made her way through the maze of bodies, seats and chairs toward her friend. Still, she received several points and stares with whispered "yeah, that's her—the hospital's chosen one" along with a few waves from some of the less cynical doctors and nurses for her to sit with them at their table. She gave the people who caught her eye a polite nod before pointing toward Towanda.

She sat with her friend and sighed. "Sorry I'm late."

Towanda shrugged. Despite having not run track in over ten years, Towanda still had the tall, muscular figure that once had her on the fast track for the Olympics before an injury ended her career. Her sienna skin was as line-free as it had been when Imani first met her, and she wore her hair in braids that were pulled back in a ponytail at the base of her neck. She looked closer to thirty-three than her actual forty-three.

"It's so busy today, but I knew you'd make it for corn dog day." Her friend grinned and pointed to Imani's tray.

"Loretta never lets this day go by without saving me one," Imani said.

"That was before you helped her daughter. I'd be surprised if she doesn't make extra just to pack up and deliver to your office."

Imani chuckled while opening a package of mustard to put on the corn dog. "I would've helped her daughter despite her support of my corn dog addiction. She was seeing a doctor who ignored all her fears. I was just happy to let her know that her concerns were valid and that I wasn't going to gas her up with fancy talk."

"And that's why you're the hospital's doctor of the year," Towanda said pointing behind Imani.

Imani didn't look over her shoulder. She knew what was there. Her face was plastered all over the hospital right now on signs, cardboard cutouts and television screens. Was she proud of being named the hospital's doctor of the year? Kind of. She'd spent so much of her life trying to become an obstetrician patients could rely on and trust. Did that translate to being comfortable as the "face" of the hospital system for a year? Not one bit.

"Can we not talk about that right now?" Imani squirted mustard down the length of her corn dog.

"Why not? It's something to be proud of."

"And I am proud. I just don't want that to become all I am. Especially when we know the hospital administration's guilt about the last few doctors of the year may have had something to do with it." She raised a brow.

The last four years hadn't included a female doctor of the year at all and only two women were nominated. Ever since

Guardian Health merged with Mid-State Health to become one of Florida's largest health care systems, the struggle to diversify prior to the merger was lost as profits and popularity became a thing. When she learned of her nomination, Imani hadn't believed she'd had a chance of winning against a heart surgeon and oncologist.

"You won because you're the best and that's all we're going by," Towanda said.

Imani shrugged. "Fine, I'm the best. Now can we talk about something else?"

Talking about being the hospital's doctor of the year meant thinking about how the obstetrics unit now pushed her in front of every camera they could find to draw more clients to the practice. Imani, who'd previously been a liked and well-respected member of the practice, but never thrust forward as the only Black doctor for diversity points, was suddenly a double commodity. She didn't like that.

Imani took a bite of her lunch. The savory mixture of the mustard with the hot dog wrapped in cornmeal batter made her groan with pleasure. "This is soooo good."

Towanda's brows rose and she eyed Imani curiously. "Can we talk about how after watching you go in on that corn dog and moan like a porn star, I don't know why you haven't caught a man, yet?"

Imani tried to glare at her friend but could only cover her full mouth and suppress a laugh. She chewed and swallowed hard. "Corn dogs, unlike a lot of men, don't disappoint."

"Chile, please. Everything disappoints eventually."

"Corn dogs never disappoint." Imani took another bite.

"Even microwaved ones?" Towanda asked.

Imani scrunched her nose and shivered. "Touché. Thanks for reminding me nothing in life is perfect."

She'd once believed in perfection. That she'd had the best

life ever. That reality had been shattered harshly and abruptly one fall afternoon.

Her cell phone vibrated in the pocket of her white lab coat. She pulled it out and smiled when she saw the text icon from her mom.

"Who is it?" Towanda asked.

"My mom. She only texts with town news or a funny video she found online."

Towanda grinned. "You still care about town news?"

Imani nodded and clicked on the text. "I mean, I don't live in Peachtree Cove anymore, but that doesn't mean I don't like hearing what's going on with all the judgmental people in town."

"The people couldn't be that bad."

Imani grunted and didn't answer. The same people who'd loved her parents together had been quick to talk about all their faults after her dad's girlfriend decided to put a deadly plan in place to separate Imani's parents for good. So, maybe it was petty, but Imani indulged in her mom's texts about the trials and tribulations of the people so eager to cast judgment on her family all those years ago.

Imani opened the text, preparing for the funny video or latest update, but frowned at what looked like an invitation instead.

"Everything alright?"

Imani zoomed in on the invitation and nearly dropped her phone. She had to read the words out loud to be sure her eyes weren't deceiving her. "You're invited to the wedding of Linda Kemp and Preston Dash. What the hell is this?"

Towanda leaned forward and tried to see Imani's cell. "Your mom's getting married?"

"No. She couldn't be. My mom isn't even dating."

At least, her mom never talked about dating. Her mom hadn't dated since the disaster that ended her last marriage. She hadn't been able to trust anyone since. Not that Imani blamed her.

Almost getting killed by your husband's mistress tended to do that to a person.

"Who in the world is Preston Dash?" Imani muttered and why was her mom marrying him? In a month! This didn't make sense. It had to be a prank. She called her mom immediately. The phone went straight to voice mail.

Imani stared at her cell phone. "Seriously?"

"She didn't answer?"

"This has to be a joke," Imani said. The watch on her arm vibrated. "Damn." She pressed the button to stop the alarm reminding her that she needed to be back upstairs in the practice in time for her next patient appointment.

"You're probably right," Towanda said. "Your mom wouldn't get married without telling you, would she?" The question in Towanda's voice was the same question in Imani's heart.

"My mom wouldn't get married, period," Imani said. She shoved the rest of the corn dog into her mouth and jumped up. She pointed toward the exit.

Towanda nodded. "I know. Go ahead. We'll talk later. Let me know what your mom says."

With her mouth full, Imani nodded and hurried out of the cafeteria. She shoved the bag of chips into the pocket of her lab coat and chewed the rest of the food in her mouth after dumping her trash into the can. On the way to the elevator, she texted her mom back.

This is a joke, right?

She watched her phone and waited for her mother's response. There was nothing as she waited for the elevator. Nothing as she boarded with a group of people. Still nothing as she tried to avoid eye contact with the others as they slowly realized the face smiling back at them from the picture plastered on the elevator doors was her. In the background the throwback song "How

Bizarre" by OMC played from the speakers. Imani hummed along and watched her phone. The doors opened, thankfully, before everyone connected the dots between her and the life-size photo, and Imani quickly got off. Her phone finally buzzed as she approached the door to the practice.

No joke. Come home. We'll talk.

What kind of response was that? Her mom wouldn't answer her call, but she'd text back telling her to come home. She'd just talked to her mom a few days ago. She hadn't mentioned anything about getting married or even given a hint of there being a special person in her life. A few months ago, her mom mentioned Imani's cousin Halle said something about getting on a dating app for seniors, but Imani had immediately shot that down. No way was her mom about to be played by some random guy online after all she'd been through. Now she was talking about marriage after she'd vowed to never trust another man again? Something wasn't right.

She was preparing to dial her mom's number when she walked through the door of her office.

"Oh, thank goodness, Imani, you're here!" Karen, the receptionist behind the desk, exclaimed.

Imani looked up from her phone to Karen. The receptionist had a bright smile on her face as she pointed to a man holding a camera next to the desk. The white guy wore a blue polo shirt with the logo from a local news station on the breast pocket and khaki's. His dark hair was stylishly cut, and he grinned a hundred-watt smile at her.

"Dr. Imani Kemp, it's great to meet you. I'm here for your interview at one," the man said.

Imani looked from him to Karen behind the desk. "I have a patient at one."

The door behind the reception desk opened and Dr. Andrea Jaillet came out. Tall, red hair, with bright blue eyes and a supersweet personality that wasn't manufactured, Andrea was someone who was nearly impossible to dislike.

Andrea beamed. "Imani, you're here, great. We've moved your patients around to other doctors so you can do this interview. Isn't it wonderful? The news wants to feature our doctor of the year."

Imani's phone buzzed again. She glanced down.

Dinner Friday afternoon. You'll meet your stepfather then.

Friday! It was Tuesday. She looked from the text to Andrea's smiling face, to the reporter and his camera. The chorus of "How Bizarre" played on loop in her head. All she'd wanted was a corn dog. What in the world had happened to her perfectly normal day?

Don't miss The Secret to a Southern Wedding,
available now!